'What a story! What a heroine... ...!'
ADAM NICOLSON

'The novel is so very impressive and so saturated with atmosphere and rich in mystery – it flows so freely, takes risks other novels might dodge and transports us into an entirely different world'
JONATHAN LEE

'Truly epic . . . The richness and enthusiasm of the prose speaks of a novelist who loves the process of spinning an unpredictable, fabulist yarn'
i

'Goody Brown is an unforgettable character and her story utterly gripping'
SOFKA ZINOVIEFF

'A swashbuckling smuggler's tale . . . Told with exhilarating colour and flair'
ECONOMIST

'Beautifully told and expertly crafted, a moving and evocative tale of longing and belonging'
PETER FRANKOPAN

'A well-wrought, satisfyingly solid romp'
GUARDIAN

Also by Alex Preston

This Bleeding City
The Revelations
In Love and War
As Kingfishers Catch Fire (non-fiction)

WINCHELSEA

ALEX PRESTON

CANONGATE

This paperback edition published in 2023 by Canongate Books

First published in Great Britain, the USA and Canada in 2022
by Canongate Books Ltd,
14 High Street, Edinburgh EH1 1TE

Distributed in the USA by Publishers Group West
and in Canada by Publishers Group Canada

canongate.co.uk

2

British Library Cataloguing-in-Publication Data
A catalogue record for this book is available on
request from the British Library

ISBN 978 1 83885 487 4

Typeset in Bembo MT Pro by Palimpsest Book Production Ltd,
Falkirk, Stirlingshire

Printed and bound in Great Britain by Clays Ltd, Elcograf S.p.A.

To Ary

Winchelsea, Rye and the Marshes, 1742

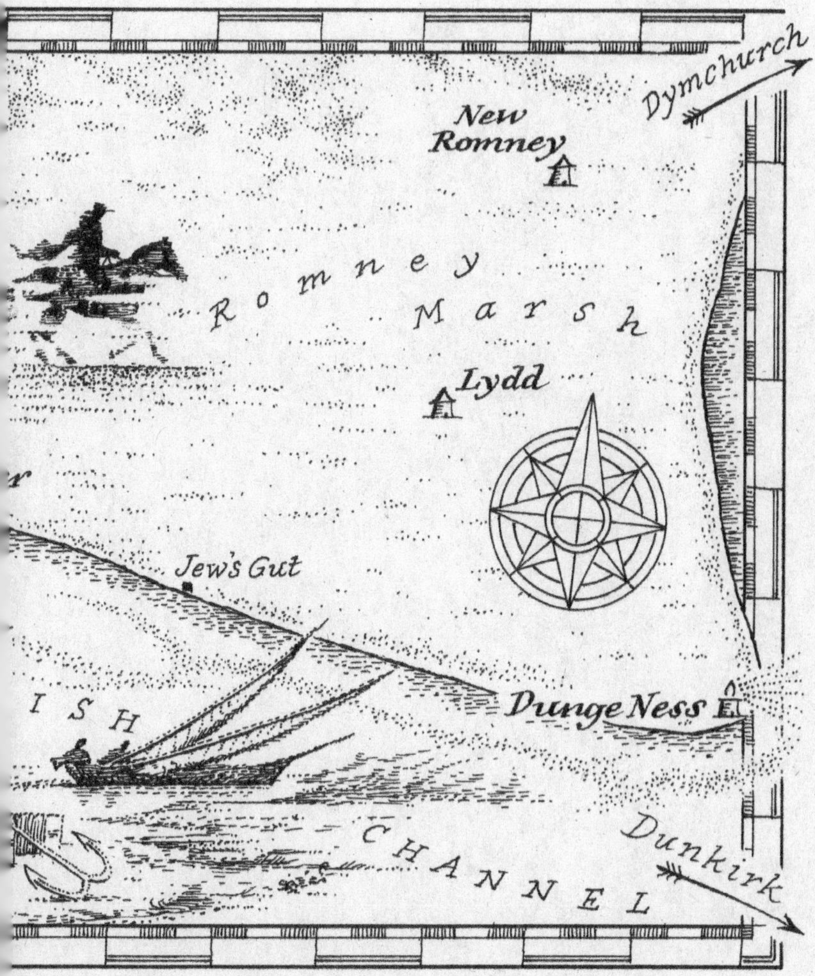

Dymchurch
New Romney
Romney Marsh
Lydd
Jew's Gut
Dunge Ness
ISH
CHANNEL
Dunkirk

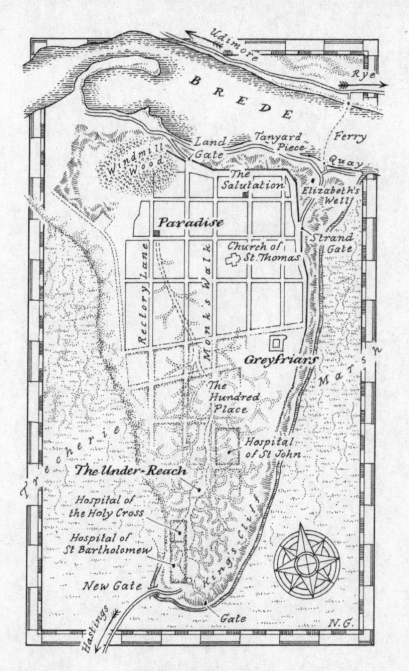

Winchelsea, 1742

'There is only one Winchelsea, and there is no place like it, no place that so effectually and so pleasantly teaches us the lesson that we most need in these days of hurry and forgetfulness. Where else can one so well realise that there were strong men before Agamemnon; so well learn that the Agamemnons of to-day are but the strong men that will fall and be forgotten at the rise of the Agamemnons of to-morrow?'

Ford Madox Ford, *The Cinque Ports*

A Letter from Goody Brown

Dear Reader,

Let us make one thing clear: lives do not take the shapes of stories. Any author who tries to tuck his subject between the covers of a book is forced to exchange reality for artifice. Certainly, I believed that what you are about to read was my story as I dictated it, told with as much truth as I was able. But writing a novel – which it appears that this tale now has become – is an act of settlement, banishing the native and replacing her with another that may seem to be her, yet is not.

The friend to whom I recounted this tale generously permitted me to edit or redact any passages I felt misprized or mangled my experiences, or whose relation caused me embarrassment. I took advantage of this license. The truth, though, was not to be found within the text, for all that I changed, for the sentences crossed through or added. In the end, I felt something like despair as I read, and wondered whether the fault lay with consigning my tale to a man, who could of necessity scarce comprehend what it is to be a woman. I discovered much greater truth in the author's prefatory sketch, which viewed me from without, than I did in that portion purportedly narrated in my own voice.

I should like also to make mention of my brother Francis, whose tale this is as much as my own. The reader will no doubt wish to know more of Francis's childhood, his life in the Americas and cruel mistreatment at the hands of the slavers. This, I recognise, is how novels comprehend the character of those who move within them: they know the man by the child. But Francis's tale is not mine to tell, and while I mention elements of his escape from the slaver-ship in passing, I do not wish to visit the same violence upon the life of my beloved Francis that my late friend, albeit with no malicious intent, visited upon my own.

I ask you, then, to read this book as you would any by a man about a woman, reckoning for it to tell you more about the mind of the man himself than about the woman who is his subject.

Signed,

Goody Brown, Winchelsea, June 1779

Preface: The Death of Jim Lawrence

THERE IS A certain device forged in the East that, when held to the eye, permits the operator to perceive time at speeds faster than the normal beat, and, conversely, to slow its march down until the world appears vitrified. I wish you to imagine viewing the Sussex town of Winchelsea through this sorcerous glass, so that the centuries might be condensed into a few short pages.

First, a thousand years back, the land is covered over by a blanket of water – the Camber, a vast inland sea. On a precarious spit interjoining the Camber and the roaring ocean, you will find Old Wynchelsea, a town known for the piratical ferocity of its sailors and the cunning of its shipwrights. Watch as the town grows and prospers, becoming the principal port of the realm, receiving wine from Bordeaux and Bayonne, Jerez and Lisbon. Cheer as French raiding parties are repelled. At its pomp there live ten thousand souls in Old Wynchelsea, with the town supporting fifty inns and two great churches. The sea is always there, though, waiting.

It is February 1287. The sea has already claimed one of the churches and a good many taverns. The town has a foot in the ocean. Now a great storm sweeps up the

Channel and Old Wynchelsea is whelmed completely, the spit upon which it sits being sucked into the sea and all who live there drowned. The morning after, watery sun on flotsam: timbers that were once houses, beds, pews; bodies that were once stubborn, buccaneering folk.

Longshanks is on the throne at this point, and orders a new town to be built upon the Hill of Iham. Iham looks over the Camber towards Rye. Over two years the new town of Winchelsea is constructed, with each house perched atop a large cellar, and these cellars interlinked by a network of tunnels, so that wine might be stored and moved without revealing it to the concupiscent eyes of French raiders or English smugglers. These tunnels, which are named the Under-Reach, sit themselves atop the ancient mines of Iham, dug by those who lived here before the Romans came, and which are said to penetrate down to the very heart of the earth.

Now Winchelsea thrives again, sitting fast within her walls, with three turreted gates safeguarding her seaward and landward entrances. As the years pass there commences an enterprise known as the Innings, whereby ingenious landowners claim first a field, then ten fields, back from the Camber. What was once the sea becomes farmland, and the Isle of Oxney is un-islanded. By the shore, though, things are less certain, and Winchelsea and Rye are moored above a shifting, transitory prospect of pools, marshes and sulphurous bogs, all transversed by three swift-flowing rivers: the Rother, the Tillingham and the Brede.

Winchelsea grows rich as England prospers. The church of her main square might be mistaken for a cathedral. Her houses become more splendid, their doorways spout porticoes, their gardens grow orangeries; many of the original dwellings are levelled and replaced by elegant, square-fronted townhouses. Her sailors remain belligerent, fellish folk, but are now named lords and admirals by grateful kings. It is the golden age of the Cinque Ports, when Rye and Winchelsea oversee the administration of Hythe, Sandwich, New Romney, Dover and Hastings, near-independent from the rest of the country. Winchelsea's population is as rich just now as that of any town in Europe, with the wealthiest calling themselves Jurats, administering the thriving ports by means of an organisation named the Brotherhood and Guestling.

Then, and there's always a then, comes the long decline: the French invasions, the plagues, the reversals in warfare and diplomacy. The church is sacked and burnt, its vaulted narthex collapsing into rubble; rubble too are the town walls, swarmed over once too often by French soldiers and privateers. The great hospitals in the south of the town are destroyed, the largest houses ruined. Winchelsea's townsfolk die or flee, and a place that once held many thousand is scarcely eight hundred souls by the time of the Civil War. Grass grows between the cobbles of her streets; pigs graze on her thoroughfares; life becomes sleepy, back-countryish. Just the sort of place a smuggler, wishing to remain unobserved, might make his headquarters.

Now the picturing-device slows. It is the eighteenth century, a time of getting and spending, of great wealth built on the backs of bloody empires. We see Goody

Brown, just a babe, plucked from the waters of the Brede by the man she will come to call Father: Ezekiel. We see her adoptive mother, Alma, and her brother, Francis, another orphan. Goody grows as a tree might grow: in short, surprising bursts, followed by years in which she hardly seems to change at all. By ten she is already larger than many of the good women of Winchelsea, who watch condescendingly as she goes by on her father's horse, her white-blonde hair a plume behind her, her clothing that of a stable lad or smith's boy, her pale eyes set on the sea, or the high ridges of the Weald. Her father still dreams of making a lady of her, forces her into damask gowns, corsets and canes. She is happiest like this, though, out in the elements, or deep in the winding dark of the tunnels.

Now let us slow that time-machine down further still until we find Goody on a September evening, just shy of her eleventh birthday. She is standing where King's Cliffs meet the marshes, below the ruined walls of Winchelsea. Goody's father, the Cellarman Ezekiel, has tasked her with checking the fastness of the gates to the Under-Reach, to keep safe those goods stored within the tunnels from thieves or excisemen. She performs this duty, rattling the gate, peering in at the murk of the caverns beyond, which she knows intimately, having played in their close darkness since a small girl. She then turns to look out to Rye. There, over the marsh, coming towards her in the long late rays of the sun, she sees her friend Jim.

Jim Lawrence is his name. Fifteen, pimply and mopish, with a voice that creaks like a gate every third word. His father died three years hence in the workhouse and he is the breadwinner now for his mother and three sisters. He has become a smuggler, as many do when there is little between them and starvation. Goody does not know him very well, but he always has a smile for her, even when he's been out in rough weather, or when there's been a close call with the Revenue.

Now, though, Jim is running pell-mell through the quaggy marsh, his arms and legs moving furiously. He skirts the ruins of King Henry's fort, turns and looks back, presses on. Goody climbs a little up the cliff to get a better view of him. She sees that three men are chasing Jim, men she recognises. Further back, she makes out another familiar shape: the squat, tub-like figure of her father, attempting to keep up.

Goody draws back against the cliff, into the cover of ferns, and watches. Nasty Face is the first of the men to catch Jim. He tackles him as if they were playing football, then takes him by his hair, pulls him to his feet and knocks him down again. Now Gabriel and Old Joll catch up with them. Her father is still some way back. They lead Jim to one of the ponds that pock the marsh. Jim tries to make a break for it, wading in, knee-deep, and Gabriel goes after him. They stand there facing one another for a few moments: the tall man with his sweep of black hair, the boy with his face a mess of tears and mud and blood. Finally Goody's father, winded, arrives at the pool and stands there, panting.

Words are spoken, mainly by Gabriel, and as he speaks, Goody sees him bind his fist in a piece of cloth. Old Joll and Nasty Face stand behind him as he hits the boy. After two punches Jim goes down in the water and comes up spluttering; but then the three men take turns to bring their heels, their fists, their elbows down on his head and his back until he doesn't come up any more. At the end, it is as if they are dancing a gigue on his poor back, trampling him into the water. When they are done, they stand there for a moment, watching over the pool as it stills, breathing heavily. Ezekiel looks on, then reaches into his coat and draws out a notebook, scribbling something within. Goody feels a taint seep from that pool and drift over the marshland, over the river, towards her.

Now we rise out from Goody, a tall, square-shouldered child with great swags of hair the colour of sea spume. Her mouth is open, her pale eyes wide. She is fringed by fernbrake and hawthorn, deep in the greenery of the hillside. We rise up, over the town, its regimental streets and squares, its ruined church, its crumbling walls. We rise out until we see Winchelsea like a dim jewel set at the throat of the sea. Then all is ocean, and the wind is high about us, and we take the device from our eye, and permit Goody, at last, to begin her story.

BOOK ONE

The Life and Recollections of Goody Brown, of Winchelsea, as Told to One Who Knew Her

PART ONE

Winchelsea, November 1742

I

I'D LEFT THE curtains open that night, the drapes of my bed too, so that the fire in the Hundred Place painted the walls of my chamber with fading reds. I lay with my feet arched around the bed-warmer, knees up, blankets to my chin. When I closed my eyes, I could still see fragments of light from the rockets, squibs and crackers fizzing off to explode over the marshes, lighting for an instant all the dark reaches of damp land.

That day the wind had swept in from the sea, tearing copper leaves from the trees. As dusk fell, Father and I had stood looking over the marshes to cold violet light edging down the sky, fires alight in Rye and Udimore, the first rockets whose colours reached us long before their sound.

We'd stayed out until the wind dropped, just past eleven, marching with the townsfolk because that was what my father's father and grandfathers had done before him. Father said some part of him felt those earlier Rejoicings in his bones, when they'd celebrated not the failure of a Catholic plot, but something more ancient: a last gesture of light and life before the coming of darkness. We were all brave on Bonfire Night.

Winchelsea sits moored most autumn nights in a lake

of mist, and when there's a full moon the hilltop glows silver. In bed, hearing the watch pass below – 'Twelve o'clock and the mist is rising' – I fanned through memories: the ten or eleven Bonfire Rejoicings I could remember. For the last four – since I turned twelve and seemed to have grown a yard in a year – I'd been taller than my father, but I always perceived the younger impressions of myself there beside him, my small hand slowly growing to fill his as we marched through a decade of fire-breathers and masked dancers, the burning Popes and the boys rolling their flaming tubs. Francis had been with us in the early years, before he and my father fell out, and I'd strung myself between them, my almost-brother and nearly-father, and been swung into the air as we walked. Mother never came, at first because she'd felt it was not her celebration, this English riot, but then because she recognised it was something we did, Father and I, this tough little doctor and the awkward, lumbersome girl who was both his daughter and was not.

Sometimes I know a thing moments before it happens, and so it was just then. I felt all at once a perturbation of the air outside, a sudden rising in my throat. I sat up with a gasp and shot my legs out straight, sending the bed-warmer to the floor. Then came the banging on the front door.

II

IT WAS A heavy fist on the oak, pounding hard and without pause, and each new thud seemed to shake the house. I lighted my candle and went out into the passage.

There stood Father, in his nightshirt, underlit by his own candle, wigless and wide-eyed. He looked tiny there, and lost, as if still caught in the net of a dream. I wanted to take him in my arms and hush him back to sleep as he had when I was small. I went to the window at the top of the staircase and peered through the mullion.

'It's Gabriel,' I said with relief. 'I'll let him in.'

'Wait,' Father said, and there was something in his voice that made me look at him, and then again through the window.

Gabriel Tomkins, my father's oldest friend, near enough an uncle to me, stood at the door, still thumping. 'Ezekiel!' he shouted now. 'Open up.' Behind him, on the pathway, were gathered others I knew: Old Joll and Nasty Face among them. But there were strangers, too, some of them in the lane, mounted on dark, impatient horses. Those at the back wore bee-skep masks, or had blackened their faces, as if ready for a run. They carried blunderbusses and brass musketoons, had cutlashes and carbines at their waists. The fear I'd felt in bed came back to me as I turned to my father.

Mother appeared and we stood all three of us on the landing as the thuds went on. Now there was the sound of an axe against the door. 'Goody,' Father said, and he reached around his neck and took his keys. 'You look after these, just until this is resolved. I'll go down and speak with him.'

'No, Ezekiel!' Mother let out something like a sob. 'Let us make for the cellars.'

'Come, my love,' he said, taking her hands in his and placing a kiss on her forehead. 'It's Gabriel. We'll be able to reach some accommodation.'

There was the sound of splintering from below. My father opened the window and leaned out. 'I'll be down presently, Gabriel,' he said. 'Call your axe-man off. I'm fond of my front door.' He was a minute or two in his dressing room, emerging in his long coat, buckled boots shining and his periwig like a great cauliflower on his head. I watched him go down the stairs and out of sight. Then I heard the door open.

III

MOTHER AND I waited, crouched above my candle. I still had Father's keys, hot and rusty in my hand. I could hear Gabriel's deep rumble, the occasional word from Old Joll on the path. My father was mostly silent, or it may have been that I didn't catch his voice. Finally he appeared again, his face peeping up around the turn of the stairs.

'Alma, Goody, get dressed. We need to go with them.'

'No, Ezekiel, we mustn't.'

'There's been a misunderstanding,' Father said. 'Someone's fouled up. I'll take Gabriel down to the cellars and we'll recount the goods.'

I went back into my chamber and took off my nightgown. I hung the keys around my neck, pulled on a shift and cloak, a pair of stockings and Francis's old boots. I dressed like a man, Father used to say, frowning. I waited for Mother, who came out in her black mantua. We surveyed each other by the light of my candle. I didn't know her well, this woman I called

Mother, not as I knew my father. She was as obscure as the potions and unguents she concocted in her jars and albarellos below, the mysterious wise woman to my father's bluff country doctor. We went down the stairs together, slowly.

Father was already standing out in the road and I saw that they'd bound his hands. Gabriel's long, lined face was set hard and he wouldn't look at me or my mother as Old Joll and Nasty Face ushered us out of the garden. I wondered what had happened to the watch, to the people who'd thronged Rectory Lane earlier, to the servants who lived above the stables. It was silent in the mist, only the hollow bark of a man in a bee-skep mask coughing, the rattle of a cutlash at someone's waist. The horses had their hooves padded in sackcloth. Nasty Face took me by the arm, and I saw only the half of his face that was pink and waxy from the scalding he'd had by his drunken mother as a boy. No hair grew on his head there, nor eyebrows nor lashes, and the eye scarcely opened. I'd had nightmares about him as a child; I had them still.

We marched down the lane without speaking, the quiet thud of the horses' hooves behind us, the clack of swords around and ahead. We passed the dying fire in the Hundred Place but there was no one around it now, and the mist above the embers glowed, flakes of light rising every time a log or branch shifted. Father walked in front, tied hands before him. They had left my mother and me unbound and I thought for a moment of reaching for the sword at Nasty Face's waist. But there were a dozen of the smugglers, and the Revenue men, if they were here at all, were by now certainly drunk and most of them already in the pocket of Gabriel and the Mayfield Gang. Even if we yelled, we'd only wake townsmen who were smugglers themselves, or who profited from the free trade. I thought of Mayor Parnell bringing up wine from the Brotherhood cellar. Or Jurat Garland, the chamberlain, who found bales of tobacco in his stables, calico and Hollands for his wife. Often I'd been the one to leave them there. It was even rumoured that Albert Nesbitt, the richest and most powerful man in Winchelsea, paid for the upkeep of Greyfriars, his vast and gloomy home, with money tithed from the Gang.

So we made our way in silence, strange pilgrims, past the canted gravestones of the ruined church of St Giles, past Deadman's Lane, down towards the south of the town, towards the sea.

IV

WE CAME TO rest beside the old gibbet on Great Gallows Hill. In front of us were all the ruins of the southern end of town, the three hospitals and bailiffs' court, the old prison and alehouses, now just roofless pillars of stone drifting in and out of the mist. I heard birds passing above us, fieldfares, I thought, their lonely twits falling down through the dark. I had hope, even then. My father had been in tight spots before, had stood up to Revenue men and dragoons, had broken wild horses and been charged by bulls. He was barely five feet high in his heeled boots, but I had faith in him, that he would steer us through whatever lay ahead.

I saw that Father was looking over towards St John's, dimly visible in the mist. There were steps down to the Under-Reach beneath a grate in the crumbling ruins of the old hospital. I felt them always in the ground below me, the warren of ancient vaults, the maze of tunnels connecting them. Often as I walked through Winchelsea I'd picture the dusty catacombs, imagine dropping through the earth to land in the close air of a cellar. 'We're not going down tonight,' Gabriel said, his voice cold as the mist. 'It's too late for that, Ezekiel. Minds have been made up.' He shook his head and turned to spit in the grass by the side of the road.

Nasty Face took Father's arm and tugged him onwards. Father stumbled now, as we picked up speed towards the New Gate, and Mother hurried to catch him, her silhouette hooded like a nun's. She took Father around the waist to steady him and I saw Nasty Face draw back, as if stung by the closeness between them. I was not born their daughter, and their blood was not my blood, but they had loved me as if I were their own, and I saw the strength it must have taken to live the lives they had, in a town whose people showed such interest in their neighbours. The Jurats hated Mother for being French, even though she'd fled her homeland when scarcely more than a child. Father drew their scorn for elevating himself, for being a university man, paid for by the Catholic Carylls. He served as the town's doctor as well as the Cellarman, and was a good and devoted physician, but he fell between worlds, being neither grandling nor peasant.

We passed over the wooden bridge that spanned the

town's dyke, through the New Gate, and out on to Trecherie Marsh, where there was no longer mist but a white fog so thick we could see but a few feet in any direction. The smugglers formed a ring around us, the horses at the rear; some of the men drew their swords, others trained their guns on us. Shepherded closer to my parents, I bent over them both, put a hand on each of their shoulders, these folk who had taken me in when I was still in my clouts, my true father unknown and my mother drowned in the Brede. We surprised a bird in the rushes and it rose up into the air, piercing the night with its alarm call. 'A redshank,' Father said, as if by instinct, that tic he had of naming everything, knowing everything. He turned up to me and spoke in a whisper. 'Goody, my love,' he said, and I could hear something catching in his voice, 'if anything should happen, go to Francis. He'll look after you.' The redshank was still calling, distantly.

Now that we were away from the town and any watching eyes, the smugglers lit their lamps. I saw Gabriel's face caught in the flare of a flint striker. Strange to see a man I'd always known to be smiling so transformed. Old Joll lit his pipe and began to sing a low shanty, his voice off-key, swagged in the fog. The horses were skittish behind, shuffling sideways. They could sense the depths beneath, the hidden pools in the marsh that would suck down a coach and four as if they'd never been. Gabriel, who knew the land better than anyone, went ahead, swinging his lantern before him, brightening the high sedge, the osiers and expanses of water, the endless mud and slub of

Trecherie. Before long I could hear the sea sucking and sighing, could feel the surge and ebb of the tide in the shifting land around us. We came out on to the beach at Pett and began to walk up towards the cliffs at Fairlight.

V

I STILL FELT a kind of serenity, even then. These men, the Mayfield Gang, had danced me on their knees when I was a child, gifted me toys and trinkets from France and Flanders. They had loved me. Old Joll had picked me up a shell on every beach he stepped upon. I kept them in a wooden box in my chamber and, some summer evenings when Father and Gabriel were drinking porter downstairs, Old Joll would come and sit at the end of my bed, pick the shells out one by one and tell me of battles against the wicked Castilians, or a night with a maid in Cádiz, or when he was shipwrecked on the Azores and had still remembered to slip a shell in his pocket for me, even though half his crew had drowned. It had given him hope, he'd said, to think of me in my bed in Paradise, while he waited for rescue on that bare and rocky shore.

My father was one of them; perhaps not in name – he was just Cellarman to the smugglers, as Browns and Brunes and de Bruynes had been Cellarmen since the town was founded – but the Gang's success had allowed him to live like a gentleman, practising his physicking as a kind of benevolence to the poor of the Marsh. And he knew, Father, and had told me many times, how much more decent the Mayfield smugglers were than the murderous Hawkhurst Gang, who ruled over Rye and had killed dozens of Revenue men, or the Groombridge Boys, who were wreckers at Birling Gap and thought nothing of luring a hundred souls to their deaths. Gabriel had been a Revenue man himself, had witnessed the corruption at the heart of the Customs and Excise, and said that he now saw free trading as a way of rebalancing the odds of a top-lofty world.

There was, though, like a shadow on my mind, the image of poor Jim Lawrence, stumbling under the weight of blows from the very men that surrounded us now. I had spoken to my father about the death of my friend; he'd wrung his hands and discoursed on bonds of trust and what it meant to break them, on the compact between smugglers and the sin of peaching. He'd had to let Gabriel deal with Jim as peachers had been dealt with since the days of Old Wynchelsea.

I turned all this over as we marched uphill in silence, past the few mean cottages that make up the village of Pett. We went single-file along a path through the furze until we were out on the bare clifftop, the sea's slow roar beneath. As we made our way along the cliffs the white fog moved in eddies about us, then lifted for a moment, and I saw the great moon over the water far below. Our little procession came to a halt at the highest point of the cliffs, above where the fulmars and Channel-geese nested in spring. Men got down from their horses and stretched.

My father stepped forward, towards Gabriel, and Mother drew close to me. Three smugglers in bee-skep masks came to hover nearby, weapons drawn. I realised that I wanted to laugh. It was absurd, this theatre of menace from men I knew loved Father. Then Gabriel began to speak, and it was as if he were reciting, his tone so low and flat.

'Ezekiel, we've paid you a tithe on our profits as the Mayfield Gang paid your father and his father, as owlers and free-traders unnamed and unnumbered paid your grandfathers going back to Edward Longshanks.' If these were not his words, then it was something close. Gabriel would not meet Father's eye, but spoke to his feet. 'We've paid you fairly and gave it the go-by when you diverted goods for your own consumption or that of your friends. You play the grand man, Ezekiel, with your Papist supporters, your Dublin degree and your travels, and yet we've been pleased to call you our friend and our ally.' Gabriel finally looked up, and I realised how it is possible not to know a man, however much you think you do. I had loved him as a child, Gabriel. Had waited at the window for his arrival, treasured the gifts and gewgaws he bestowed on me. Now I saw cold in those dark eyes. I saw how much he wished Father dead, and I knew that Father saw it, too.

'Gabriel,' my father said, holding out a hand towards his friend.

Gabriel pulled a sheaf of papers from his jacket. 'You know what this is? You think that because we aren't university men we don't know how to take records, how to keep our accounts? We've known for nigh-on six years. I want you to think about that, Ezekiel. Six years I didn't say aught, but sat and watched the sums grow, our profits shrink.' He threw the papers down at Father's feet. 'Do you even know how much it was? You must think me so very stupid – your old friend, who confided so much in you.'

'Gabriel,' Father said again. 'You don't understand . . .' I was behind him, and couldn't see his face, but I saw his shoulders begin to shake, and Mother went forward to embrace him. He lifted an arm to put it around her, the two of them drawn close within the circle of lights and men.

'Now,' said Gabriel, 'I understand well enough. You spend sufficient time with high folk, you begin to believe you deserve all the exuberances of their lives. You become graspy, place things before people. We were your path to gilded greatness and you took all you could take and more. And soon the sawbones was a physician, and you took to looking down on your own kind, on us, and when you look down on folk it's easier to guggle them.'

Nasty Face came up to whisper something to Gabriel, who turned and looked westwards, towards Hastings. An owl shrieked somewhere in the night and I pictured it sweeping low over the furze and heather, great eyes like lanterns. I offered up a prayer then, for Father, and I realise now that it was the last prayer I ever said, mouthed to the mist, to the owl, to the God I half-believed in. Then, without saying anything more, Gabriel took Father by his bound hands and dragged him away from Mother. Nasty Face seized her around the waist as she screamed and struggled, holding out her arms to Father, who was led quite meekly by Gabriel towards the cliff edge.

I still didn't think it would happen – the drawn flintlock, Father taking one step, another step, one more, and then absence. Just mist where he had been. I think I cried out, but it may have been the screams of Mother, who was being held by Nasty Face as Old Joll did something to her that made her twist and writhe. She was turned away from me and my eyes were on the space where Father had been, on Gabriel coming back, his face moist with mist or tears. My mother made a terrible retching sound, then she was down on her knees, her face in her hands. Before her, on the grass, I saw the long, wet shape of her tongue.

Gabriel came very close to me. I had dropped to a crouch, crippled by a pain that was like fretting or the worm: a griping, wrenching feeling that near gashed me in two. He took my hair in his hand and came close enough that I could taste the rankness of his breath, the stench of his body. 'A fortnight hence, we'll want to move the wares on. You'll be there, Goody, and you'll lead us through the tunnels, and you'll open the doors and you'll do everything your father did, but with less thievery and more deference. You're the Cellarwoman now – the first there's been. And if you give us one mote of trouble, we'll wring your liver out.' He let drop my hair and then the smugglers were gone into the mist, and Mother and I were alone on the clifftop.

I ran to the edge, lay on my stomach and looked downward. The tide was high and a procession of waves dashed themselves against the cliffs, their spume mixing with the roiling fog. My father was down there some-where in the water, struggling with his fettered hands, feeling the weight of his coat, desperate for breath. I was seized by a compulsion to throw myself after him, to dive into the waves and coil and jag like a seal until I found him. I'd rescue him as he had rescued me, all those years ago, from the swift waters of the Brede. I owed him as much. Then I felt a presence behind me and turned to see Mother, all in black, her hood down and her black hair about her face. She had her hand pressed to her mouth and through the fingers came a steady stream of dark blood.

VI

How WE MADE our way back home, I scarcely know. The mist had cleared and the first birds stirred in the hedges as we climbed up from the marsh. I remember that dawn was not far off when we passed through the New Gate, grey tinting the air over towards Rye, an equal light from the moon in the west. We walked like the survivors of some terrible war, Mother leaning against me, stopping every few steps to spit dark gules. The house was cold and still inside, as if it might have been empty for years. I called for the servants to come and tend to us, but they did not. All the fires were out, and it was only then, my mind hurrying over imagined conversations, threats and importunities, and settling upon the night-time flight of the servants I'd loved, that I recognised how alone we were, Mother and I, and that life had changed utterly for us.

I helped my mother into her glass-house, where she lay down very still on the bench while I began to rig about amongst the jars and vials, arranging the contents on the mixing bench. I pinched small clouds of spiders' webs from a jar and placed them in a mortar as I had seen my mother do. I added dried yarrow and marigold, strips of a bark I did not know but which, when I pounded it together with the cobwebs and yellow flowers, gave off a high, styptic scent. I took a gobbet of the paste, went over to my mother, and put it in her mouth. She began to chew. I sat myself beside her supine, death-white body, amid the plants and the vials, the flasks and retorts. As the light rose outside I could see us reflected in the long glass walls, our faces smeared with mud and blood. The only sounds were my mother wetly champing and the mad call of a storm-cock, somewhere off in the orchard.

The world had taken a dangerous tilt and we needed time to learn to walk in it. Those first few days after my father's death, I tended Mother, sitting with her in the glass-house, twisting and unknotting the threads of my feelings. I dusted and swept, I fed my father's horse, who whickered sadly in his stall, and all the while my grief became blacker and harder in my chest. In waking dreams as I went about the business of helping my mother regain her health, I saw my father, the green water all about him, caught by the grasping arms of weeds, sucked down, the frantic struggle, the moment between the letting go of air and the drawing in of water. I saw the stream of bubbles as he sank from sight. He was strong and weak all at once, my father. Like all fathers, I suppose.

We don't question enough, when young. It is clear to me now, looking back on my early life, that we

lived beyond the means of a doctor in a thinly popu-
lated village at an impecunious time in that bloody
century. We had a half-dozen servants, an equipage
and a library of rare and costful books. My father
went often to London to the theatre. He had noble
friends and set off to dine with them in the finest
clothes from the tailors on Jermyn Street. Our house
was large and well-appointed, with Dresden on the
tables, bottles of the choicest Burgundy lining the
steps down to the cellars. I had more dresses than I
would ever wear (indeed I would have happily burnt
them all, so little did I like it when my father fashioned me as a doll for balls and feast-days). I did not
ask from whence this good living came, for I knew
not the ways and wiles of the mercantile world. I
knew only that my father loved me, provided for me,
taught me near all I knew. And now I wondered
where I would find another father like my father, for
I had need of him yet.

VII

ON THE THIRD day, Albert Nesbitt came to visit. He
was the town's Magistrate and Justice of the Peace, the
Chief Jurat of the Cinque Ports, and at his waist and
jowls you could see all the luncheons he'd consumed
in the acquirement of those titles. He'd been a lawyer
in London, a speculator in grain and wool, and was
now second to his friend Henry Pelham in wealth and
influence in Sussex. He told anyone who asked (and
many who did not) that he intended to restore

Winchelsea to the prominence it had once enjoyed as the principal port of the realm.

Nesbitt brought his son Arnold with him, a wigless, fleshless version of his father, not yet five-and-twenty but as gravous as an undertaker, all black linen and full of the seriousness of the university man. I showed them into the parlour where Albert sat with a heavy exhalation on the sofa, Arnold perching beside him. The older man said, 'Very good,' and from the younger issued a nasal, 'Just so.'

Mother was still in her glass-house, laid out on the bench from which she had not moved since our return from Fairlight. I had arranged some blankets upon her, a pillow beneath her head, and made her as comfortable as I was able. Conscious that I was now the woman of the house, I went off to brew some tea — we had nothing else to offer, no dainty bites nor sweetmeats; indeed we had barely eaten since my father's death. When I returned with the pewter pot and Mother's Sèvres teacups, the room was silent. I poured and served the Nesbitt gentlemen and everything seemed over-loud — the rattle of the china, the 'Thank you, miss' of Arnold, the 'Very good' of his father. The older man drew a watch from the pocket of his waistcoat, tutted, replaced it, and scratched at his wig. 'Dreadful business, what?' he said at last, looking closely at me. 'Your mother is . . . still with us?'

'Yes, sir,' I said, sitting in my father's chair, my back straight. Every word I spoke threatened to unloose the tears that had lodged themselves permanently behind my eyes, giving everything a muffled, bunged-up feeling, as if I were addressing the world through a cloud.

'I'm glad. I liked your father. I was sorry to hear of his passing. Jacobite, wasn't he? Papist? But none-theless . . . This is no good, no good at all. You may depend upon it that I will be taking it up with the Jurats at the next meeting of the Brotherhood and Guestling.'

The sound of Arnold Nesbitt's spoon in his teacup, circling.

'You needn't do so on our part, sir,' I said. I knew that the men who had killed my father would furnish the meeting with tea and wine, and that his killing would have been sanctioned by the Jurats with a nod, a grimace, as if such grubbiness were beneath them. They would then return to their Burgundy and their Nevers faience, their tablecloths and Virginia tobacco, all of it uncustomed. 'It is not to the Jurats that we will look for restitution, with respect, sir. There is too much partiality amongst them.'

Albert Nesbitt placed his hands on his knees and leant forwards, face all brows and dark, calculating eyes. Looking at him, I saw all at once the formidable man he must have been in his London days, the ruthlessness that still lurked beneath the luncheons. 'You show a deal of spirit, young lady,' he said. 'Perhaps too much, given your circumstances. We of the Brotherhood want only what is best for the Cinque Ports, for our town. Your father, I believe, was intercepting funds destined for more laudable ends. I hope you will prove more trustworthy.' He pivoted forward on the silver point of his cane and rose to his feet.

I showed the two men to the door. Albert pressed my hand to his lips and I felt how hard-set they were.

Then Arnold bade me farewell. In the glare of the entrance lamp I could see he was angular, strung too thinly over his bones, his face dainty as a girl's. I was taller than him, but not by much, and so when he leaned to speak with me, I felt his lips brush against my ear.

'Miss Brown,' he said, 'you should take steps to ensure your safety. I know the men who did this to your father. Who acted with such barbarity to your mother. I notice your servants have forsaken you. I could recommend replacements who would also act as your safeguarders.'

'My mother and I will do quite well without servants, thank you, Mr Nesbitt,' I said, drawing back a little. His father harrumphed on the pathway.

'I hope, then, that we might see you at Greyfriars before too long. You and your mother would be most welcome.' He bent his lips to my hand and I saw that his hair was thin at the crown and that he'd swept strands of it over to hide the circle of scalp. I watched them until they turned out on to Rectory Lane and then shut the door.

I went in to sit with my mother, who raised her head and attempted a smile from a mouth that was livid with bruises. 'It's time for us to call on Francis,' I told her. 'I'm going to Dymchurch.' She nodded and then lay back down and closed her eyes once more.

VIII

I RODE HERO, my father's horse, to Romney Marsh later that day. I'd left Mother sitting in her glass-house, leaning forward to the long window like a plant reaching for light. I had placed a bowl of bread soaked in milk, some stewed apples on the table for her – a still life that glowed in a bar of sunlight. I tied my bonnet, wrapped my travelling cloak about my shoulders and took some money from the drawer of my father's desk. I saw his pen there, his pipe, sheaves of paper covered with his small, familiar writing. It was too soon, and I felt my grief billow like a dark sail above me. I stumbled out to the stables and saddled Hero, then set off through the Land Gate and down the hill out of the town.

We crossed by the ferry. The ferryman poled us over the Brede, his blind dog curled in the prow of the boat while Hero snorted in the damp air, shifting his weight as the ferry crossed. Hero was an old grey, patient as a physician's horse must be, accustomed to waiting saddled outside the hovels of the marsh whilst my father went in to bleed or birth or commiserate. It was Hero he'd been riding sixteen years earlier when, in the early darkness that a summer storm brings, he'd seen my blood-mother jump into the Brede at Tanyard Piece, had galloped alongside the river until he reached the little beach by Elizabeth's Well and waded in. He'd tried to save us both, Father said, but my mother's dress weighed her down and her skin was slippery, as if she were already a sea creature, abandoned to the deep. She'd been holding on to me, my father said, but when she saw he had me, she let go.

I came into Rye over the marsh, the red-brick town rearing up before me in the afternoon light. Smoke was rising from the clustered chimneys of the town and I could hear the call of fishermen down by the river.

I trotted up Cinque Ports Street, feeling a kind of shame in the pleasure I took being out in the wide air after so long cabined with my mother. Then the town was behind me and the flatness of the marsh spread out on all sides; I allowed Hero to break into a lumbering Canterbury gallop as we cut across the damp land to the sea. We saw nothing move but the sheep and the geese, heard no sound save the wind in the reeds, Hero's bellowed breaths, the thud of hooves on grass.

When we reached Camber, the tide was far out, sand blowing across the beach in lines. The dunes were covered in spiky clouds of buckthorn, whose orange berries I had a great taste for, and I stooped to pick some as we went by. I loved the sea, particularly here where it met the long sweep of sand. It was where I came to swim, and had done since Francis had taught me as a child, the two of us plunging into the ocean in all weathers.

The further you get into the Marsh, the meaner the dwellings become, as Camber unravels into Jew's Gut, then Lydd, then New Romney, then, finally, Dymchurch, perched on the edge of the land just past the bill of Dunge Ness, as sorry a village as you'd care to see.

I first tried Francis's house, a tumbledown cottage overlooking the ocean, fishing nets strung up in the little garden, a wind-beaten look to the weatherboards and windows. I knocked and entered. It was dim and quiet within and I stood and surveyed the detritus of my brother's life: a fire burnt out in the grate, bottles upended on the earthen floor, a rude collection of coverlets heaped on a paillasse in one corner. Everything was shrouded in dust and grime and stank strongly of fish. There was nothing on the walls save, above the pile of bedding, a series of three cameos: myself, my mother and my father.

I left Hero chewing marram grass in the garden and walked along the coast road until I came to the centre of the village. A tavern named the Ship sat there on the front between the boarded-up butcher's shop and the shipwright, as ravaged by the elements as Francis's cottage. I pushed open the door and stepped inside. There was no one to receive me in the dark and slovenly saloon, so I went through a narrow passage to a room at the back of the tavern. There, face-down on the bar, his arms wide-spread, was Francis.

IX

I PLACED MY hand on that familiar shoulder, and he stirred, turning his head on the bar and mumbling something in his sleep. I looked at his face, or the half that was turned to me. He'd aged even since last I'd seen him, a few twists of white in that coarse dark hair, a certain roughness to his cheeks above a scratchy beard. He wore a golden star pierced into the lobe of his ear which I had not seen before. Francis opened his eyes and I perceived bafflement, then pleasure as he rose straight-wise. I saw myself as he must see me, in my travelling cloak and dimity bonnet: a woman.

'Goody!' he said, and there was wonder in his voice. Then he looked at me and his own face darkened in reflection of what he saw in mine. 'Goody,' he said again, and I stumbled towards him, and it was as if all that had been held inside since the night of the Bonfire Rejoicings was loosed from me. I felt myself sobbing, heavy in his arms, breathing in the familiar scent of him. Such relief in feeling weak again. I know not how long we were pressed together like that, but finally the tears abated and we moved to a bench in the corner of the saloon.

Francis held my hands in his as I spoke. 'Our father is dead,' I said to him, surprised at the ease with which the words escaped me. I watched him, this man who had been my brother, who had been my parents' child long before me and had carried me swaddled on his shoulder as a babe. I read his face like a landscape changing under passing weather. We had lost something together, Francis and I, and it seemed to call up all those originary losses, the deep sorrows we also shared. He, too, was an orphan.

I should say a few brief words about his past here: born on a plantation in the Brazils, shipped to Antwerp, escaped from the slaver-ship off Dunge Ness Head, rescued by Ezekiel. He was Winchelsea's first dark-skinned resident, much admired by visitors, accepted by the locals for his good humour and dexterity on land and at sea. Even though he was now past thirty, even though he had quarrelled with our father and drawn himself away from us, I could see rising in him at the news of our loss the abandoned waif he once was. Gradually, though, I saw his sorrow replaced by something else: a hardness, fury, resolve. I recognised it because I felt these things myself, felt them in all the chambers of my heart.

'And Mother?' he asked.

'She is . . . Francis, they cut her tongue from her.'

'Aye, that is their way. Dumb folk don't peach. I must go to her.' He rose to his feet. I had forgotten how large he was, the power of his heavy arms and shoulders. 'You have a horse? I am currently . . . between horses.'

'That sounds uncomfortable.' I smiled through my tears. 'We can walk together.'

We went through the town, past its sad-appearing church, the vicarage and many smaller, rougher homes, hastily built, all facing on to the beach and the rolling waves. Boats were resting on the shingle on their keels and men stood here and there, unknotting their nets and smoking in silent groups. When we arrived at the cottage, Francis went inside and came back out with a haversack over his shoulder. He wore a long dark coat and at his waist hung a pair of pistols. With the gold star at his ear and his hair wild in the sea wind, he looked for all the world like a privateer. I collected Hero from where he was still cogitatively cropping the grass and we set off together.

We left the village and went along the dunes at Camber, then skirted to the south side of Rye. It was market day, and stalls had been set up at the bottom of the cliff upon which Ypres Tower sits. This was the place where free-traders unloaded those goods they did not move on to London: crates and barrels of uncustomed tea and brandy stood beside the stalls, while all about unspeakable-looking men carried out whispered negotiations, overseen by the Jurats and other representatives of the Cinque Ports who stood in ceremonial robes and stamped transactions with their seal of approbation.

Just as we were coming round to where the river

bends beneath the cliff face, I saw, aside from the general mass of townsfolk, a man mounted on a fine black horse. He was blade-slender, handsome, and wore a midnight-blue coat with gold brocade, a silver sword at his waist and buckles on his boots that were large and faceted in the Paris style. I figured him around five-and-thirty; he wore no wig but a profusion of dark hair fell down from under his hat, which was also blue and trimmed with filigree. As we passed before him, he lifted this hat.

'Good morning, Francis, miss.' His voice was low and rich and tinted with Sussex.

'Arthur,' my brother said.

'I heard about Ezekiel,' said the man. 'My condolences. The Mayfield Gang are a rough bunch.'

'No rougher than your own.'

'Come and call on me, Francis, once you've done your obsequies. We have much to discuss.'

We walked on a little and, looking over his shoulder, Francis said a name: 'Arthur Gray.' I knew him as the chief of the Hawkhurst Gang and a most fearful villain. We went on in silence, crossed the Brede at the ferry and then climbed the hill to Winchelsea. We paused for a moment at the gate to Paradise while I stabled Hero, and then I watched Francis gather himself for the meeting ahead.

X

MY BROTHER LET out a low sound, of recognition or sorrow I knew not, then walked before me up the path between the rows of lacecaps, their flowers like the grey ghosts of summer. I saw the door open when we were halfway up the path, and there was my mother, stooped, robed in black. Francis hurried, almost ran, dropping his haversack and bending to take her small frame in his great arms. I found myself thinking how strange it was that the tiniest of couples had adopted unto them two such swanking young people. I saw tears on my mother's face when at last she emerged from his embrace. Mothers love their sons with a special fierceness, and for all her inscrutability, I knew this of Mother: she adored Francis.

I felt I'd been long gone from Paradise, far longer than a few hours, although the house was just as I had left it, but colder now. The food lay untouched on the table. No fires burned in the rooms and the only sign of change was in my mother's glass-house, where jars balanced in profusion along the length of the table; there were powders in mortars, liquids bubbling above candle flame, albarellos of unguents and potions pitched hither-thither. Francis lit a fire in the parlour and sat upon the sofa beside my mother, compassionating gently with her. I busied myself in the kitchen, preparing a stew for our supper. I had not been called upon to cook much previously, but had watched the maids at work many times, and I sliced and stirred and simmered in mimick of them.

It grew dark early and we sat ourselves at the dining table in the hallway, where my father's empty seat was like a reprimand to the pleasure we took in being together. The warmth slowly spread through the house from the fires that Francis and I had lit, the glow from the candelabras on the table. Francis had poured porter for us, although my mother didn't touch her glass. She took delicate, wincing bites of food – the stew was not over-good and I fancy her mouth troubled her greatly – but Francis ate heartily, going back into the kitchen to scrape the pan for more. He made many appreciative noises, then leaned back in his chair and lit his pipe. The smell of tobacco, the fire-blaze, the sight of Mother and Francis in the gentle after-supper hour – all of this seemed snatched from another, kinder time.

Francis finished his pipe, banged out the embers on his plate, and drew near to speak, his face all light and shadows from the candle flames. 'I will need to spend some time with Father's papers tonight. Then, tomorrow, I will go to Rye. The next run is ten days hence?' I nodded. 'So we have time. Now I must take myself another glass of porter and retire.' He pushed back his chair, stood and crossed to the door of my father's study.

Mother went to her glass-house, where she proceeded to illumine many candles, so that the conservatory became a beacon attached to the house. I knew not what draughts she concocted there, whether sanatives or deleteries, but only that when I went abed an hour later, having kissed Francis and selected a book from my father's shelves, Mother was still crouched over a bubbling pot, the candles around her lower now, the black shawl wrapped tightly about her shoulders. I stood awhile at the door, watching. She ran a finger along a row of jars, before pulling out an urn and emptying its contents into the bubbling pot before her.

I walked slowly up the stairs, the book under one

arm, my candle held out in the other. It was dark in my chamber, and cold. I disrobed swiftly and, realising anew that no servant was present to fill our washbowls or heat our bed-bricks, pulled on a pair of stockings and my thickest nightdress and stooped to light my fire.

XI

MY ROOM WAS next door to my brother's and as I lay abed, I could hear him moving about his own room, the occasional whistle or sigh. I had slept little the previous nights and the room was now warm and my bed well-decked with coverlets. I was drifting into sleep when there came a gentle tap on the door. I lighted my lamp and called out, 'Enter,' and there stood Francis in his nightshirt.

'I wished to bid you goodnight,' he said, coming further into the room. I sat up straightly, suddenly flustered by his presence, by the size and proximity of him. 'I realise that you have borne a great deal these past days,' he said. 'That you have taken upon yourself more than a young person should. Your father loved you more than he loved any thing in this world.' I nodded, and felt tears, which I allowed to flow without check. I looked up at Francis, who saw me, I felt, in all my distress, and he came and sat on the edge of the bed and took my hand in his rough, dry one very gently, as if it were something broken that required mending. He didn't speak, but allowed me to sob until I was exhausted and had pushed some of that dread away.

His voice, when he spoke again, was so soft and low that I had to lean towards him to hear it. 'We must discuss upon something, Goody,' he said.

'Anything.' I was still hiccoughing. Francis passed me a handkerchief.

'Father and I talked a long time hence about the likelihood of some such calamitous stroke befalling him. This was before he and I broke ways, but I made a vow then and I'll keep it now. I swore both to vouchsafe you and Mother and to do my best to ensure the continued supply of funds to Father's affairs.'

'His affairs?'

'He did not speak to you of his activities? You didn't think he was keeping all the gain for himself?'

'I knew little of his business dealings.'

'The more can wait. For now, you must have confidence in the justness of his cause, in the great necessity of our maintaining our control over the cellars, over Winchelsea.'

'Is this about the King Over the Water?' I felt something tingle at the words. My father's adventures in the Jacobite cause had about them the nature of a fairy story for me. I remember the wistfulness with which he'd spoken of the Old Pretender, the sheen on his voice when he recounted some memory of Paris or Rome.

'Aye,' he said. 'The King is returning. Not James, but his son, Charles, whom Father knew when he was but a lad. And this time he will come with all the might of the French behind him. And the English will rise up and the Scots sweep down, and the German despot be chased into the sea. For now, though, all I wish to know is whether you desire me to find some quiet and distant refuge in which you and Mother might evade what danger is to come, or if you will remain at Paradise. Father counselled the former, but I know you are a girl of strong sentiments and will wish to do your own decidement.'

I gave him a hard look. Firstly, that he had called me a girl, when everything that had passed since Father went over the cliff had made me feel my grown-uppedness, but also that something had discovered itself to me in those last few days. The world had been unkiltered by my father's fate and only through action would balance be restored. I knew I could not effect this requital without the help of Francis, but that he might attempt it without my participation hadn't occurred to me.

'I will stand beside you,' I said. 'I'm no girl, Francis. I shall be seventeen ere long. I'm strong and I'm clever. I warrant I know Winchelsea above as well, and below better, than you do. So no, I shall not burrow for safety like a vole. I am doughtier than you think, doughtier than Father held me to be.'

My tears had stopped and I felt calm. Francis let go my hand and sat regarding me for a time, his weight down-pitching the mattress, a quizzical smile twinkling his eyes.

'Why did you break with Father, Francis?' I asked, and then held my breath, for I was feared as to what might rush into the silence I'd made.

My brother looked at me, looked away, then spoke.

'Do you remember Jim Lawrence?'

I nodded.

'He was a friend of yours, as I remember it.' He stood, tapped out his pipe, pocketed it, then came to sit beside me on the bed again. 'I was a smuggler from the day I came to live here, when Father found me on the beach. Sailing or spiriting the goods away on shore, it didn't matter to me. I wished for him to be proud of me, and he was. But I saw too much killing when I was a child to countenance it here. Jim Lawrence was just a lad and Father ordered him murdered, and I've never forgiven him for that. Not even now that he's gone.'

'Tomkins killed Jim. I remember it. I saw it.'

Francis looked sharply at me. 'You did?'

I nodded.

'It was Father who discovered that Jim had been peaching,' Francis said. 'And Father that ordered Tomkins to kill him. It does that to you, the free trade. Makes you lose sight of what's important. He was a good lad, Jim. I said things to Father that night that were hard to come back from. I went to work for the Hawkhurst Gang for a time, then I took up as a fisherman. I'm poor now, Goody, but I sleep. To speak of which, we have much ahead of us. I am glad to be back in this house, in spite of the tidings which have brought me here. Now I must think. There are testing times ahead.'

Francis stood, smoothed my hair, and leant to extinguish the lamp. I saw the shadow of him pass across the room in the firelight, then heard the door close and the creak and sigh as he entered his own bed. I lay sleepless for a long while, turning over my thoughts like stones, examining them in turn, attempting to understand the world in the light of the information I had acquired. It was not a shock, this revelation of my father's part in Jim's death, and it was this that sat most ill with me – the fact that somewhere in my heart I had known that he was more intimately concerned in that dreadful act than he'd admitted to me. I'd been a child when he'd told me, but children see the truth of things better than older folk, or so it sometimes seems to me. When I slept, I know not, but I slept sounder for my brother being there on the other side of the wall.

XII

THE NEXT MORNING I was up early, before even my mother. It was still dark outside, the storm-cock calling in the orchard, the wind gusting in the chimney as I lit a fire in the scullery. I pulled a shawl around my nightgown and went out into the damp air to draw water from the well, the metal of the windlass cold against my skin, my clogs echoing in the courtyard. I fed the horses, picked one of the last apples, bit into it and looked around the garden. Ivy snaked along the ground and twined around the lower limbs of the apple trees and the quinces, some of the dark vines still bearing their tiny chandeliers of flowers. I couldn't have slept for more than an hour or two after my encounter with Francis, but I felt extraordinary energy within, stirred by the dying life of an autumn garden.

I put a pan of pottage on the stove to simmer and sat waiting for Francis to descend. In fact, it was my mother who came first, in her nightdress, hair crazing about her head. She took my face in her hand, nodded, and placed a kiss on my forehead. We sat in companionable silence for a half hour, communicating – if such a word can encompass what passed between us – with a series of smiles and frowns, a language that was all our own and seemed more eloquent than when we'd had the luxury of words. Then she rose and went off to her glass-house from whence, soon enough, I heard the clatter of jars, the pounding of her pestle. It was past nine of the clock, and I went to dress, taking a bowl of water with me to clean my face and feet. On the way up the stairs, I met Francis, who appeared much excited.

'I have received communication from Gabriel,' he said, holding a letter up to the light. 'He wishes to move swiftly. We must be swifter. I suggest we parlay with Arthur Gray at Rye. I have arranged a meeting at the Mermaid at six tonight. Make sure you're ready.'

As it was, Francis and I spent the day together, mostly sitting in the parlour, watching the minutes tock by on my father's old clock. The house still struck me as unnaturally quiet, without the bustling enterprise of my father, without the tuneless whistle of the stable boy, or the fussing of the other servants. Francis told me no more of his plans, and I chose not to ask. Instead we spoke of practicable things: the horses, the marketing trip I must make before we departed, the question of Mother's soundness of mind – this last in low voices. She was again in her glass-house, pistillating, brewing. Weird mists and miasmas emanated from her chamber: the scents of earth, vinegar, blood. Her hair she wore unkempt, her skin was dull and smutty. She had always been unconventional, offering the townsfolk her herbs as an alternative to my father's university-learnt medicine. Now, though, it was as if she were lost in her lores and receipts, only able to find meaning in the combination of roots, leaves and powders.

'I fear for her reason,' Francis said. 'Her senses have been unmoored by it all. There will be time enough after all is done to tend to her. And knowing that we have achieved our reckoning, that her husband is venged, this may go some way to righting the vessel of her mind.'

I put on my calash and cape to go marketing. The roads were miry in the mizzle; pigs rootled in amongst the tufts of grass and florets of dandelion that grew along the middle of the road. Winchelsea had about it a bleak, ill-used air that day, with dark clouds overhead and the threat of more rain. I made sure my bonnet was well-tied over my head, and leapt between puddles all the way to the butcher on the High Street, thence to the grocer by the Strand Gate. I talked as little as possible to Mr Webb the butcher, nor to the interchangeable girls who worked behind the counter in the grocer's, who were bedazzled by my presence and the scandal of death. They asked me question after question, calling me 'Miss Goody' as if we were acquaintances of old, but I answered laconically and beat my escape as swiftly as I could.

It was already growing dark when I returned home, discharged my marketing bags and fetched together a light supper for Francis and Mother. When we'd eaten, Francis and I rose from the table and made our way upstairs to dress. I wore clothes that obscured my sex, and marked me neither as servant nor master: a tunic of dark linen, a black jerkin, black hose and boots. I tied my hair up and fitted it beneath a black tricorne hat. I looked at myself in the glass for a moment and was pleased to see a stranger, one who might do anything, if called upon, even unto murder. Francis was waiting for me at the bottom of the stairs when I descended. He looked as dashing as he had when, as a young man, I'd seen him fligged in the latest fashions, dancing the *passepied* with a host of beauties at the Hastings Ball. He too was decked out in black, save for a shirt of crisp white linen and buckles on his boots. He smiled when he saw me.

'You are ready?' he said.

'Aye,' I said back.

'I'm glad to hear it. You look like a highwayman. Now wait, I have one last accoutrement for you.' He turned to retrieve something from the table and, quite reverentially, handed me my father's sword. It was a beautiful rapier with bronze quillions, its scabbard engraved with oak leaves. It was very old, so my father had told me, having been with the Browns since the wars against the French, since the days of Old Wynchelsea, perhaps. It had hung on the wall of his study and I had crept in there sometimes when he was out on his rounds, to draw it, silently, and admire the keenness of its edges, to see myself in the blade. 'I've sharpened it for you,' Francis said. I attached the scabbard to my belt, took a few steps, drew the sword and replaced it. 'Pray God you won't need it, tonight at least. Let's bid farewell to Mother and be off.' I saw, as he turned, that beneath his cloak Francis did not wear a sword, but rather his flintlocks, with long muzzles like the beaks of wading birds.

I stood at the door while he went into the glass-house and embraced our mother, told her we'd be back that night, that she wasn't to worry, but that if we failed to return by the morrow, she should go to West Grinstead, to the Carylls. She nodded like a child at these instructions, then gestured for me to enter. I stepped into the room, feeling the weight of the sword at my waist. When I leant to kiss her, she held out to me a spoon upon which sat a pale green paste. She pointed to her own mouth and smiled. The paste was chalky and bitter-tasting, drying as I chewed. I swallowed it and felt at once a great warmth and strength spreading within me, as if a fire had been lit within. I squeezed her hand and followed Francis out into the evening.

XIII

WE RODE DOWN to the ferry, side by side on the empty streets. There were enough left of the day's dregs to make out the shadows of coppices on the hills as we descended. I sat atop Hero, Francis on one of my father's piebalds. There was no one about but we could hear music and voices from the Salutation, owls echoing forth and back in Windmill Wood, the breath and clop of the horses. When we came around the bend by the King's Cliffs, where the road drops sharply down to the marsh, we saw the lights of Rye, a half-moon low over the water, fast-moving silver clouds. Francis was silent, his wide-brimmed hat drawn low over his face, his cloak long and black, so that he gave the air of a great night-bird flapping above a stream. I carried a lantern on my pommel, but had trimmed the light low. We dismounted and picked our way carefully down the steps to the ferry.

The water was flowing swiftly that night, in streaks of black and silver, frowning every so often under a gust of wind. I never crossed the Brede without thinking of my mother – my real mother – swept away in its currents. It was perhaps her watery end that made me the swimmer I was, a means of drawing closer to her. I trailed my fingers in the water as the ferryman poled us across, feeling connected to the woman who'd birthed me, who'd almost drowned me, and whose blood beat in my veins.

We mounted and set out upon the road through Trecherie Marsh, so-named because of the number of men and horses that had lost their lives within it. Now it sat under a low blanket of mist. We rode side by side, our eyes fixed on the town ahead of us, islanded in the mist. I'd always used a man's saddle, not having any time for the niceness of side-riding, despite my father's imprecations. I remember Mrs Nesbitt, the Magistrate's wife, coming to remonstrate with my mother about my unladylike gadding about on Hero. They had commiserated together at how provokingly I did insist on unwomaning myself. The Nesbitt woman was dead now, my father too, and I rode tall with my sword clacking at my waist.

Rye loomed up ahead, windows and house-lanterns glowing. We could hear the creak and slop of the boats in the harbour, the shouts of sailors on the quayside, the rumourous hum of the town. Francis leant over and took my elbow for a moment, gently lifting my hand from the hilt of my father's sword. 'Are you ready, Goody?' he said, a note of humour in his voice, but serious too, so that I became suddenly very sober, and looked at him in his eyes.

'Yes, I am,' I said, not quite sure of it and gripped by a lurching feeling at the thought of what lay ahead, although this was as much excitation as fear.

'We shall not require bravery so much as wisdom this night,' he said. 'Our bravery will be needed later.'

'Let us go, then.' We rode together over the bridge, past the quayside and up Mermaid Street, between houses that leaned their facades from either side as if bending the ear of their neighbour. Moonlight silvered the cobbles and the street echoed with hoof-beats. We dismounted outside the Mermaid, the smugglers' tavern, a place that lived for me only in the world of rufflery and ill-report.

XIV

WE LED THE horses through the coach passage, a narrow tunnel within which rang shouted conversations, shanties and the clash of tankards. I paid the ostler, a swarthy, narrow-faced man, who took the horses with a curse and led them across the yard to the stables. Francis and I walked up the back steps of the public house together, then he opened the door and we were inside. A sudden and discomfiting silence: the shanties stopped, the man at the spinet played a closing chord, then turned on his stool to regard us. Now only the sound of the bartender's wheezed breath, a dog scritting itself, a fart.

I surveyed the room, larger than it appeared from the outside: a sprawling, low-slung saloon with many small declivities and recesses. Never had I seen so many scars and skin prints, eyepatches and ear-drops. Every table bore sufficient flintlocks and muskets to double as a gun show; great fowling pieces and bayonetted matchlocks leant against the tables or hung by their straps with assorted bandoliers over the backs of chairs. It was a den of brigands, no question, an air about the tavern as if violence were on the cusp of breaking out, or had only just abated. There was not another female within the place.

Near the door sat a group of long-haired men playing cards, their eyes fixed narrowly on the game. By the window a couple of jagged clerks in dark vestments were bent over a hand-bill. In one corner I espied a vast man made vaster still by the horse-hide coat he wore. He sat holding an enormous musket, more like an arquebus, across his knees, and as we came further in he turned towards us, glowering through his beard.

My attention was drawn finally to the large table in the centre of the room. Here, surrounded by a brigade of sinister figures in leathern jerkins, each of them decked in jewels and bangles, sat a man with a face like a glazed ham, complete with fatty scar drawn down one side and peppercorn eyes. I could smell the rum about him from three yards. It felt as if the room were waiting for him to speak.

'Francis Brown, if I'm not a blind cur. Come back

to haunt the beast that birthed him. Join us, boy. And bring your lady friend. Grog for Francis, Ketch, and swift about it. For both of them.'

Chairs were pulled back for us and I found myself between Francis and a young man with a ratty beard who was chewing on a thin briar pipe. He took it out to nod at me and said his name was Smoker. I made myself look the men around the table in the eye, aware that I was being judged and measured. Our grog arrived and I made as if to draw down a gulp whilst allowing but little into my mouth. Even the tasting brought water from my eyes. The ham-faced man noticed and laughed a high squeal. 'Wenches can't hold grog like we can, eh, Francis? Now introduce me to your friend, will you?'

I watched Francis smile, sip his grog, could feel the whirl of his mind as he looked from the man to me and back again. 'You heard of the death of my father,' he said.

'Your stepfather. Yes, I did. Sad. My condolences.'

'Thank you. This is Goody; she is my sister, if not of blood then of deeper stuff'n that. We are settling up our father's estate, tying those threads that are loose when a man goes before he expected to.'

The man looked closely at me. 'I'm sorry for your loss, young lady,' he said.

'Thank ye, sir.' My voice came out low and foreign-sounding.

'He was a good man. Fell in with the wrong crowd, those Mayfield villains, did Ezekiel, but always dealt fair by folk, he did. Didn't deserve what happened to him. My name's George Kingsmill. Mayhap you've heard of me.'

'Mayhap I have, sir. I believe you're with the Hawkhurst Gang, sir, and are brave or bloodthirsty depending whom you're listening to.'

'P'rhaps a touch of both, young lady. Like your brother here. A dandy and a fop on land, but once you got him on a ship he was monstrous. I've seen him hack wenches and bairns apart without blinking. The deck like a butcher's apron . . .' This last brought hacking laughter from Smoker and the others. 'Lookin' at you with that sword at your waist, I reckons you share some of your brother's viciousness, if not the colour of his skin. Do you also share his love of a gigue? Let's have some music, boys! Another round of drinks, Ketch! Rare to have a friend like Francis back.' The man at the spinet began to play again, and Kingsmill bellowed along with the rest of the room, crying, *O for the sea and the fast-flung spray!* Francis sang as loud as our host, and soon they were both standing, arms around one another's shoulders, and even the clerks by the window were roaring along.

An hour later, or five hours, I knew not, for I was drunk as I'd never been drunk in my life, I looked around as if waking from a reverie. It was far from pleasant, this drunkenness, and I was haunted by the feeling that I'd betrayed myself as I'd sunk further into my cups. As a Cellarman, my father had warned me of the dangers of spiritous liquor, but had allowed me to taste some of the choicest wines of the Winchelsea store, although never in sufficient quantity to give me this sensation, which came and went in waves, of being breathless and dry-mouthed and barely in command of myself.

Francis and Kingsmill were in close confabulation, their chairs pulled out from the table and turned towards one another. They hunched their shoulders over their tankards, and would shake occasionally, laughing at some shared memory. I didn't know this Francis, who seemed suddenly rougher and more man-like than the brother I knew. I didn't believe for one instant the slander that Kingsmill had aimed at him – my Francis was no child-murderer; indeed it was the killing of a child that had caused him to break with my father. I'd seen him on runs when I was a child and he was cool and deviceful and cunning, but never over-bold or hard with the men. If there was word of the Revenue, he'd be for snaking back into the tunnels rather than risking confrontation.

Yet looking at him now, matching Kingsmill tankard for tankard, a devilish air about him as his earring caught the firelight, I found myself conjuring other dark pasts for him, ones obscured rather than revealed by the closeness that lay between us. For who may say how well we truly know even those closest, when the heart is such an improvidential and obscure thing, and our secret desires and midnight acts may remain half-hidden even from ourselves?

Smoker kept pawing at my arm. 'The thing is,' he said, 'the thing is, you ladies don't un'erstand the sea. You've got no feel for it.'

I pictured myself far out in the bay, the feel of the godlike currents sweeping me out and back, landing me on the shore salty and breathless. I allowed myself a moment resting my head on my hands on the table. I didn't sleep, but rather dreamed, of swimming.

When I stirred, Smoker was lolling back in his chair, his head skewed to one side, a whistling snore escaping every so often. I stood, adjusted my sword, then walked over to the window where the two crow-like clerks had put away their bills and now sat in silence over their mugs of porter. I looked past them and out into the lamplit streets. The cobbles were newly wet from a passing squall and the town now bore a burnished aspect, the moon reflected on wet stones. It was twelve of the clock, I saw by one of the clerk's pocket fobs, and I felt a great weariness sink over me; then, as had now become a habit, I called to mind the face of my father, set my teeth against one another, and commenced to make silent, if still half-drunk, vows to the brave, silly self I saw reflected in the glass.

XV

THERE WAS A perturbation in the window, a movement that appeared at first like a flaw in the glass, but which I then perceived to be the reflection of the door on the far side of the saloon opening. A new hush fell upon the room. The gentleman who'd entered had left the door ajar and icy air rushed in after him, sobering those closest. The clerks beside me rose and pulled on their capes, then shuffled over to the corner of the room, so they might wait for the man to pass before effecting their departure. The gentleman was tall and black-haired, dressed in his dark blue jacket. It was Arthur Gray. His eyes appeared to fix upon me for a moment, although I could not read whether in recognition or curiosity. All who had been sleeping were now awake, Smoker rubbing his eyes and an older man, nudged awake by some foot, climbing up from the floor on to which he'd fallen an hour since. The room held quite still as the gentleman walked to the bar, where the keep had already poured out a glass of sack and was now busying himself arranging his tankards. The gentleman removed his three-cornered hat, swigged back the drink and turned.

'It appears that I have missed the celebration of your arrival.' He crossed the room and put a hand upon Francis's shoulder. 'Welcome, friend. Shall we repair to somewhere a little more private? I've been wanting to share a few words with you.'

'Certainly,' and Francis's voice was hard and cool again, the voice of my brother. 'You'll want my sister there too,' he said, gesturing towards me. 'This is Goody.'

'Yes, I rather think I shall. A swordswoman? Delighted.' A smile on thin lips. I saw that his dark hair was tied at the back with a velvet ribbon of the same blue as his coat and hat. He looked once around the room, gave a series of nods, and then ascended the narrow wooden stairwell that rose beside the fireplace.

Upstairs was a private dining room with a broad dark table and a dozen chairs. Candles had been lit upon it some time ago and were now dribbling in little pools on the wood. Francis and I sat either side of Gray, who was at the head in a chair somewhat more throne-like than the others. Soon, jangling up the stairs and filing into the room with the air of schoolboys feigning sobriety, came a selection of the men from below. Kingsmill was the last to enter and sat at the far end of the table, facing Gray. The keep came in carrying glasses, which he set on the table before returning with bottles of sack and Burgundy. Gray lifted his glass, inspected the wine. He sipped, looked faintly perturbed, then set it down.

'You know everyone here, I think, Francis? Perhaps young Smoker is new to you. Has Miss Brown been introduced?'

'I've met Smoker,' I said, 'and Mr Kingsmill.'

'Well, Goody,' and he said my name as if testing some new conjecture, 'here we have Diamond, Perin and Poison. And I'm Arthur Gray, of Seacox Heath.' Perin was the older man who'd been stretched out on the floor downstairs. Diamond had a stone set into one of his front teeth and grinned it at me. Poison was the giant I'd seen on first entering the Mermaid. He pulled at his beard when Gray said his name and looked my way with inexplicable ire. 'People have called us all sorts, Goody, but you'll no doubt have heard of us as the Hawkhurst Gang.'

'I know who you are, sir.'

'And no doubt you're much aggrieved at what befell your father.'

'Yes, sir. He did not deserve such a fate, nor did my mother.' I watched something flicker in his eyes when I said this.

'I knew Ezekiel. I was distressed both by the news of his passing and the manner in which he was so cruelly dispatched. The Mayfield Gang are indeed our countermates in the business, and yet you must believe me when I say that they are a black-hearted bunch, with Gabriel Tomkins the very devil at the helm.' I saw a look pass between Gray and Kingsmill. 'We would willingly put ourselves at your service if there were any way to remedy such a dreadful wrong.'

'I thank you, Arthur,' Francis said. 'I know that we have not always been likeminded on the finer points of our mutual enterprises, but I have watched the multiplication of your successes with no little admiration.'

At this, Kingsmill, who had eschewed the wine and continued to drink from his tankard, clanged it down on the table, spilling a pool of beer foam. 'Hark at him,' he said, looking towards the giant Poison, and to weaselly Smoker, and to the black-jerkined Diamond. 'Hark to the airs and graces he puts on.' Kingsmill's face was glowing brighter than ever now, the glazed slabs of his cheeks quivering with excitement. 'This is a fellow who swam to shore from a slaver-ship, who was to be sold in the Antwerp markets, whose father was a slave and his father a slave before him. And now he jaws on as if he'd been up to the universities and swallowed every book he'd lighted upon. We know what you're here for, Francis, so let's wear our hearts on our tongues and stop this speechifying. I liked your step-sire, or whatever it is that you call him. I didn't trust him, though. And whilst I've seen you brave, I've not yet seen you honest. Seems to me it's likely black is as two-faced as Brown was.' At this, Diamond snorted and Smoker let out a pip. Then there was silence. Gray stared coolly ahead. I sensed again the weight of the sword at my belt and thought of Francis's flintlocks. Everything felt provisional, ready.

'George,' Francis spoke, his hands flat out on the table before him, a smile in his eyes that didn't quite

reach his mouth. 'We've had time tonight to speak of
the past. There's much good that comes of having
known a man for an age and a day, but bad comes
with it too. You and I were younger men when last
we stepped shipward together. I was a hot-blooded lad
and I made decisions I now regret. Tonight I come to
you seeking help, surely, but also to submit to you a
proposal that will be to our mutual benefit. I hope
you'll hear me out.'

'Of course we will,' Gray's voice was all warmth,
and I realised that I'd been clutching the handle of my
sword under the table, and let it go. 'Come, dear
Francis,' Gray went on, 'have a cup of Burgundy and
tell us your plans. We were all foolish as little shavers.
Kingsmill there was just bones once upon a day and
had a head of hair as fine and fair as any maiden, you
remember, George? And now will you look at him?
He's sorry, Francis, for any offence, doubly sorry for
speaking ill of your late father. Now charge your glasses,
men. To Ezekiel Brown, to Francis, to Goody.' Kingsmill
scowled a little, then raised his tankard, and I sipped
at the wine, which was good, as good as any I'd tasted
before. I saw Perin lift his glass with quivering fingers,
and Diamond, Smoker and Poison theirs, and we all
drank, then turned to listen to Francis.

XVI

'I HAVE HAD word from Gabriel Tomkins,' said Francis.
'A week hence, he and his men will clear out the
cellars of Winchelsea. There's the spoils of the run

from a sennight ago and much more besides. He's mayhap expecting me to stir up trouble and will hope to act swiftly and move on the goods before we can get our house in order. He's not slow-witted. I know you've clashed with him in the past, Arthur, and not always come out best.'

'Right enough, but he had the advantage of the land and the jump on us then.'

'Still, I don't doubt he'll come with a greater force than usual and hope to bluster it out. He won't imagine me coming to you Hawkhurst boys, but rather he'll be expecting me to inform the Revenue and will rustle enough men to put the frighter on them. Now young Goody here knows the cellars as well as any, having been down there since she was knee-high.'

Gray turned to regard me. 'Is that right? Are you brave, Goody? Can you handle that sword? We've not had a wench in our number before. How old are you, by the by?'

I felt something thrill within me, to be spoken to by a man such as this. 'I'm sixteen, sir,' I said. 'And while I am no great fencer, I know the Under-Reach like you know this tavern. I wish to venge my father. Beyond that there is but little that interests me just now.' I was not sure that I was brave, and I worried at what might befall my mother should Francis and I come to trouble, but I knew the role that was expected of me just then, and how difficult it would be to persuade them to put any trust in a mere girl.

'Strong words, young Goody,' Gray said. 'If we plan on whelving over these villains before they expect us,

like as not you'll have no need to test the lick of that
blade. Am I right, Francis?'

'Dead right,' my brother said.

'And on the night, we can count on your help?'

'And that of Goody.'

I saw Gray and Kingsmill exchange another glance.
'And if we assist you here, then we can rely upon the
Winchelsea trade in future?'

'You have my word.'

Then there was silence save for the wind, which had
begun to bluster, whipping from the sea, over the
marshes and up the streets of the town.

Gray spoke again, not to any of us, but rather to
the table, to his men. 'We have known for some good
while that Tomkins was seeking to extend the ambit
of his undertakings and that ere long he'd rub up against
us.' Here he looked around for a place to spit, finding
none convenient. 'Winchelsea is as good a battleground
as any, and if young Goody here knows the catacombs
under the town as well as she says she does, and if our
friend Francis here is a man of his word, then we ought
to carry the day. Now, you cutthroats, you villains of
sea and main, are you with me? Are we ready to scribble
a new chapter in the history of the Hawkhurst Gang?'

'Aye,' said Kingsmill at once, and then Poison growled
and Smoker muttered, 'I'm in,' while Perin merely
rapped his knuckles on the table.

'We're decided, then,' said Gray. He raised his glass
and there was a solemn moment before we all stood,
filed back down the narrow stairs, and returned to the
now silent saloon where only a single candle burned
on the bartop, the landlord gone abed. We said our

Godspeeds and then Francis and I were out on our horses on Mermaid Street with the wind whipping about us.

The flame of my lantern kept blowing out as we rode down through the town, and out across the marsh to the ferry, and for much of the journey we made do with what light came down through breaks in the fast-scudding clouds. Francis didn't speak once as we rode, and it was only after we'd rung the bell for the ferry and were looking across the water to where the ferryman was finally rowing himself across that he spoke. 'You did well this night,' he said. 'There will be sterner tests ahead, mind. I know now, though, Goody, that I can reckon on you in whatever lies ahead.'

XVII

IT WAS PAST three of the afternoon and the Rye Mop Fair was in full sway. Looking at the three of us, standing apart from the crowd, you might have taken us for part of the fair: the black-skinned man in fine clothing; the large and clumsy-looking girl in a dress she'd begun to outgrow; the mother, almost a dwarf, neat and self-possessed in black.

Bunting fluttered above Cinque Ports Street, and all the windows of the houses were open, with locals selling gingerbread and plum pie, strong ale and cider. Music came to us from many sources, meeting discordantly over the slanting rooftops and mingling with the buzz of conversation, the shouts of men hawking penny toys. The crowds were packed so thick along the narrow streets that, stepping into the throng, we found ourselves having to jounce and jostle to keep abreast of one another. We were spewed out into Market Square, where there were stalls and entertainments among the stands for hiring labour. Everywhere the high scent of close-packed bodies, animals and beer.

Men seeking employment were dressed in their Sunday best, each of them carrying an implement betokening their trade. In one corner of the square, men leant on shepherds' crooks while the sheep-farmers of the marsh, or more often their agents, mixed among them, stopping now and again to subject them to questions of character and capability. Fishermen congregated down towards the quay with their nets, while farriers and blacksmiths stood holding horseshoes by the town stables on Rope Walk. I watched a man being hired; he was passed a fastening penny by his employer, which was in fact three shillings.

'He looks relieved,' I said to Francis.

'He's secure of his living for a year. He'll spend it on a new pair of boots and the settling of bills.'

'And getting riotously drunk in the Mermaid?'

'With any residuum.'

There was a hubbub of excitation about the place as fate passed over the crowd, turning fortunes to the good or the ill, dividing lovers and sending others to the farms and fields where they would find their future loves.

A troupe of Morris dancers took to the square, their faces blacked. They leapt and cavorted to the music, the bells on their heels tinkling merrily. 'Moorish dancers,' Francis said, looking over at them with a kind of wince. 'They dance as they believe Africans dance.' I looked at them again, these men I'd thought as much a part of Old England as the May Pole and Jack-in-the-Green. I saw that they were an affront to Francis, to the people from whom, via Brazil and Hispaniola, he was descended. In truth I knew little of his life before he came to England, only what my father had told me: of a slaver-ship bound for Antwerp, of a desperate leap from the deck and of the teenage Francis, naked and half-drowned, washing up on the beach at Pett Level.

Walking up the steep cobbles of Conduit Hill, outside the Friary Chapel, we came upon the dignified figure of Winchelsea's portly Chief Jurat Albert Nesbitt, with his son Arnold following behind him. Both men bowed deeply, while Albert took my mother's hand in his and pressed it to his lips. Arnold had on the outfit of the dragoons, somewhat lost in a jacket of fine, new and very red cloth, his elaborate gorget gleaming at his throat and his sword at his waist.

'The boy has taken up arms,' Albert said. 'Partly as a result of what happened to Ezekiel, no doubt. He'll be a captain at Hythe, lead the sorties against these ruffians, what?' He clapped his son on the back and Arnold swayed at the blow, wincing. 'Very good, this may be the making of him. They're going to need all the soldiers they can get to enforce the Indemnity Act. With luck this will finally break the hold the blasted free-traders have over us. I've always said we should hang the swine first, ask questions after.' Here, it was as if he all of a sudden became aware of Francis's presence beside us. 'I don't know that I've had . . .'

'Francis Brown, sir. Mr Brown was my adoptive father.'

'Ah yes, the blackamoor. You departed Winchelsea before we arrived, I believe, but I've heard talk of you. Drop in and see me sometime. I'm at Greyfriars, you know. Indeed, you must come and festivate Arnold's commissioning. I've a mind to throw together something grand.'

'I'd be delighted.'

Now Arnold fell into step beside me. 'Do you enjoy the fairs, Miss Brown?' he asked in his schoolboy's voice.

'I do,' I said, and then thought more upon it. 'I like the way they measure out the passage of time for you. We come together at the hinges of the year, the moments between seasons where things seem to wait, readying for the next.'

'The hinges of the year,' Arnold said, smiling. 'Just so.'

Francis and the older Nesbitt were in conversation ahead and I tried to make out what they said. We turned on to the High Street.

'I enter the army with a degree of trepidation,' Arnold said, and I shot him a sideways glance, saw his thin hair beneath his three-horned hat, the sense of one not prepared for an arm-wrestle, far less a battle. 'Father bought the commission for my twenty-fifth birthday. It is today, my birthday.'

'*Multos et foelices* to you,' I said, remembering my Virgil.

'*Gratias ago*,' he replied. 'It is time for me to strike out on my own, I recognise this. And at least, stationed where I am, I shall be close by this corner of the world, and shall be able, God willing, to address this scourge of smuggling.'

There was the noise of a parade approaching along the High Street, a group of those hired who would be blowing whistles and banging drums and dancing as the bystanders cheered them on the way. The Nesbitts here left us, turning up Lion Street towards the church, issuing before they left further imprecations requiring our presence at the celebrations they would host at Greyfriars in a fortnight's time. I thought about what was to come between this moment and that and felt a kind of giddiness overtake me. I inclined my head towards the door of the George. 'A drink?' I said, and my brother nodded.

XVIII

A SERENE WHITE building with ballroom and parlour, the George was fitted out as befitted Rye's principal coaching inn, with fine paintings on the walls and Turkey carpets on the floors. It was where the Jurats of the Cinque Ports came to sip their Madeira and conceive their intrigues, where business-folk down from London or merchants over from Paris sojourned. We established ourselves in the saloon, and soon Francis was back with a glass of wine to brace my nerves. He took a tankard of beer himself and set before my mother a pitcher of water. The room was busy with wigged and portly men and their plump, flustered wives, with landowners and agents come to escape the rowdiness of the fair. The place danced with a different sort of merriment to the wildness of the hired men outside; here was the feeling of satiety and congratulation that comes from having a great deal and seeing the prospect of making more of it.

'So Nesbitt junior is now a Revenue man,' Francis said, 'while his father enriches himself with his share of the free trade. They speak from both sides of their faces, these folk.'

My mother narrowed her lips, whether in agreement or otherwise I could not say.

'Why does Albert trouble subterfuging such antipathy towards the smugglers?' I asked.

'Because he has set his sights beyond Winchelsea, beyond the Cinque Ports. He wishes to become a great politician, and must be seen to support the Act of Indemnity. Perhaps he has intrigued his mollycott son into the Revenue precisely so that the force remains toothless.' All of a sudden, Francis seemed to stiffen, his hand tightening around his glass. 'Don't look,' he said in a hard, low voice, his eyes on our mother. 'Finish your drinks and we'll depart.' He swallowed his beer in a long gulp and, scarcely able to heed his advice, I took a sip of my wine and from the corner of my eye saw Gabriel Tomkins at a table across the room.

The Mayfield Gang drank in the Ypres Inn, this was well-known. Local wags claimed they'd established themselves there for the close convenience of the gaol. But here they were – Gabriel, Nasty Face and Old Joll – in close confabulation with Mayor Parnell, a rotund man of five-and-fifty or so in a coat of green twill. It was at this moment that Tomkins happened to look up. Our eyes met and I saw something like fear in his face before he rose, said a brief word to Parnell, and then crossed the room to where we sat.

'Francis,' he said, 'I'm glad to see you. You received my note?' He was smiling thinly and placed a hand on Francis's shoulder, who lifted himself from his seat and turned to face the man who'd killed our father. Gabriel looked tired, his skin sickly-sallow, his eyes protuberant. He appeared suddenly small-shouldered and washy beside Francis, who loomed over him as some great oak will overshadow a willow or alder. 'I was planning to pay a visit to you later today, so that we might discuss the clearing of the cellar,' he went on, and I was afeared at that moment that Francis would do him harm, right there in front of the great and good of Rye. I realised at the same moment that I wanted him to do so, to take Gabriel's long, wan head in his hands and crush it like a marrow. But my brother was very calm, his face devoid of expression. I could see that the other members of the gang had their eyes on us. Parnell, stolidly unconcerned, stared out of the window.

'You were over-hasty,' Francis said. 'I understand you were vexed with my father, but our long association deserved better patience.'

'I hear you,' Gabriel said. 'But you're a business-man, you know that difficult decisions needs must be taken. There were powerful forces, elements beyond my control. It were him or me, Francis, surely you can see that.' There was a kind of desperation in his voice as he looked swiftly over at the table, at the portly mayor, who smiled. Gabriel lowered his voice. 'I hope you're not here to cause trouble for us.'

'I have come back to Winchelsea to get things straight for my sister, my mother.'

'We were thinking they might move on after the cellars are cleared. It's not a wench's game, this. You know that too.' Gabriel looked down first at my mother, then at me, and I shot back at him all the hate in my heart.

'They will remain,' said Francis. 'I'll assist Goody in carrying out the duties of the Cellarman until such a point as she can manage the concern alone.'

'Right, then. As you will.' Gabriel shook his head.

'Listen, Gabriel.' Francis, too, had lowered his voice, and I had to lean forward to hear him. 'We understand that we must demonstrate our own degree of accommodation. Tomorrow night, we will be at your service. You can bring the goods up through Paradise. Goody and I will open the gates to you; we'll light your way through the tunnels just as my father did.'

'And what in return?'

'That once this run is completed, we sit down together and find a more equitable manner of dividing the proceeds. I want to ensure that Goody and my mother can continue to live at Paradise, to have the lives they would have had if my father were still with them.'

'Truly, friend, I am sorry he is not.'

It was agreed that Gabriel and the Gang would be let through the gate in King's Cliffs at midnight on the morrow. By this time, Francis and I would have amassed the goods in the cavern beneath St John's, ready to be taken through the Under-Reach, up through the cellar at Paradise and then over the river to Knellstone, an ancient farmhouse on the Udimore ridge owned by a certain Thomas Freebody. From here, they would be spirited away along the thousand lanes and holloways of the Weald, first to Mayfield, then London.

Francis and Gabriel shook hands, and I wondered how he could bear even to touch the man whose guilt was visible in the sweat that pearled along the line of that lank black hair, in the way his eyes darted about. I watched him walk back to his table, to the Mayor, to the malformed Nasty Face, to Old Joll, who'd brought me shells from distant beaches and cut the tongue from my mother's mouth. I saw my mother looking at the man who had so grievously wounded her, and I realised that the vengeance I'd carried in my mind had been of an abstract sort, with retribution meted out but with no definite scope nor substance to the violence. Now I knew that what I wished most was to use my own fists upon them: these monsters I'd once thought of as family.

My mother rose first, scurrying past the table at which the men sat without turning their way, though I could feel the white rage burning off her. I followed, my head high, while Francis stopped for a few words before joining us out on the street, which was now largely empty of people; a thin rain had set in while we were at the George, driven by a wind that carried in it rumours of the winter to come. I drew my shawl about me and we walked back down to the Tillingham Bridge, then on to the marsh road, where a few straggling fair-goers were weaving their way homewards. We went in silence, until we were about halfway across. The daylight was fading, and Francis turned back towards Rye, where lamps were being lit. At this point, under a low sky, we could see the mouths of the three valleys – the Brede, the Tillingham, the Rother. We could see, too, the rival towns, Winchelsea and Rye, like twin moons rising out of the marsh.

'At least we now know that Parnell is well-mixed in all this,' Francis said. 'He is implicated in anything that might serve to elevate Winchelsea's fortunes, and his own.'

'I wonder that he will meet them so brazenly,' I returned.

'It is a time for brazen men,' my brother said. 'A time for the shameless, the vulturous, the shillers and undercraft-merchants to thrive while honest folk struggle and starve.'

We came to the Brede and rang the bell for the ferryman. There was a group of farmworkers and farriers waiting already. We went across in silence, and I watched the farm boys head off towards the Salutation. My mother took my hand in hers as we climbed the road up, past the jagged ruins of the town wall, through the Land Gate and home.

XIX

IT WAS QUITE dark outside. My mother sat in her glass-house, a dim flame burning in the brazier. I watched her quick hands scrimmaging among the vials and cruets, here a flash of something thrown in the fire, there the clashing of jars and pounding of pestle in mortar. I had exchanged my dress for a smock and jerkin, breeches and a pair of Francis's old boots. I'd removed my bonnet and my hair went off at odd angles. A trespasser in the garden, pressing their face against the window, would have had trouble naming me man, wench or devil, but I cared not. I felt a great deal more myself thus attired, closer to the person that lived under my skin than when rigged out in long skirts in front of the townsfolk.

Seeing Gabriel earlier had started a breathless rhythm in my chest and I was eager to move. I was testing my father's sword against my thumb when Francis came downstairs. 'Do you have Father's keys?' he asked. I drew them out from around my neck. 'Then we shall go down.'

The entrance to the Under-Reach was through a small oak door that stood beneath the wind of the stair. I went in search of my lamp, lit it, then joined Francis beside the door. I noticed he had his pistols buckled around his waist, their two long muzzles reaching almost to his knees. I inserted the key and the door opened with a dry creak, revealing stone steps coiling into blackness. I went first, Francis following. I hadn't been down for several weeks, the longest absence from my subterranean world since I was a child and the cellars had been out of bounds. I took a deep breath of the air, which smelt of brick and must, mice and earth. At the bottom of the steps we came to a narrow passage, both of us forced to bend near-double. I went along with one hand holding the lamp ahead of me, the other braced against the brickwork. We shuffled in this fashion, stooped like old men, for some moments before the quality of the air changed: a fresher note, the tang of the sea.

The main tunnel of the Under-Reach ran beneath Monks Walk, the principal street of Winchelsea, so-named because it joined the religious institutions and charity-houses of the seaward half of the town with the dwellings, shops and taverns of the landward side. The passage from Paradise gave on to this tunnel, which was dead straight and large enough to drive a carriage through. We both now stood, stretching. The flame in my lamp danced in the breeze.

We walked south in silence and, as we did, I remembered my younger self: the girl who, a few weeks after her tenth birthday, was first permitted to come down to the Under-Reach on the night of a run. I recalled the ceremony with which my father wielded his keys, as if he were working under the eye of his father and forefathers who'd safeguarded the cellars over the centuries. Francis had been with us during those early runs, and I remembered the anticipation, standing holding his hand at the King's Cliffs gate, the sight of muffled lights coming towards us across the marsh, and how his presence beside my pint-sized father had made me feel safe then. It made me feel safe now, too.

The tunnel ran downhill slightly, following the slope of the land, and I could tell by subtle altera-tions in the colouration of the earth above us when we passed beneath the open space of the Hundred Place. Here the smell of the sea was stronger still, and I could feel the strange breeze that seemed always to be moving in the cellars, carrying within it a warm wetness, as if it were blown up from the very belly of the world. We stopped for a moment as we came to the stout iron door that marked the end of the town cellars. I reached down to unlock it and heard, distantly, the growl of the sea. The lock was stiff: I had to place the lamp on the floor and, with Francis helping me, grasp the bars and pull until it opened.

The tunnels yawned upwards when we passed through the gate, although it was more a case of the ground beneath us falling than the roof rising. We were in the first of the large chambers that lay beneath the southern end of town, each of them echoing as a church. In one corner of the cavern, stone steps wound up to the ruined Hospital of St John. It was here that we saw the first signs of the free-traders' work: bales of tobacco raised on planchers; stacked tubs of jenever; piles of Hollands wrapped in hessian. Francis lifted up some of the cover-cloths as we went by, nodding. 'He'd have moved a good deal of this on, had he lived,' he said. 'Always sought to lose a certain portion of the goods while they waited here.'

We continued southwards, passing through the mouth of an arch on the far side of the cave and into the next chamber, larger still, which sat beneath the Hospital of the Holly Rood, the oldest and most extensive of the charity-houses. These hospitals had been less intended for the treatment of the sick than as almshouses for the aged and destitute of the parish, those who would now find themselves in the poorhouse, for the hospitals above ground were roofless ruins, with only these vaults remaining.

Here the goods were piled higher than before, with a path passing between stacks of linen, tubs and ankers of spirits and hogsheads of wine. There were strange clusters of organ-like eminences rising from the floor of the cave, while from above stalactites hung, glimmering in the torchlight. This was my special place. Often in my childhood I would come and sit here with a book, curling up on a pile of Hollands and imagining the world above altogether gone. It was here that I lost myself in tales of desperate smugglers and ruthless privateers, feeling I was in some way implicated in their adventures, cloistered among goods from Dunkerque or Middelburg or Ostend. And all the time I would hear about me the roar of the wind and the sea, booming in the deep hollowness of the earth, which honeycombed the hill far beneath these caves, shafts and voids that were the relics of ancient excavations by the Romans and those who were here before them.

The walls of Holly Rood cavern were pocked with smaller caves and tunnel mouths, in which lay racks of wine and other nameless spirits. One of these passages was the only known entrance to the warren of mines beneath, which my father had called the Deeps. There were boards nailed across it after my father's father, years earlier, had caught his son waist-deep in water in one of the passageways that lay beyond, preparing to plunge down in the hope that he'd emerge among dwarves and elvish folk, or alongside Arthur and his sleeping knights. Iham was our Caerleon, my father told me, and as a child he'd imagined that the Deeps beneath Winchelsea were connected to other dwarf-hewn caverns and passages across Britain, through which the ghostly knights of Camelot would ride, and into which the elves, horrified by the industrious bustle of man, had retreated.

Finally, we passed through another vaulted archway and into St Bartholomew's cellar. It had once been larger, but the western half of the cave had subsided long ago, and the space that remained was now used as the initial repository for goods brought in from the marsh. The gate that opened on to the foot of King's Cliffs lay in a declivity on the far side of the cave. To get there, we had to pick around the tubs and crates which remained from the last run. I opened the gate with my keys and we stepped out through the concealing brown fronds of dead and dying ferns. The night was blustery, the air cold on our skin after the closeness of the tunnels. I shivered.

'There is work to be done,' Francis said.

We spent the next hour moving tubs from the first cellar up into the northerly caves, to clear space for the goods that would arrive on the morrow. I found my father's tub carrier and slipped it over my shoulders, allowing me to balance a tub on my chest as I walked. Francis hefted a barrel under each of his arms. It was hard work, and thirsty, and when we finished Francis broke open the neck of a bottle of wine and passed some my way. It was bitter stuff and served neither to slake my thirst nor steady my mind, which imagined shadows moving in the dark corners of the caverns.

At last the cellar was clear and Francis and I sat on the earth, passing the bottle of wine between us. I'd taken off the tub carrier but still breathed. Francis reached out and put his hand upon my hand. 'We must scheme out the actions of the morrow,' he said. 'But first, we should school you in the usage of your sword and pistols. You must not meet the dangers ahead without some measure of preparation.'

XX

NEXT MORNING, FRANCIS and I stood out in the orchard, a gentle mizzle about us, and he instructed me in the martial arts. He taught me the correct manipulation of my father's sword: how to thrust and parry, the lines of attack and defence, how to make use of deception and the feint. We then charged and fired the pistols at targets he'd painted on to the garden walls. Using his pocket watch, he noted the time it took me to load both my barrels with shot and discharge them, and by the end of the morning I felt myself growing increasingly dexterous and confident in my abilities.

Later in the day we took delivery of a dozen horses: mangy, spiritless things, who stood in the yard before the stables chewing hay and shitting watery squits on the cobbles. I went up to my chamber and attired myself in my highwayman's garb, affixed my father's sword about my waist, and then walked down the stairs to where my brother awaited me in the hall.

Francis and I talked through the necessary actions of the night ahead: how we would let the Hawkhurst Gang down the St John's steps, how they would conceal themselves until Gabriel Tomkins and his men appeared at the King's Cliffs gate. I would shut and lock the gate once they were inside, with Francis leading them into the trap. Once the Mayfield Gang were subdued,

I'd ride over to Knellstone to tell Freebody that the run had been postponed. It was all planned with great meticulousness.

Darkness fell, and it was time to descend to the Under-Reach once more.

XXI

FRANCIS AND ARTHUR Gray stood at the King's Cliffs gate, looking out into the roaring darkness. I was behind them, holding the only light in our party, alone but aware of the men that lurked in the shadows about me, the greater numbers concealed deeper in the caverns. It was nearing eleven o'clock and a wild night to be abroad, worse to be at sea. I went up to stand behind Francis, who turned and shook his head at me. 'Nothing yet, sister,' he said. 'It will not be long, though.'

'Miss Brown,' Gray said, turning to regard me from under the brim of his hat, dubiously. 'Are you quite sure you want a part in this?'

'Quite sure,' I said, although I was not sure, not by any means.

'And you are clear of what is asked of you?'

'Quite clear,' I said, and this much was true.

'I like it not, but I can see that having a maid to front for us may increase our chances of surprise,' said Gray, then he turned back to the gate. 'There!' he said, in a fierce whisper. 'Do you not see it?'

I did: a flicker in the black heart of the night, the blue light of a spotsman's pistol charged with powder. The two ketches were lying far out, beyond the sandbanks, the smugglers rowing goods to shore in fishing boats. Closer by, I saw the retort from the landing-man, the spark of a tinderbox to indicate a clear coast.

'They're on the way, lads. Ready yourselves.' There was something like joy in Gray's voice. I sensed it too, this surge of excitement. Before we'd descended, my mother had fed me another spoonful of her green paste, and I'd felt within the same wondrous warmth as before, a strengthening that began in my heart and reached outwards. I pressed further forward, pushing some of the fern fronds aside better to see out into the blackness, to watch the enemy approach.

'Get back, girl, damn it,' Gray said, pulling at my arm. 'Into the caves with you and your light. There may still be the Revenue men to contend with.'

I retreated, my heart loud in my chest, my breaths coming fast and shallow. I felt another hand on my shoulder, pulling me further back still. It was Kingsmill. The scar on his face shimmered in the bright embers of his pipe before he tapped it out against the wall.

'There'll be a moment yet afore they come nigh,' he said. 'You stay back until we have the word.'

It was indeed an age that passed there in the light of my lamp, the only sound that of Kingsmill's breathing beside me, the wind howling through the gate and the deeper roar of the sea. I had never before smoked tobacco, but watching Francis and Gray in the gateway, their pipes cupped carefully in their palms to shield them from outside view, I wished I had something to do with my hands to fill the time. Finally, though, I saw Gray knock out his pipe, turn and mutter something to Francis, and then move towards me.

'Don't lose your nerve. Don't make me regret having you down here. Shut the gate when they're through. We'll do the rest.' He linked arms with Kingsmill, something jaunty about him, and they disappeared back into the caves.

I was left with Francis. He came and stood before me, placing his hands on my shoulders. 'You remember everything we said?' he asked. I nodded. 'Lock the door well,' he said. 'We are strong in numbers, and they will not be expecting attack from within.' I nodded again. 'It is midnight. They will be here soon. Luck be with you, sister.' We went together to stand by the mouth of the cave, where the ferns thrashed about in the storm and rain cut the air in seams.

Below, coming slowly across the marsh, I could see the clothed lamps of the smugglers. There were a good number of them, most carrying tubs, but others – more than usual, it seemed to me – ranged alongside, batmen bearing clubs and flails. They picked carefully across the pools and ditches, well used to the perils of the damp and shifting land, although as they came nearer I perceived that there was something unnatural to their slowness, as if the whole train of men had been hobbled. They came to the bend in the Brede, just where it widens before flowing into the sea, and I could see in the glow of their lamps that, at the tail of the procession, one man was being supported by another. They ascended the slope to the gate that sat at the foot of the cliff, and then they were inside and I could perceive on their faces that something had gone very wrong with the run. Gabriel Tomkins came in, half-draped around the shoulder of Nasty Face, and I saw the blood coming through his dark trousers, the pallor of his face.

'Make a space for him, come now, look lively!' Nasty Face said, and two tea crates were moved together. While this was happening, not having forgotten my duty, I went to the gate, pulled it shut and locked it as quietly as I could. When I came back into the cavern, the men – Francis included – were standing around Gabriel, who was spread out on the crates panting, his injured leg extended. A black pool collected beneath it. Old Joll held a flask of some spiritous substance to Gabriel's lips. He drank and then raised his head.

'I'm fine, damn you all,' he said, a crack in his voice. 'Are the horses ready? The Revenue will have alerted the riding officers. We'll need to move swiftly.'

'What happened?' Francis stood beside Old Joll.

'A Revenue sloop-of-war, an eighteen-gunner,' Old Joll said. 'Caught us broadside. We took a blast from a fourteen-pounder in the gunwale. It's the splinters that have made such a mess of him.' He lifted a piece of Gabriel's torn and tattered trouser leg, just above the knee, had a look beneath, winced, and put it back. 'He'll need a physician.'

'You killed the physician,' Francis said flatly.

'Take me to Alma, then,' Gabriel said. 'She always knew more than her husband in any case. She'll see me right. The rest of you start moving the goods up into the tunnels.'

'The horses are in the yard at Paradise as you requested,' Francis said. 'The ferryman is in the Salutation, being stood kopstoots until he passes out. The ferry is upstream and Freebody forewarned.'

'You've done well, Francis.' Gabriel rose, swinging his injured leg around, looking for a moment at the gouts that stained the tea crate. 'I'll take Goody with me for support,' he said. 'She's a big lass, she'll manage it. The rest of you get on with moving this up to the cellars. I want to clear this run and a deal of what remains before the night's out.'

Francis shot a quick, desperate look over towards me. I stepped forward, held my arm out to Gabriel, felt him move his weight on to me. 'Come on, damn you.' He turned to Nasty Face, who was gawping stupidly at us. 'Get moving!'

XXII

I CANNOT TELL you what it was to have my body pressed so closely against that of the man who'd killed my father; to feel his heft upon me, his breath mixing with mine. I held my lamp in one hand, while the other I passed around his back and clasped in the damp hollow of his armpit. We made our way into Holly Rood cavern and I could sense the presence of the Hawkhurst Gang there in the corners and declivities, behind tea crates and hogsheads, watching us. We moved on, beneath St John's. Gabriel's breath was coming quicker and shallower. When we paused so I might open the gate into the Under-Reach, I saw him look down again at his leg.

'It needs just a bit of binding,' he said. 'I've survived worse.' He gave a chuckle that unravelled into a barking cough, then draped himself once more over my shoulders. We staggered together through the tunnel until we came to the passage to Paradise. Here, it was necessary for me to go before, while Gabriel came on his hands and one knee, trailing the damaged leg. I waited for him at the bottom of the stone stairwell that wound up to the house, listening to the heaviness of his breathing as he came, aware that he had lost a deal of blood. I held the lamp down over him as he rested on the first step and saw how white and wan were his cheeks, the manner in which his chest rose and fell, the sweat that sheened his forehead and made his hair fall in strands about his face. I could hear the men moving tubs in the cellars, the clanks and echoes coming to me distantly, eerie above the groaning of the wind, so that I could well imagine why some thought Winchelsea haunted on moonless nights.

'We are all but there,' I said to Gabriel. 'Give me your hands.' He did and I grasped them – they were cold and damp – and half-dragged him up the stairs, not minding that I jounced and jarred him as we went, paying no heed to his cries and exhortations. At last we were at the top of the steps and through the door, Gabriel on his hands and knee, moaning gently. I turned to shut the door and that was when my mother appeared from behind it carrying a skillet, which she brought down with some force on Gabriel's head.

We got him into the glass-house and lowered him into the armchair that sat in one corner of the room. It was cold and the rain fell hard on the glass roof. The fire that burned in a small grate on the mixing table appeared to give out no heat, but instead emitted a greenish light that caused me to imagine for a moment that we were underwater. I watched my mother – bustling, concentrated – bind Gabriel's hands behind him, then coil the rope about the chair, so that he was held fast. She reached over to the mixing table beside her, drew out an albarello and spooned a little of a dark, resinous substance into his mouth. He began to blink, moved his head a little to the side, then, cognisant of the constriction of the ropes, he let out a feeble cry. Now my mother reached a hand into a drawer beside her and drew out some other object. I saw it glint in the subaqueous light, and turned my head away, not wishing to witness what was to come. Looking out upon the darkness of the garden, trying not to perceive the reflected movements in the glass, I heard Gabriel scream more energetically, and then a wet sound, a terrible retching, followed by silence, and the wind and the rain.

Finally, I looked. Gabriel's head lolled to one side, a runnel of blood issuing from his mouth. His body appeared strangely contorted, held in place by the ropes. I saw that his chest still rose every now and again, but was unsure if this was a sign of ongoing life or merely part of his progress to death. My mother was cleaning her blade with a cloth, staring off into the green light. I heard the church clock toll two of the morning. Kneeling down in front of Gabriel, I looked at him, seeing but few traces of the strong, violent, loving man he once was. I picked among my feelings, discovering joy that my father was venged, but not unequivocal joy. My nerve wanted ruthlessness, I realised, placing my hand on Gabriel's blood-drenched trouser leg and twisting the flesh where it was jagged with splinters of wood. At this he opened his eyes all of a sudden, and then his mouth, which was a dark and gaping thing. He began a low, gurgling howl, and I stumbled back, knocking into the mixing table from whence a jar overbalanced and hit the floor with a smash.

It was in the moment after the crash that I heard, over the sound of Gabriel's blarting and the patter of the rain, the echo of footsteps coming up the stairs from the cellars below. I struggled to my feet, looking over at my mother, who was standing quite still in the green light. I went out into the hall, drew my father's sword, and waited for the heavy steps to come nearer still. I summoned all the courage I had, knowing that surprise was with me, but that strength was likely with my opponent. I saw the shadow first, then my brother, who grinned delightedly when he perceived me.

'They are quelled below,' he said. 'They gave in with barely a brickbat.' A pause. 'What is that sound?'

We went together into the glass-house, where Gabriel whimpered still, his white shirt front now red with gore, his hair matted with blood, his eyes wildly rolling in his head.

''Swounds, sister,' Francis said.

'It was our mother,' I said, and as if to confirm it, she turned then, the small, composed woman, and held out in her hand the long pink protrusion of Gabriel's tongue. A broad smile spread over her face. She jubilantly placed the tongue in a jar and then set about scrubbing bloodstains from the floor while Francis hefted the quiet form of Gabriel on to the floor and dragged him unceremoniously by his bound feet.

'He lives yet,' Francis said. 'Now we must reunite him with his cronies.'

Francis went down first, whopping Gabriel's head against each step as they descended, leaving a long dark trail on the stone. In the tunnel of the Under-Reach, Francis hoved him on to his shoulders, as if the man weighed nothing at all. When we came to the Holly Rood cavern, I saw that many lights had been lit, with lamps on the floor and candles disposed on tea crates and hogsheads. A space had been cleared in the centre of the room in which the Mayfield men now sat bound and fettered, black hoods tied about their heads. Francis deposited Gabriel – what remained of him – on to the earthen floor, and at once Perin and Smoker trussed him like the rest.

'Ah, Goody.' Arthur Gray came towards me from where he had been crouched inspecting a pile of linen. He was high-coloured and jubilant as he grasped me by the hand. 'You have informed Freebody of the delay? The horses await us still?'

Here Francis cut in. 'Goody was forestalled by Gabriel's arrival. Freebody can wait in ignorance a while longer. We will go now to fetch the wherry. You march these curs down to the river.'

XXIII

I let us out through the King's Cliffs gate and Francis and I went down the path together. It was still raining, the wind coming in great gusts, the reeds and osiers of the marsh flattened with each new buffet. We walked northwards, away from the sea, for some minutes, our hats clamped to our heads. We came to the wharf where the ferry would usually stand. Instead, in the lee of the willow that grew on the bank, a wherry was moored, its sail furled. The boat bobbed and bounced on the chops of the river, creaking now and then when it came into contact with the stanchions of the quay. Francis and I got into the boat and I cast off, pushing us out into the stream with a heel.

I'd not been much on the water, my father having no sea legs, and my own preference being for swimming over sailing; thus the ease with which Francis took control of the boat surprised me. I knew he was a fisherman, and that he'd been on runs in the past, of course; that he'd seen the ports of France, bargained in Ostend and Brügge, watched the moon rise over the harbour in Spaarndam. But to see him now, moving the tiller like it was an extrusion of his own body, sailing with thoughtless facility, was to have a new facet of my brother's life revealed.

It was not easy going, with the darkness near-complete, the wind against us, the waves higher as we came to where the river widened. Francis, though, seemed to have some special feeling for where the channel lay, and steered us carefully into the bank just by where the cliffs rose up from the marsh. We could just make out the ragged procession of the Mayfield Gang, surrounded by their captors who lit the way, prodding them and slapping at them as they stumbled, hooded, hobbled, down the path to the river. At the back I saw the bulk of Poison, a slack shape flung over his shoulder. Then they were on the bank, and I threw a rope to Gray, who held it fast as the Mayfield men were urged and enjoined and then compelled by force to enter the boat. I stepped on to shore and assisted in shepherding our prisoners on board. There was not room for them all on deck, nor were they able to arrange themselves, blinded and bound as they were. They lay in places three-up-piled, or sprawled out on the bow-deck. The boat sat lower and lower in the water as its cargo was loaded, cursing and imprecating, aboard.

Poison was the last to convey his load, lowering Gabriel's limp form abaft, near where Francis perched, one foot on the gunwale. Gray now stood on the bank, saluting. 'You'll be right, Francis?'

'I'll set them fair for Boulogne.'

'Then be off with you.' With that, he kicked the boat away from the bank. I watched from the land as Francis paid out a little more sail and the wherry gathered speed towards the mouth of the river, where the waves from the sea surged in. Francis's lamp was by the tiller and I watched it for a while, bobbing madly until it disappeared into the wind and high water. Gray let out a celebratory yell, while Kingsmill swigged from a pocket flask. Smoker shot his pistol into the air. And although the sound of it was near lost in the wind, I saw in the flash from its powder the drenched, enraptured faces of the Hawkhurst Gang all about me. I knew then, with a blaze of certainty, that these were to be the principal players in my life to come.

'I will ride up to Knellstone,' I said to nobody in particular, and nobody seemed to notice as I slipped away, round the winding road and up the hill to Paradise.

XXIV

I CAME IN just past four of the morning to find Francis sitting at the table in the hall in his nightshirt, a bottle of porter half-drunk before him. I had not expected his return so soon, and bent to embrace him, too tired and confounded by the events of the day to feel anything other than the relief of having my brother back. He went to the pantry to find another glass for me and we sat facing one another across the flicker of two candles, sipping the dark beer. I told him how I'd taken Hero across the Brede to Knellstone. I told him of the clattering branches in Slut's Wood and how Thomas Freebody, a balding, pigeon-chested man in whom the battle between nerves and avarice was ever visible, had seemed relieved when I sent him abed with the information that the goods would be delivered on the morrow. I'd galloped Hero home through the dankness of the night and then fed him and the dozen meaner horses who still stood, doughtily unconcerned by the weather or the wait, in the stable yard.

'What of you, brother?' I asked. 'How did you fashion such a swift return?'

As the storm blew itself out in the tail of the night, replaced by a dripping stillness, Francis recounted his tale. He told me how, in the mouth of the Brede, he'd jambed the tiller to the south-east, so that the sails of the wherry billowed large with the wind. He'd lashed the boom to the toerail and dealt the prone form of Gabriel a final cuff about his hooded head. Some of the men were still shouting, struggling against the bonds of wet rope, cursing Francis and Gray and God. Then, just as the wherry came past the spit of shingle that marks the western rim of the entrance to the river, he'd leapt for shore, finding himself only waist-deep in water. He'd trudged to land and turned in time to see the white sail of the wherry one last time rise up and then disappear into a valley of water, swallowed by the blackness.

'Are they whelmed, then?' I asked him.

'I doubt it. Hard to sink a wherry. They may be grounded on Goodwin Sands, if they get that far. More likely they'll hit the banks off Jew's Gut. If that's where Gabriel breathes his last, there'll be a measure of justice in it.'

'Why so?'

'He never boasted to you of the pirate Gustave Tonkin, whom he claimed as an ancestor?'

'No.'

'I'll give it to you as best I can, then,' he said, refilling his glass and leaning back in his chair so that his night-shirt stretched tight over his chest and belly. 'It was in the early days of New Winchelsea. The storm had three years since swept the old town into the depths, and the new settlement on the hill of Iham was a place of bricks and ballast. On the sea, however, Winchelsea was still in her pomp: three-quarters of the wine drunk in England came through her. The men of Winchelsea were pirates and brigands then, sailing up from Bordeaux and Bayonne, guarding the mouth of the Channel, as hungry for gore as any in the Spanish Main. Gustave Tonkin was the most wolfish and sangui-nary of them all.'

At this point there was a creak from upstairs, then

another, then the sight of my mother, also in her nightgown, descending the stairs. She came shuffling, placed her hands on each of our shoulders in turn and smilingly laid a kiss upon our heads. Then she went and fetched herself a beaker of some yellowish unguent from her glass-house, sat down at the end of the table and listened to Francis.

'I was telling Goody of Gustave Tonkin, Mother,' Francis said. 'Gabriel is now headed for the sands off Jew's Gut.'

She nodded, sipped, folded her hands on the table.

'This all happened when Longshanks issued the Edict of Expulsion, exiling all Jews from the land. Their principal trading post in Sussex and Kent was at Jew's Gut, Jews being then prohibited from entering Rye or Winchelsea or, for that matter, any other of the Cinque Ports. If a man from hereabout wished to borrow money at that time, he went to Jew's Gut. So it was that when the order came for the Jews to leave the land, there was a great gathering of them down there, where the sea meets Dunge Ness. Gustave Tonkin sailed right up to the beach and, after striking a bargain with the elders who spoke for the hundred or so men, women and children who stood there, shivering against the sea wind, he agreed to take them across to Dieppe.

'They loaded aboard their possessions – no doubt a good deal of gold and silk, linens and other finery, which they often took as surety from those to whom they lent. Tonkin led them aboard, hovered a mile offshore for six hours while the tide dropped, telling the elders that the wind was not right. Then he and his men turned their swords on the Jews, hacking some to death, forcing the others off on to the sandbar that sits there yet, and is near revealed at low-tide, but covered by depths of ocean when the water is high. They all drowned, and Tonkin sailed back with the loot.' He refilled both of our glasses, emptying the bottle in his own, then swirling it in the glass, a long look upon his face.

'It was on that same sandbar that I landed, just as I was about to give myself up to the ocean, all those years before, when I worked my leg irons loose and jumped from the deck of the *Emmanuela*. I rested only minutes with my feet on the sands beneath, but it was enough to give me the courage to press on, towards the lights that I had thought so much closer when I saw them from the galley of that benighted vessel.'

My mother rose, went into the scullery and began to make familiar breakfast noises – the lighting of the fire and the pouring of water, the stove-pan clanging on its chain. Francis and I talked on as Mother put first strong, milky coffee, then porridge-oats before us. We spoke of the need to move the goods that night, and the securing of feed for the horses; we spoke of the Hawkhurst Gang, and how we would never trust them, but would choose to work with them – at first just this night, then, perhaps, on other runs, other nights to come. I felt the future stretching out before me then, as the light rose and I saw my brother – tall, strong, credible – opposite me. Birds began to sing wintery songs as a pale sun rose over Winchelsea. I went up the stairs with dreams of the world to come bright in my mind, took off my clothes and slipped between cold sheets to sleep.

PART TWO

Winchelsea, April 1743

I

I STOOD AT the parapet of the terrace with Greyfriars behind me, the cliffs and the marsh before. It was evening, the end of April. The low sun which had been blazing over my shoulder was now gone, leaving a pink smudge along the horizon. There was the sound of a string quartet, a gavotte, and tinkling conversation, while in the ruins of the old monastery to my right, a barn owl hissed and spat. Arnold Nesbitt came down to join me. I heard him first: an awkward clearing of the throat, the rattle of the sword at his waist. He was dressed in the gaudy red jacket of the dragoons, a pair of white linen trousers and riding boots polished to a shine. His hair had thinned more since the last time I'd seen him, and he had attempted to compensate by sweeping it over his pate.

'I don't much enjoy balls,' he said, standing beside me, looking at the marsh and then raising his eyes to where the sea stretched away to clouds. 'My father insisted on felicitating my return.' He picked with his toe at a divot of grass, looking sidelong at me and then out again to the sea. 'I thought much of you when I was gone, Miss Brown,' he said, and I could hear a tremor in his voice. 'I hope you didn't take it amiss that I wrote to you. What happened to your father was so much involved in my taking up arms that I thought you should like to know how it was passing for me.'

'I did. Thank you for the letters, Arnold.' I realised, with a touch of surprise, that I meant what I said to him. The letters, written in a fussy, feminine hand, had contained but little to interest me – the niceties of military conduct, the intricacies of drills, a series of brief and unrevealing sketches of Arnold's fellow officers and the men they would command. There had, though, been something touching in the regularity of their arrival, in the knowledge that he had composed his life to right a wrong I had already revenged in the bloodiest fashion.

'I am pleased now to be back in Winchelsea,' Arnold went on. 'I was hoping that I would be posted to the Sussex watch, but scarce imagined that it would be at my home.'

'I understand that the riding officers will be stationed in the ruins.'

'And a dozen dragoons. My task over the coming weeks is to effect reparations on the old chapel, to erect lodgings, a scullery for the men, a watch nest in the tower.'

'It sounds like a great deal of work.'

'I have been furnished with sufficient funds. It appears that the government at last recognises the necessity of meeting this smuggling scourge with force. So great is my father's wish to see the free-traders vanquished that I'm certain I shall not want for more if I require it.'

There was a pause. It was that hour when the day birds pass over their song to those of the night. A dewfall-hawk began to churr somewhere in the scrubby trees at the top of King's Cliffs, a hundred yards to the south of us. As we both listened to the low, liquid notes, I wondered how much the coming of the dragoons would trouble our operations in the Under-Reach. Arnold Nesbitt was as unformidable a personage as one could imagine, but to have dragoons and riding officers in Winchelsea rather than the aged Revenue men would demand a little more subtlety in our actions.

'Goody,' Arnold said, turning towards me. 'I may call you Goody, mayn't I?'

'Of course,' I said.

'Why did you not write back to me?' He held my eye for a moment here, before looking again at the divot beneath his foot.

I gave a little laugh and then, seeing his face, grew serious. 'Forgive me,' I said. 'It did not once occur to me to do so.' I felt a kind of exasperation at how circumlocutory conversations must be, how I could not state out loud all of the thoughts that spiralled through me just then. Or rather, I wished he would just be silent, this nervous, spindly soldier standing beside me, so we could listen to the hawk and the night wind in the trees. 'You must remember, sir,' I said, 'that I have not had the advantage of your education. My father schooled me at home, it's true, but I never learnt the accomplishments of a young lady. The only manners I got were from Plato and Pliny. My father tried hard to make me grand, but I fear that blood does tell in these matters. I was pleased to receive your letters, but recognising the great gulf in breeding that lay between us, I thought you would consider it a presumption to reply.'

'A presumption? Not at all! And please, you must call me Arnold.'

'I will,' I said. At this, he reached out and took my hand. I let him clasp it for a moment and then gently withdrew my fingers from his. 'Arnold, your father will not wish to see you hand in hand with a girl from the town. I'm sure he has great designs for you.' There was a burst of applause from the house, the sound of laughter, then more music. 'It is your party, you must go in and dance with the Honourable Misses that have been ranged up for you. And look, here comes my brother.' Francis walked unsteadily towards us down the lawn, a glass of champagne overfilled and swilling in his left hand. 'You have come for some air, brother? Mr Nesbitt was just going back inside to his guests.'

Arnold shot me a desperate look, bowed curtly to Francis and then strode up towards the house.

'What's that noise?' Francis said, his voice slurring a little.

'A dewfall-hawk. A night-churr, they call it, some places.'

'It's awful,' he said. 'Hellish.'

'I think it's beautiful.'

Francis sat down on the parapet, swinging his feet over the edge and letting them dangle. 'I figure we have little to fear from His Majesty's reinforcements. Nesbitt is a feeble creature, don't you think?'

'I like him,' I said. 'And he's far from stupid. We

will do well not to underestimate the difference that he and his men will make when they're established.'

We stayed there together, Francis dangling his legs and sipping his champagne, me with my shawl pulled about me, and although we did not speak, our minds, I was certain, turned upon the same object. We had become smugglers, Francis and I. Not in the way that my father was a smuggler, merely aiding in the conceal-ment of goods, but rather we had been taken up by the Hawkhurst Gang as two of their own. Although several of the men had expressed their displeasure at having a girl assume her place among them, I had been grudgingly accepted on board the sloop *Albion*, sailing out twice to Boulogne, once to Dunkerque, coming back in under cover of darkness and unloading on to the shingle at Pett. I'd seen the ease with which my brother had fallen in with these brigands and I'd tried to be as hard and hellbound myself. He had continued his schooling of me in the orchard, and I had proven myself gifted with the sword and pistols, able now to disarm my brother one time in every three, and could charge and fire my pistols in ten seconds flat.

I put my hands on Francis's shoulders, rubbing his knotted flesh with my thumbs. If in the colder months Winchelsea was like a ship floating on an ocean of mist, in spring and summer the hill of Iham was moored in a green sea, with every approach covered in a galloping profusion of chestnut, oak and thorn. Now, though, with the light almost gone, all that greenery was grey, the breeze drifting whisperingly about the branches of the trees. Francis looked up at me.

'The guinea run . . .' he said. 'You think it doable?'

'Arthur Gray thinks it doable. I think that, should we succeed, it will be the making of us.'

'It will that.' He stood then. 'I need more champagne. Come dance with me, sister.'

II

I WAS NOT nimble of foot, nor did I seem able to arrange my limbs with the grace of some of the young women who turned about Greyfriars' ballroom. I was discomfited by my gown, with the stays of my corset jutting into my ribs and the cane-hoop skirt rattling like bones as I moved. I thought, nonetheless, how proud my father would have been to see me in the beau monde, and how much I missed the fact that I could not make him proud any more. I plucked a gull egg from the table beside me, dipped it in salt and bit into it.

Albert Nesbitt sat on a kind of raised throne at one end of the ballroom, his cheeks red and hectic, a group of Jurats and their wives arranged about him. My mother was seated up there also, apart from the rest, tapping her fan on her knee in time to the music, which was provided by a quartet in the corner. There were officers from Hythe in their red-breasted finery, a number of naval types from the ships at Rye and Deal, some grander gentlemen at a table behind Nesbitt, looking faintly bored. Amongst them, I saw Mayor Parnell. He caught my eye for a moment and I wondered if he recollected my presence in the George in Rye all those months ago. He was one of a number of those in positions of power in the town I had named in my heart as being in some way responsible for my father's death. I would come for him as I had come for Gabriel.

A table stretched the length of the ballroom's back wall, whereupon were arranged all manner of plates and dishes of the most delectable nature. There were large silver punch bowls at one end; beside them were bottles of champagne upon which customs-house stamps were ostentatiously displayed. There were whole salmon shimmering beneath their dill fronds, rolled calves' heads glistening with liquor, a steaming battaglia pie, asparagus dressed in the Italian fashion, fricassees and curries and a water-souchy soup, all much of the mode. There were trifles and kishchaws, syllabubs and brandied cherries, and a sparkling sugared heap of other candies and sweetmeats.

Francis was a fine dancer, even when in his cups, and with a little tutelage and steering he had me take my place in the bourrée and Allemande. I never strayed far from him at first, feeling his hand in the small of my back correcting my missteps, watching the movement of his black shoes, his gloved hands. Then Arnold Nesbitt walked from the dais, where he had been in conversation with his father, bowed and kissed my hand, and asked me to dance a gigue with him.

That gigue became a gavotte and I kept step with Arnold, who was a sprightly and energetic figure on the parquet, his leaps and prances full of Continental flourishes. Soon I was flushed and panting, but very happy. Francis danced with Mayor Parnell's wife, a plump woman of five-and-forty who had to fan herself after each dance and kept looking over to her husband for approbation. He was in close confabulation with Albert Nesbitt, though, and barely seemed to notice his wife's evident pleasure in Francis's company. The young ladies of noble birth who had come in their fine gowns and perukes stood watching us, their faces white with powder and displeasure, their lips rouged and pursed. When I finally begged Arnold for the respite of a dance or two, so that I might regain my breath, he delivered me to a group of these fearsome women.

'May I introduce Miss Goody Brown, a dear friend? She's done dancing for the moment. I, however, have not. Isabella, may I?' He and a pale girl with a very splendid wig danced off together, and I was left with two young ladies of perhaps two-and-twenty. One of them, whose sardonic countenance I rather liked, had red hair and wore a satin gown with a pearlish sheen to it. The other was more homely, her mantua over-elaborate and frilled, a dark mole drawn in above her lip.

''Zooks, aren't you large?' the first girl said. 'You're terribly brave to dance like that.'

'Isn't she?' the other said, mimicking her friend's tone. I felt my smile fading.

'I haven't had the pleasure, I don't think,' I said, looking over desperately towards my brother, who had Mrs Parnell clutched tightly against him as they turned circles of increasing speed.

'I'm the Honourable Elizabeth St Leger,' the first girl said, 'but you may call me Lily. This is Miss Abigail Maddox.'

'Charmed,' Abigail said, pausing to cast a demure look at a passing officer.

'Our fathers are business associates of Mr Nesbitt Senior,' Lily went on. 'My papa is the Member for Winchelsea. We come but little to the country, though, unless it is to stay with my father's close friend the Prime Minister at Stanmer, or with the Trenchards at Coverton Magna. But the London season takes so much out of one and it is charming to come down to a rusticated outpost like this. Now, tell me, Goody – it was Goody, wasn't it? – have you ever fucked anyone?' She looked at me, then at Abigail, who was with trouble restraining her laughter, then back.

'No,' I said, leaning towards them confidentially, 'but I have killed a man.'

Lily's eyes flickered for a moment. 'You've what?' she said. Abigail's mouth had opened to reveal a supernumerary collection of teeth.

'I was in Boulogne in February,' I said. In my mind's eye I saw the floating dock frozen over, the rigging of the ships festooned with icicles, the slushy river heaving past. 'I was on the wharf. It must have been past ten of the evening and I was walking towards our ship, which my companions were just then attempting to work free of the ice. Coming towards me along the empty quayside, I saw the man who'd cut my mother's tongue out, a man I'd believed already dead.' All this I gave to them in the most matter-of-fact fashion. The colour had now drained entirely from Abigail's face.

'Go on,' said Lily.

'I was carrying my father's sword. I do when I'm abroad.' This last as an aside. 'He was drunk, my mother's molester, and walking unsteadily in a horsehair coat that had become damp in the driving ice and snow. I recognised him, though.' Like a hand around my throat. I recalled again the particular kindnesses he had shown me as a child, the shells he'd brought, the stories I'd listened to as he perched on the end of my bed, conjuring for me the vast complexity of a coral reef, the steaming of submarine volcanoes, a procession of fierce pirates, tribes and blood-thirsting navvies. I apprehended just then that it was the stories that Old Joll told me, as much as the books I read, that made me dream of becoming a smuggler.

'He didn't perceive me at all until we were very close. When he did, there was no sign that he knew me.' I had taken to wearing a greatcoat that winter, with a collar that I turned against the cold so that I was oft mistook for a man. 'I reached beneath my coat, drew out my sword and, feigning to stumble against him, I plunged it hard into the space beneath his ribs, thrusting upwards until I encountered the resistance of his lungs, his heart, all the other soft organs that conspired in his survival.'

Here Abigail, a hand pressed to her mouth, ran past me, fleeing the room. Lily was all eager attention, however, her blue eyes avid. 'And he died?' she said. 'You were revenged?'

'I pulled the sword out and he was shouting, frothing blood from his mouth as he yelled for help in English and French. I couldn't attract attention to us just then, given other things that were transpiring, so I gave him a hard shove and he went over the edge of the dock. It happened that the ice was thick there, and while the fall stopped his clamour, it being some twelve feet from the wharf to the ice, he lay there in full view of any who might pass by. I don't know if, perchance, you have visited Boulogne?'

'I have not.'

'It is a cheerful kind of place, with the port and the floating dock on the starboard side as you come up the Liane – that's the river there – while the town itself rests on an incline on the larboard bank. But it so happened that the lights thrown from the town cast themselves upon the ice just where the man lay. He was leaking prodigiously by this point, both from the wound I'd opened in his stomach and further injuries done him in the fall.'

'He was dead?'

'Oh yes. I hurried over to where the men were cutting the ship from the ice, called down to my brother, who was no little displeased both at the disturbance and when he understood the cause. We both of us took the man's body and dragged it over the ice to where dark water was visible around the hull of the ship. We bundled him in amongst the shards and slush. His horsehair coat performed the task for us in the end, dragging him down so that all that remained was a long red smear on the ice.' I remembered that the weight of the coat turned him, so that his face was visible beneath the water for a moment, that kind old face, and I wanted to reach down and take his slack cheeks in my hands, tell him I was sorry, and that I forgave him. It was but a passing sentiment, and very swiftly I was aboard the ship, and Arthur Gray came to tell me I had done well, and that likely Old Joll was there in the employ of those who wished our failure.

'How is it that you live like this?' Lily said. She took my hand and we went out into the grand entrance hall, where the stairwell curved down from the upper floors. We crossed the hall, past a table where flowers floated in a bowl, then followed a wood-panelled passageway until we found ourselves in a book-lined salon whose windows were open to the night. Low lamps burned about the place, and we sat in a flickering corner, the music drifting through to us distantly like the music one hears in a dream. I liked the way the shadows fell on Lily's face. 'Tell me,' she said again, 'what it is that you have done to escape the impediments they place upon us? I myself am half-mad with life, most days.'

I shook my head. 'I cannot say now, not here. But I believe we will be friends, you and I. And perchance a time will come when I may be more forthcoming in my answers to you.'

'Do you swear it?' She clasped my hand again.

'I do.'

'And I may come and visit you, whenever I am in Sussex?'

'Of course.'

'Mr Nesbitt wishes me to marry Arnold. I fear that he may possess sufficient money to persuade my father of it.'

'Arnold is not so bad as you think.'

'He is a dreary milksop. You're more of a man than he.'

'There is a hardness in Arnold; a goodness, too. Do not give up on him yet.'

We were quiet for a moment.

'You dance like a man, too,' Lily said. 'Here, let me instruct you a little. I have had sufficient lessons to establish my own dance school. But hold, will you unlace my stays? I loathe constriction while I dance.'

She turned her back to me and I undid first the lace of her dress, then of her stays beneath, then pulled aside her shift to reveal skin so pale it was almost blue. I placed my hands there, on the skin of her back where it was marked by the stays, and rubbed gently at it with my thumbs. She stiffened for a moment, then relaxed. We stood there for a time, my warm palms on her cool pale skin, then she turned to me, taking my hands in hers. Though the music came to us faintly, the rhythm was clear enough. Lily bowed her head. 'I shall be the man,' she said. 'Now curve your arm round like this, as if you were opening a fan. That's right. Take my hand. Lift your feet more gently.'

We danced, Lily and I, for another half hour. At first we were nervous lest we be discovered, but nobody came, and after a time we stopped speaking and there was only the sound of the music, the half-drawn curtains breathing in the night, the occasional churr of the dewfall-hawk. We regarded each other frankly as we danced. I saw that she was not beautiful, but had that particular alertness of expression that is more attractive than beauty, a face that in its fineness conveyed the vitality of her mind. Her palms were cool and dry. When I mistook my step, she'd stumble against me, laughing, and I felt the softness of her body beneath the satin and tulle of her dress. I felt flustered each time this happened, but also delighted, my emotions butting up against one another until I felt quite light-headed.

Finally, the music abated and she leant forward against me again, breathing hard. I held her in arms that had become strong from hefting barrels and crates, from hauling sheets through halyards. I placed my hands again through the loosened laces of her dress, beneath her stays, on to her skin. I could feel the fast skip of her heart, the shallowness of her breath. Every part of me tingled.

She in turn reached up to place her cool hands on my cheeks, then she moved her hands up and into my hair. Her lips were parted a little, her breath audible in the stillness after the music. 'I love to dance with you,' she said, moving her head closer still. Then we heard the sound of carriages upon the gravel, footsteps coming down the passageway towards us. We leapt apart and then stood there, unnaturally posed, as Arnold came into the room.

'Goody, I was searching for you. And Lily! I am so pleased that you are not already departed.'

'Indeed not,' said Lily. 'Goody and I have become friends.'

'I must go,' I said, suddenly flustered, feeling the blood in my cheeks. 'My mother will be waiting.' I bade them both goodnight and scurried back into the ballroom, where servants were already collecting up the platters of food and ramassing glasses. My mother stood at the French doors with Francis. I went to stand with them, my family, as we looked out over the moonlit sea and the dewfall-hawk sang on.

III

I⊤ WAS THE day before May Eve, which they named
Walpurgis Night in Germany and France, and which
my mother celebrated each year with a fierce private
joy. We would not be with her this time, though, for
Francis and I were bound for the Continent, for the
guinea run, to make our fortunes. We stood just past
six of the evening on the wharf at Rye, watching the
cabin boys strip weed from the hull of the *Albion*.
They'd had their pockets loaded with shot to weigh
them down and each was suspended on a length of
rope upon which they'd tug when they wished to rise
for breath. Smoker held one rope, Diamond another,
Poison the third – although this last was busy cleaning
his collection of knives with a shammy cloth and was
remiss in pulling his lad up, so that the boy's face was
bluer with each new surfacing, his panicked breathing
painful on the ear. I watched the boys down there,
moving along the flanks of the ship like lampreys, their
hair mingling with the weed and drifting in the same
strange currents. There was the smell of fish all about
the wharf, the fouler stench of the tanneries and the
dark water they pumped into the river. Gulls hung
lazily in the evening air, terns arrowed towards their
roost-islands in the bay. The *Albion* rose and fell gently
in the water, the breeze singing in her rigging. Gray
and Kingsmill were already aboard, so Francis and I
walked up the gangplank to join them.

They were both on the poop deck, bent over a chart.
Kingsmill looked up when we mounted the steps and
Gray came to embrace us, clapping me on the back

so hard that my hat fell off. I cursed him and the men laughed at my saltiness. After just three sorties, I already considered myself a rogue, and the men seemed to have accepted me as a kind of entertaining oddity, as much tied to the ship as the figurehead on the cut-water. I bent to retrieve the hat and Kingsmill spoke.

'Caleb Ruddy said he saw the *Amelia* out patrolling this morning. She was eastward-bound. Worth bearing in mind.'

Gray nodded. 'We'll get the guns on deck as soon as we're under sail.'

At that time, the Revenue had but little power, being still distinct from the more puissant forces of law and state; moreover the waiting officer at Rye, Barnaby Dengate by name, was ineffectual, a sot, and corrupt. Only the chance of encountering one of the three naval vessels – of which the *Amelia* was the most swift – tasked with preventing the free passage of goods across the Channel hindered us from operating in daylight. As it was, Arthur Gray's commercial activities – his mother's family, the Lambs, imported customed wine into Rye – provided ample cover for our undertakings.

It had come to Gray's attention that the central counting house in Ostend was in possession of an unusual amount of gold bullion. Several years earlier, a combination of English and Dutch pressure had obliged the Austrian Netherlands to cease their commercial ventures. The short-lived Ostend East India Company had flourished for a few years, trading both in the Indies and the New World. Now, it was said, the last of its profits – the fruits of an investment in South Sea pearls – had been repatriated and was awaiting transportation to the mint in Brussels. With the help of the jeweller who'd brought the news to his attention, Gray intended to carry out a raid on the counting house: a guinea run, as the smuggling of gold was known.

Having a girl aboard appeared to be a source of both comedy and shame for the smugglers, but I was tolerated mostly for my brains. I'd let slip that I spoke French, as well as a little German and a smattering of the Dutch language. This facility for strange tongues, which had been fostered by both my parents, seemed to strike Kingsmill in particular as absurd. He shook his head at the folly of such knowledge – 'In a wench, what's more!' – while grudgingly recognising its use as we bartered on foreign quaysides.

I was mainly consigned to the Captain's chamber, where Gray spent his time plotting the ship's course with compass and sextant. He worked with remarkable care, knowing, perhaps, that Kingsmill was the captain proper, had worked as a merchantman and a privateer – had even, as a young man, fought in the navy at the Battle of Syracuse, although the circumstances of his departure from the service were, Gray forewarned me, not to be discussed.

I was also respected by the men because, despite my age, I was willing to work. This was one thing I'd discovered early in my time as a smuggler, viz. men weren't as strong as they liked you to believe. I was large for my age, but I had not beforehand considered myself brawny. As it was, I could heft as much as many of the men. Francis, of course, would carry three tubs merely to make show of it, but amongst the others there were few of similar strength. The older men complained of their backs and their joints, coughing their stale tobacco coughs and hawking up great globules of green spittle that they'd shoot through their tongues over the side. The younger ones, when not subject to the strict rhythms of the ship, the sheets and sails and hawsers, were a dissolute and listless bunch, over-fond of grog and whoring.

When they sailed, though, as they were sailing now, out of the protection of Rye Bay and into the open Channel, they were like an intricate machine, each of them understanding clearly his place in the mechanism. I knew little of sailing then, less of the particular terms by which each part of the ship and its operation were described, but I appreciated the effortlessness of it all, the way the sloop seemed to absorb both wind and waves, transmuting them almost as if by magic into motion. Those first few journeys, Francis took it upon himself to explain to me the lore of the ship. Like any language, I picked it up quickly, and Gray would take great pleasure in testing me upon the difference between by and large, between bowsprit and sternpost, between luffing up and bearing away, as we sat in the comfort of his cabin at the ship's stern, the mullioned windows open to the night air.

That evening of the guinea run, as the sun disappeared over the western horizon and the stars began to emerge in the deep twilight, the *Albion* underwent an extraordinary transformation. From a well-manned but unexceptional commercial vessel, she became a fighting craft. Guns were brought up from below deck: heavies, which required six men and a system of ropes and pulleys to hoist them through the scuttles; swivel-guns, which were lighter and arranged to allow firing at angles other than broadside to the enemy. Subsequently, all manner of musketry and other firearms were brought up on to deck, along with boarding pikes and grappling irons, hand axes, marlinspikes and other sharp-bladed instruments of close combat. As soon as we were well clear of land, Gray ordered a firing of the guns, and it was a marvellous thing to see the speed with which the men sponged and rammed the pieces, the care they took in cupping their matches and lighting the fuses, the synchronicity of the balls which landed in close succession, sending up dimly visible spouts in the distance.

I stood for a while with Francis and Kingsmill at the helm, looking at the night watch in the crow's nest, the billowing topsail, the vast sky of stars above and the full moon which seemed to cast a path on the water before us as it rose. Gray would shout up instructions from his cabin below which Kingsmill would then relay to the crew through his speaking-trumpet. There was nervousness amongst us, certainly, but it was happy: that of a crew with faith in our captain and our prowess, knowing that a successful run would make rich folk of us all.

When, just after three of the morning, lights became visible in the darkness to the south, we prepared to go about, and then began a kind of cabotage along the French coast. At four, the watch changed, and Francis and I slung our hammocks in the forecastle where we slept amongst the snores of the other men, the groaning of the ship's timbers, the slap and shush of the waves.

I slept lightly, and dreamed of Lily St Leger when I did. She had been scarcely from my thoughts since Arnold's ball. I saw no likelihood of encountering her again any time soon, so far apart were the paths of our lives, but I felt a slow power seize hold of me each time I thought of her wide and mobile face, her soft white skin. I could only hope that she felt the same and would employ her greater years, freedom and ingenuity to effect another meeting between us.

IV

THIS IS WHAT your heart does before you kill a man: it hammers in every fibre and tissue of your body, it is loud in the drums of your ears, pulses fast in the corners of your eyes. Then it stops. And as you squeeze the trigger, everything narrows to the point of the rifle and even your heart holds its breath. Then, into that vast and dreadful stillness of time, everything rushes, and your heart pounds again, and you watch the boy – for he is only a boy – fall first to the cobbles and then, as if slowed in time, off the side of the quay and into the water.

But all that was after. At first, the guinea run went smoothly to plan. We sailed into Ostend harbour, behind the long arm of the great stone mole, just after five of the afternoon, having tarried offshore to wait the changing of the tides. It was a bright day, and the yellow flags of empire fluttered from the turrets of the old town. The port bustled with merchants and fishermen, urchins running from one end of the quayside to another, carrying messages, making mischief. The jeweller, Van de Venter, was waiting for us on the dock in a long, dark robe, such as folk wear in those parts. He had a shifty, ingratiating look to him, as if he were a man who traded confidences as easily as he traded diamonds.

We followed the jeweller into the city, with Perin taking charge of the ship. We must have made a peculiar sight, with the giant Poison, the dark-skinned Francis, myself in my unwomanly garments, and Gray, immaculately attired amid these ruffians. We carried burlap sacks and, covertly, rifles and pistols, swords and daggers. It was a boisterous place, Ostend, with troops from the Austrian wars thronging about, soldiers of the Empire and mercenaries alike, and we were certainly not alone in bearing arms. There was a holidayish air, bunting strung between the high, shuttered houses. Van de Venter, in a voice of accented but precise English, told us that the town would be riotous with Walpurgisnacht festivities, dances in the town's squares and a feast hosted by the mayor. In the darkness that night, he said, all eyes would be turned elsewhere, and we might return to our ship unmolested.

We came to the counting house, a grand, porticoed building in a wide square, where Van de Venter went inside for a moment to speak with some accomplice, then emerged from a smaller door along an alleyway that ran down one side of the great edifice. He gestured us through it. We lit our lamps and went down a narrow corridor to the strong-room, where we were to wait until the clerks had left for the evening. Then Van de Venter departed, with much bowing and benediction, and we were left in the close candlelight.

The gold itself was not, as I had imagined it, piled high in the centre of the room as if in the treasure hall of a Norse king, but rather stored in strongboxes set into the walls. Smoker lit his pipe and soon the small room was foggy with fumes. Diamond, Francis, Poison and Kingsmill each found a corner to lie down in. Gray and I both made our way back out into the low-ceilinged corridor, where we sat ourselves facing one another.

I could smell in the air the sweet scent that Gray carried about him, of orange blossom, and it made me think of my mother's glass-house, and how this was the first May Eve I had spent away from Winchelsea. We were quiet for a time and then he began to speak, in a low voice, almost as if he were talking to himself.

He told me of his past. He spoke of his mother, Ellen, the youngest daughter of the powerful Lambs of Rye, who had fallen in love with an Irishman, Pádraig Gray, Earl of Inishmore, whose title turned out to be as fictitious as his fortune, and who disappeared in the months before Gray was born, sending Ellen back to her family, where she was accepted with a degree of resentment as a kind of maiden aunt, young Arthur occupying a role somewhere between the children of the servants and the offspring of Ellen's brother, Gilbert Lamb.

'Then, one by one,' Gray told me, 'Gilbert's children, my cousins, died. Two girls of the sweating sickness, then the only boy drowned in the Rother. I proved myself quick at my lessons. My uncle Gilbert paid for my education, for my time at the university. I thought I might be a London lawyer, or a political man. I found myself missing the sea, though, and over-sensible of the closeness of bodies in London, the filthiness of the streets and the air. I came back to Rye, met up with Kingsmill, who was not long returned from the Spanish war, and we set about playing pirates. My uncle Gilbert's fortunes were at a low ebb and he was glad of the contribution my efforts brought in. The Hawkhurst Gang had existed for some centuries previous, but in a lilyish, half-hearted fashion. Kingsmill and I figured that there were fortunes to be made, and we have been blessed with luck thus far.'

We were silent again for a while, then we heard the sound of the great oak doors at the front of the building being closed and locked. Gray sprang to his feet. 'Let us be at it, then,' he said. We went back into the strong-room, jostled the others awake, and began to open the boxes.

I'd never held a guinea before, but now I took up handfuls, surprised by the weight of them, by the slipperiness of the coins when rubbed together. I charged my burlap sack three-quarters full, leaving sufficient room that I might twist its neck and swing it over my shoulder. I filled another, and was about to comment that I was ready to depart when there came to us all the sound, very distinctly, of the doors at the front of the counting house opening once more.

We stopped what we were doing and I saw a look pass between Francis and Gray. My brother now crept out into the corridor, coming back several moments later with a wild look in his eyes. 'Guards in the entrance,' he said. 'Van de Venter is with them. We've been guggled.'

V

GRAY STARTED UP and drew his pistols, looking round with the air of a cornered fox. 'Bastard, I thought as much.'

'Fuck 'em,' Kingsmill said, continuing to fling handfuls of gold into his sack. 'We takes what we wants and if the sons of bastards want skewering, we'll skewer 'em.'

We gathered up our sacks and, weighted down with them, proceeded to the side door. Francis went out first and I heard a shout, quickly silenced. Darkness had fallen outside and I saw, lying back on the ground, two young men in the dress of the Swiss guards, their necks yawning beneath their chins, blood seeping on to the moonlit cobbles. The town was loud with cele-brations, fireworks bursting over the jostling rooftops. Francis wiped his blade on the hem of his coat.

'We run,' Gray said. 'Fast and low. Francis, you lead.'

With the sacks hefted over my shoulders, the gold pieces biting into my skin, I ran, both unable and unwilling to look behind me. I heard the sound of what I thought at first was more fireworks, but then, as a musket ball whistled close past my face, revealed itself as something more deadly. Now the shooting began in earnest, and we each of us ran for our lives, impeded by the great sacks that we carried with us. I followed Francis down first one alleyway, then another, the footsteps of soldiers pounding behind us and regular explosions of musket fire. One shot passed so close that I was covered in brick dust from where it struck the wall beside me. Then, rounding a corner, I heard music in the distance and headed towards it, yelling at my brother to follow me.

There was a procession of masked revellers making its way noisily down the principal commercial street of the place, with several carts pulled by gaudily accoutred horses. There were jugglers and fire-eaters, musicians playing discordantly on the backs of the carts and from windows above. I forced my way out into the stream of people, brought the bags off my shoulders and swung them at my sides as if they were so much marketing, keeping my head down, my hat pulled low over my face. Then Francis took my arm and led me suddenly off down a side street, through a public garden in which couples strolled and courted, and then we were finally at the gates of the port. There we encountered the others: Gray insouciant, Kingsmill panting, Poison furious. We felicitated one another on our escape and set off for the quayside.

We heard the shots before we saw the soldiers. They were visible by the flare of their muskets and by the light cast from a fire that had broken out on the deck of a frigate moored between them and the *Albion*. The soldiers had ranged themselves along the mole, thinking to prevent our ship leaving port, and I counted two dozen of them at least. They lay on their fronts on the curved promontory, rolling to reload their weapons on the seaward side. We made our way down the quay in the cover of the customs house. The soldiers had their fire turned on the *Albion*, upon whose deck the crew were moving in frantic shadows. I saw that already the mizzenmast was badly damaged and a fire burned on the poop deck. Partly from the benefit granted by their elevation, partly because the crew of the ship were not in the main fighting men and handled their weapons with a degree of nervousness, the soldiers appeared to be besting the fight. I watched as Perin, seeking to repel a boarder on the foredeck, took a faceful of shot. He went stumbling over the edge and into the water, where he sank into blackness.

Gray gestured to a point further down the wharf where it ran up against the mole. We piled the gold on the cobbles and scurried hunkerwise until we were couched in the shadowy corner. From where we stood, we were looking down the line of the mole, side-on to the soldiers. Each time they fired, I saw young faces illuminated, ghostly cameos of concentration and fear. Poison was already busy over the mouth of his rifle, issuing occasional curses into his beard as he fumbled in the darkness. The soldiers, apprehending our arrival, turned their fire upon us. I heard a cry as, close by me, Diamond was hit. It was not a clean kill, the ball having struck him in the shoulder, from which a good deal of blood was now spouting. He turned to me, his face twisted into the most horrible grin, and I saw the stone in his teeth glint in the moonlight. Then there was another volley from the soldiers and Diamond's entire head seemed to leave his shoulders in a great eruption of blood.

It was at this moment that I felt strong arms forcing me to the ground. Gray was on top of me. His breath was hot on my cheek, his body heavy upon mine. 'Keep down,' he said. Then he brought his rifle up in front of me. 'Take it.' When I did so, tucking it up under my chin, he folded his cool fingers over mine.

I felt my breath coming quickly and willed it slower. 'Your brother seems to think you could be a great smuggler, Goody,' he said. 'More than just a passenger. I thought I'd see if you were up to it. Now close one eye.'

I looked along the barrel of the gun and my heart was loud.

Everything narrowed to the face of a boy, eighteen or nineteen, in a helmet that was too large for him. I noted the quiet joy in that face, the excitation that came with his first taste of battle. I saw the way that, even now, as the air of a musket ball passed close by his cheek, he felt himself invincible. I could see in that sweat-sheened young face the inner workings of a placid provincial mind, and how he was already recounting the story of the skirmish to his sister, a few days hence, of how they'd chased the Englishmen from the town, and those they'd not killed had been direly injured, and how he'd shot dead ten, perhaps twelve of the pirates himself. I knew that even as he was fighting he was imagining his return home, his father's pride, his mother's embrace, and the bright enraptured eyes of his sister. At that moment, I cocked the frizzen and pulled the trigger of Gray's rifle. There was a crack in the air, a burst of powder, and the boy, in the flickering flames and the cool light of the moon, slumped forward.

Now Poison fired his weapon also, and Smoker and Kingsmill began to pick off the enemy one by one. The soldiers panicked, rose to their feet, running first one way, then another, finding that the mole they'd moments earlier considered a stronghold had become a trap. Francis and Gray were up now, firing. I drew my father's sword, not trusting the flintlock in my pocket. Men ahead of me fell left and right under the combined attack of my brother and Gray, plunging into the water like Channel-geese. I saw that Poison was running along the wharf below with Smoker, hurrying to get the gold aboard the *Albion*. Kingsmill, huffing and cursing, trotted behind them.

While we'd been on the mole, the fire that had been raging on the frigate had leapt to a sloop-of-war, whose gunpowder went up in a great eructation, so it appeared that the whole of the harbour was aflame. Fishing boats seemed to pass the fire between them like a gift, while a series of larger ships had all of their rigging alight, and crackled and blazed merrily, casting flickering shadows on the walls of the city. I saw that the *Albion* had raised her jib, which was her only functionable sail, and now moved haltingly through the flame-lit water. Kingsmill was at the tiller, steering a course as closely as he could to where we stood at the end of the mole. As the ship passed, Francis took a running leap over the bloodied remains of the soldiers, over the wide gap of dark air, landing on the topsail rigging. I went after him, finding myself attached further down than him, with my hands and fingers stinging, my breath knocked from me. Gray waited for the mizzenmast, and landed in its shrouds awkwardly, letting out a loud curse. But then we were out in the open sea with the flaming harbour behind us, and all the gold aboard; the mainsail was big-bellied with wind and men clambered up the rigging and into the crows' nests and on to the gunwales and every one of them let out a halloo to the wide and moonlit night.

VI

I WILL NOT here recount how limpingly we jib-sailed our way back to Rye, nor will I speak of the further moments of danger that we experienced on that passage – but I'll say we snagged our keel on one of the outer banks of the Goodwin Sands, and the whole ship shuddered and groaned until we broke free; and a navy cutter that appeared coming up fast out of the west forced us into the lee of the Dunge Ness spit, where the great light turned its endless revolutions. We watched the ship go by through our glasses, ready to beach ourselves if we had to, the gold we were carrying being worth twenty or thirty *Albions*.

I sat on the deck that night, my senses all roiled and perplexed, and I thought of the distance I had journeyed from the genteel young lady my father had hoped to raise. I remembered him telling me how important it was for me to embrace the delicate pleasures of womanhood – in other words, that I ought to submit to a future of burping colicky babies, infantile prattle and a distant, reproving husband. He'd had great plans for me, my father – greater perhaps because his son had forsaken him, and if I had to bury my true nature in order to achieve them, this, it seemed, was a price I ought to have been willing to pay. I wished he could have known, though, the joy that filled my heart, to be out on the ocean, with his sword at my waist; to be living a life that was full and unconstrained.

Finally, we were round the headland and into Rye Bay. It was now a soft spring evening and the fishermen were on the riverbanks as we made our way up the

Rother, folding and repairing their nets in the day's last light. They stood and watched us, broken-masted and hamble-shanked, tack effortfully up the river, until we were finally at the wharf. We were silent as we unloaded into the great Lamb warehouse first what remained of our powder, sailcloth and victuals, then the gold, cached inside water butts that necessitated three men to heft them down the plank and across the cobbles of the wharf to the warehouse. There was the long, customary process of distributing the share: first to the cabin boy and loblolly boy, thence to the common sailors, then a sombre moment, when Gray set aside in a solemn pile what was owed to the families of the six who had died – a greater share due to Diamond's father and to old Mrs Perin, who lived over on the marsh towards Hythe with their son, and imagined her husband a hero, and would be quite undone by his death. Finally came the turn of the gang itself. On previous runs, my portion had been calculated as one half of Francis's, and had been added to his imbursement, but this time Gray placed his arm about my shoulders.

'Six thousand guineas in all. A good night's work. Has any man an objection to Goody being given a share? She showed no more fear than the rest of you; less than some. And we have two fewer now to consider.' There was a heavy silence. Poison cleared his nostrils on to the ground. But no one spoke and, after a moment longer, Gray's eyes met mine. 'So be it, then. We've had no wench in the gang before, but there's nowt to stop us.'

Our gold was placed into saddle bags ready for the

trip back to Winchelsea. 'Be mindful of footpads, now,' Gray said, grinning. The sailors disappeared swiftly into the night, back to their wives and children, many doubtless swearing never again to put to sea with smugglers.

The rest of us – the Hawkhurst Gang, of which, it seemed, I was now a member – took our leave more slowly: sending up for horses to the Mermaid; loading and securing our gold; allowing ourselves to feel, as we stepped out into the evening, which was mild and sweet, a brief sense of having pulled off something magnificent. Francis and I finally departed, our horses so loaded that we had to lead them. I turned back when we reached the Tillingham Bridge to find the gang still standing in the lamplight outside the warehouse, looking after us. Smoker was puffing brown clouds from his pipe that drifted before the lamp; Poison scritched at something in his long, matted hair. Kingsmill and Gray kept their eyes on us, and I felt a moment of unease. Kingsmill said something and Gray shook his head. Francis called me on, and as the stars came out over the marsh and a slow moon rose, we went home.

VII

MY MOTHER WAS in her glass-house when we returned at just past eleven of the clock. She was sitting with her back to us, looking out upon the garden where, amid the shadows of the orchard trees, the embers of a fire dimly glowed – she had festivated Walpurgis

Night in our absence. She turned when we came into the room, and took first Francis's hands, then mine, squeezing them as if to confirm that we were not ghosts. She looked tired and old, and I bethought myself of her life, one in which she had waited for my father, for Francis, and now for me, fearing all the time that we might not return.

We went through to the hall, where my mother bent to light candles upon the table. I caught sight of myself in the looking-glass by the door and saw my hair, falling in a candlelit wave about my head, more silver than blonde, shimmering. My face was pale and grimy; I had grazed my cheek, I knew not precisely when nor how. I gently pressed the back of my hand to the raw place, and found that the salt on my skin stung the wound. I turned to where Francis now sat pouring two tankards of porter, a small glass of my mother's favourite liqueur already poured for her.

When we had supped a little, we went to discharge the horses. The gold we placed in the strongbox in my father's study, and when this was filled, in the trunk where he had kept his liniments and unguents, his bandages and splints. These relics of his doctoring my mother scooped up in an armful and took through to the glass-house. Francis now sat down at my father's desk with a familiarity that I couldn't bring myself to begrudge him, and made a series of notes in a ledger-book. My mother came and stood beside him, as she used to with my father when he was working, and I saw her look over the figures and place an approbatory hand on Francis's shoulder. He swigged at his porter, patted her hand and returned to his figuring.

'Do we stop now?' I said. 'We have more gold here than we will ever require. We came breath-close to death and saw those who sailed with us die. It felt as if last night was a warning, brother.'

Both my mother and Francis were looking at me with a deal of intensity. Then I saw my mother reach down and pick up the pen with which my brother had been making his accounts. I stood and watched, upside down, as she formed the words in her slow, ungainly hand.

TELL HER

Francis turned and looked first at our mother, then at me, then back at the ledger. He shook his head, then shook it again, as if trying to loosen a thought. He stood heavily, reached for his bottle, stumbled to the door.

'Not tonight,' he said. 'I am dog tired and know not how to phrase it all yet. Perhaps on the morrow, sister. I must see my bed through the bottom of this bottle.' He came and placed a kiss upon my cheek. We listened to him clumping up the stairs. It struck me then what a noise a man makes, merely getting about the world. We heard him stomp into his room above us, piss loudly into his commode, a fart and a sigh halfway through. Then the creaking of a heavy body hoisted into bed. Finally, the silence of two women.

My mother went to sit at my father's desk. I stood in the middle of the room, as I had done when, as a child, my father had chastised me for spending too long in the cellars, or up in the wildwoods, or swimming out in the bay. The lamplight flimmered as my mother picked up the pen and began to write, casting shadows across her face. It was painful to watch her; each letter seemed forced from her with a pang. She was not lettered, my mother, and although my father had taught her to read – and indeed she was well-versed in the books of herbalism and old lore in her glass-house – she had never written easily. Since she had lost her tongue, we had developed between us a mode of understanding that employed, in the place of words, the raising of eyebrows, the pursing of lips: a silent language of the face.

After a time, she held up to me the ledger, on a blank page of which she had written:

YOUR FATHER WAS A SPY

I nodded, shifted my weight from one foot to the other, watched her write again. She raised it to the light and I read it.

FOR THE KING OVER THE WATER

I nodded again, feeling something knot within me. My love for my father was boundless, stretched eternal by his death, but at the same time, none of this struck me as surprising. Indeed, it felt like something I'd known long-while, somewhere deep within.

FRANCIS MUST TELL YOU OF THE ASSOCIATION

She looked up at me, and our eyes met; hers were small and hard and full of some obscure but puissant sentiment. I recognised there were things I ought to have asked her long ago, and that I needs must seize the opportunity to question her.

'Tell me about my mother,' I said. 'My real mother, who died. Did you know who she was – her family, her home?' I was half-tempted to write my own questions on to the ledger, it seeming an unbalanced way of communicating, that I should speak while she struggled with her pen.

SERVANT GIRL, my mother wrote. *IN RYE. BEAUTY. NO FAMILY.*

'And my father?' I asked, coming towards her, stepping into the circle of light by the desk lamp. 'What do you know of him?'

GENTLEMAN, she wrote. *BUT A BOY.* Then – and this haltingly, taking so long that I was tempted to swipe the pen from her and complete the words that I knew were coming, even upside down and in my mother's crabbed and quavering hand, words that sprung tears to my eyes – *I LOVE YOU*.

I went around the desk then, and she rose, and I took her in my arms and we stood there, both breathing. She scarcely reached my chest, this little woman, and I knew I'd loved my father to her exclusion when he was alive. For, whilst he had been as diminutive as she, he had seemed bigger with his passionate enthusiasms, and had cast her in the shadow of his learning and ideas. My mother now rose up on her tiptoes and stretched to place a kiss on my shoulder. I bent to return it, encountering the tousle of her short, dark, musty-smelling hair.

Then I went up to my chamber. I removed my clothes, which had become so sweat-smeared and salt-crusted that they were stiff, and here and there stuck to my body. I stood for a while, letting Old Joll's shells fall through my fingers. I thought to myself of what I had learnt, trying to wheedle out the right and wrong of things, to see my father in the dim light of my mother's scrawled information. When I slept, I slept depthlessly, though I dreamt not of Lily, but of the ruined face of the boy I'd shot.

VIII

FRANCIS WAS CALLED away to Rye early the next morning to meet with Gray and Kingsmill. They would go together to visit Perin's widow out on the marshes, take her the gold, and speak to her of her husband's heroism, of the esteem in which they all held him. Perin had an indigent, rapscallionish son, who lurched from one down-at-heel marsh tavern to the next. Francis would speak to the son, let him know his responsibilities now that the old man was gone. I pictured broken fingers, a bloodied nose, a snivelling commitment uttered through burst lips.

It was a fine day, and we watched Francis set off, his back straight, his pace brisk, trotting up to the top of Rectory Lane, then round the corner and out of sight. My mother and I spent the day in the garden, which was now entirely given over to riotous nature. Dancing swags of ox-eye daisies and cow parsley swayed, while grasses reached up to the lowest branches of the trees, all of them rustling and whispering in the breeze. The careful regularity of my father's garden had been replaced by a different kind of order, where everything seemed to glow with an especial intensity, in quite the same vivid green as the paste my mother made for me. Ivy grew all about the place, wrapping itself protectively around every tree, snaking up the red-brick walls, twining up the white sides of the house itself.

Francis did not come back until late that night, when we had gone to our chambers. I heard him pass my room, cannon from one side of the corridor to the other, then upend himself on his bed. I rose, lit my candle, and went along to find him face-down on the counterpane. He smelt of port and pipe smoke and had pissed himself, quite recently. I removed his clothes, eliciting from him a groan or two, and stood him by his bed. He grasped one of the stanchions and leant against it. I then took a sponge from his washstand, where a bowl of water stood, and cleaned down his long, muscled shanks, between the ovals of his buttocks, his veined pizzle. Finally, I stripped the pane from the bed, found that the piss had not dampened the linen beneath, and helped him between the sheets. At once, with his head upon the pillow, his face achieved a kind of beatific look, so that it was possible to see how he must have appeared as a child. I kissed him and went back to my own chamber. I could not sleep for some time, but thought about my brother, about the horrors he must have endured as a little one, about the extraordinary luck and fortitude that had brought him to Winchelsea − to my father, to me.

In the morning, Francis came down late, his clothes from the previous night heaped beneath his arm. He placed these on the floor of the scullery, fetched himself a bowl of oatmeal, and came to sit beside me at the table. It was a while before he spoke.

'We go to Seacox Heath tonight. Arthur is celebrating our success. It will be a grand affair. With Arthur, it always is.'

We spent the day practising swordcraft, aiming and firing pistols and muskets at the targets in the garden. Then it was six of the evening. I went to my chamber and dressed myself in the dark tunic and hose that had become my habitual attire. These manly weeds felt to me as close an expression in outward apparel of my inner self being neither one thing nor the other, and imbued every movement with a freedom that was at once physical and symbolical.

I knew not what kind of night lay ahead, but I guessed it would be neither so formal nor so staid as the Nesbitts' ball. I kissed my mother goodbye. Francis had already saddled Hero and a new horse, a Belgian dray with shaggy ankles which he'd named Mariana, and we went clopping out into the warm afternoon. When we'd crossed the river and were making our way slowly up the hill towards the Udimore ridge, I thought it time to raise the subject of our father with Francis. 'Mother scribbled some revelations in your ledger the other night,' I told him.

'I saw them,' he said, moving a stalk of grass from one side of his mouth to the other as he spoke. 'You must believe me, there was no attempt to misuse you here. I'm certain that Father wanted to tell you – would have done so, as soon as he felt you prudential enough to keep your counsel.' He slapped a fly on Mariana's flank, looked about, and continued in a more confidential tone. 'You have heard talk of the Association of Gentlemen?'

'No,' I said.

'Well then, you know of the uprising that took place in Scotland these thirty years hence.'

'The King Over the Water.'

'The very same. Father was there. He and Baron Caryll fought together at Inverness and Gordon Castle. He was in it for adventure, but also for the riches and titles on offer should they have succeeded. As it was, they failed, and Father fled to Europe. He would return there often in the years that followed, to sit in the court of the Pretender at Rome. He met Prince Charlie there, became a kind of mentor to the boy.'

I pictured my father, who had always been swayed by titles, by the fallalery of the high life, by beautiful things. I imagined how taken he would have been by the image of himself as a peer of the realm, in close confabulation with the rightful Prince of Wales; a confidant of the court. My father was a good man, but he was vain and he was avaricious. This love of good things had brought him to his watery end, just in a more roundabout fashion than Tomkins had suspected.

'Tomkins accused Father of drawing off funds from the Mayfield Gang to support his extravagancies,' Francis said. 'He was correct. Certainly, Father bought books and wine and paintings. But the main share of his expenditure was upon the Jacobite cause. When he returned from the defeat in '15, he was initiated into the Association, a group of English gentlemen who sought to ensure the success of the next Jacobite uprising. They met in secret at West Grinstead, or at one of the other great houses where dreams of the old regime were harboured. When Ezekiel found me on the beach at Camber, a year after the failure of the Spanish invasion, he took it upon himself to instil in me a Jacobitism as pure and unshakeable as his own.'

'And did he?' I asked, aware that while my father had told me stories of his adventuring past, he had never seen fit to inculcate me in the Jacobite cause, presuming, no doubt that there was no place for a woman in politicking.

We had now quit Peasmarsh and were climbing up on to the ridge that lay between the valleys of the Rother and the Tillingham, the woods all spread out around and below us, their leaves glowing gently as evening fell.

'No,' Francis said, carefully. 'What I did perceive, and swiftly so, was that there was deep love of the King Over the Water amongst many of the most powerful gentlemen of this land, and of course more so still in Scotland. I recognised then, as I believe now, that with the help of France, Jacobitism has a fair chance of success, and that our fortunes will be substantially altered if we play a role in hastening it. Father and I worked out the manner in which we would levy a tithe from the Mayfield Gang's operations in the cellars. Then we waited for the Prince and his allies to make another essay. We wait still.'

We were silent as we went over the Rother – a much narrower river here – at Newenden. There was a game of cricket finishing in the long late rays of sunlight, the fieldsmen crouched close around the bat, the bowler charging to the wicket before skimming the ball wickedly at the batsman, who despatched it with a *plock* into the river. Another ball was found, the bowler barrelled in again. As we rode up past the church and around the corner, I heard the dry sound of the wicket falling, and a great cheer that went up from the men. We kicked the horses into a gallop as we passed the Tenterden road, went through Sandhurst and up Megrims Hill towards Hawkhurst, towards Seacox Heath.

IX

GRAY HAD BUILT his new home on a stretch of moorland to the north of Hawkhurst, the place after which the gang was named. There was little about the village to suggest its dangerous associations: an almshouse, a cobbler sitting out on the street mending a pair of riding boots, a group of children playing huzzlecap beside the road. There were a few well-dressed women at the crossroads who called out as we went by; Francis raised a gallant hand to them. We left the village and were soon climbing again. It was nearing eight of the clock and the sun had gone down quietly into a bank of cloud, so that the country about us became grey-blue in the gloaming. Finally, we saw a place where two torches stood flaming in the ground, lighting pillars on which a pair of lions rampant stood. We followed the path under a canopy of inter-reaching trees until we came out on to a crescent-shaped driveway that led up to a house of extraordinary size and splendour.

I scarce had time to appreciate the great gloomy mass of Seacox Heath – the way the darkness of its stone was accentuated by the lights that blazed in every window, the turrets that pointed up at each of its corners – before a liveried footman appeared and helped me from my horse. I gave Hero a pat, linked my arm through that of Francis and we went together up the scroll of steps at the front of the house and into the loud vastness of the hallway.

Everything within was too much – the windows, with their stained glass and intricate lattices of lead mullion; the parquet of the floor, which dizzied the eyes with its clever interstices; the lighting, which was principally a series of enormous chandeliers dependent on long chains from the ceiling. In each one, perhaps three dozen candles burned. There was a company of musicians at one end of the room playing a rollicking hornpipe, while nearer by I saw a table laden with exquisite pyramids of sweetmeats and pastries.

We went through the hall, Francis and I, as if we were in a walking dream. Many of the close-pressed guests wore masks – some that covered only the eyes, others that hid their whole faces. The dresses of the women were of the most sumptuous and finely wrought materials, although their bodices were cut lower than any I had seen before. As the dancers spun and clasped and jumped and whirled, flesh and ringletted hair rippled and jounced.

Regular doorways opened off that cavernous central hall on to smaller rooms, each of which was packed with figures. And where the central hall blazed with the light of the chandeliers, these side rooms were low-lit, shadowy; like secret, shameful thoughts pushed to the outer edges of the mind. In one, I glimpsed writhing bodies, naked as babes, intermingling in such a variety of ways that they seemed like some great fleshy beast: a groaning, swiving, undulating thing that bucked and shuddered and swelled.

'It's scarce past eight of the evening,' Francis said with tug on my elbow, 'and you are too much of a child to witness such things. Come, there's Poison; let us take a stroll on the terrace with him.'

But I looked into the room as long as I was able, neither repelled nor much excited by the vision, but rather fascinated, as when at the Mop Fair some sad and freakish figure was paraded in the tents for those willing to fling a ha'penny their way. Then we were at the far end of the hall, past where the company of musicians stood on a raised platform and fiddled and drummed as if the devil were after them. I recognised Poison by his bulk, of course, although he was dressed in a long cloak of dark velvet, and upon his head wore a golden mask from which a pair of antlers protruded. The bush of his beard beneath the mask gave him the look of a *wolpertinger* or *rasselbock*, or one of those other strange deer-creatures that haunt the pages of German folklore. He raised his tankard towards us and leered, the gold in his mouth glinting in the candlelight.

I saw, gathered around Poison, others of the Hawkhurst Gang, less recognisable until I perceived that they all wore the same cervine masks, the same golden antlers thrusting from their foreheads. Kingsmill had a young woman on each arm, red-faced things, their breasts spilling from their bodices. Smoker chewed on his pipe, then swigged at a bottle of sack. Behind them, at the high casement windows that stood open on to the terrace, was Gray. He was attired in a long black cloak, a huge white ruff around his collar that called to mind a Dutch priest. With the mask and the horns and his long dark hair swept back behind it, this hieratical impression was devilish unsettling. He grinned at us, then gestured to one of the footmen, who scurried off upon his order.

'Come, let us step outside,' said Gray, bowing us through the casement window and out into the night. We followed him on to the terrace, which stretched the length of the building and then curved down at each end to the lawns below. The night was clear, with a waning moon illuminating enough of the landscape to show that the lawns led down to a lake, then woods rolling away into the distance. We stood at the stone balustrade, along which were posed more flaming torches. I was on one side of Gray, Francis the other.

'It is for this that I am brave,' Gray said, nodding his head back.

'For the house,' Francis asked, 'or for the orgies?'

Couples walked and frolicked in the dim light beneath us; others strolled along the terrace, some of them masked, others with their masks in their hands, inspecting the faces of those they'd danced with or tupped within.

Gray laughed. 'A little of both. To be in possession of a home that makes the place in which I grew up appear fiddle-faddle in comparison. But also to throw a thrash like this, in which the daughters of noblemen felter with farmhands, and where you don't know if the wench beside you is a common drab or a magistrate's wife as you play her. What about you?' This last in a suddenly sharper tone, all the humour gone from his voice. 'Why is it that you risk it all, Francis?

'Or you, Goody? Avenging your father I could understand, but why then stick at a life which will see you either gibbetted or murdered or drowned afore you're old?'

I threw back the rest of my punch, took a breath, then heard Francis speak. 'You and I have disquisited upon this subject before, Arthur,' he said. 'You know my motivations as well as any.' We were interrupted at that point by the footman, who returned with two of the golden masks. I removed my hat, laid it on the balustrade, and affixed the mask. The antlers made it rest heavily upon my face, and all about my vision was a new dark halo, as if I were peering up from the bottom of a pit.

'Very good,' said Arthur. 'You could pass for a man with your mask and your highwayman's get-up. Bravo. So, Francis is a Jacobite and that's where his money goes. And what about you, young Goody? Are you as wedded to your brother's Popish ways? How do you intend to disburse your profits from our ventures? You comprehend a man when you perceive what he will die for. A woman, too.'

Now both Gray and Francis were looking at me: two inquisitive, gilded deer.

'I can only tell you this,' I said. 'That before the ships, before the night-runs and the fear, I lived a life that was solitary, circumscribed, comfortable. Now I am pressed close to the dangerous edge of things and it makes my blood run fast. I was not born to be a gentlewoman.'

There was a shout from within. A brawl had broken out in the hall and Kingsmill was calling in a jocular voice for Gray to come in and adjudicate. Francis went with him. Soon there were more raised voices, the sound of breaking glass, a cry. The music struck up again, although there was a kind of forced jollity to the gigue now.

I remained outside, my attention suddenly drawn to a pair of young women strolling along the terrace towards me. They wore masks about their eyes, but I recognised the nacreous sheen of one of the dresses, the intricate frills of the other. I saw also the way that one of them moved, and remembered how that body had felt in my arms, the beat of her heart under the skin of her back, her cool hands against my face.

X

I POSITIONED MYSELF to interrupt their passage towards the hall. They were looking downward as they walked, lost in the kind of secret feminine conversation that always fired a dart of envy into me, knowing I had never had such confidence from a friend, nor ever would, it seemed, given the shape my life was taking. Finally, the girls stopped, looked up and saw me. It is difficult to read eyes deprived of their faces, but I saw something like fear in their parted lips and the quickness of their breath, and in the way Abigail darted a glance towards the hall, as if she might make a run for the safety of the crowd.

'Sir,' said Lily, and I realised that in my black tunic and mask I might easily be taken for a man. 'You mistake us for acquaintances, I fear. My companion and I are waited upon by friends within.' I stood longer, suddenly unsure as to my next move. 'Please, sir, we are in debt to you and your comrades for the spectacle this evening, but I pray you, let us past.' I could perceive a slight tremor in her voice. As if picking up on her friend's disquiet, Abigail set off at a brisk trot past me. Lily attempted to follow, but I reached out for her hand; said her name, first low, then louder.

'You know me?' she said, her eyes wide beneath the mask.

'We have met,' I said, 'under different circumstances.' I watched happiness flood her face.

'Goody?' she said. 'I had hoped to see you here.'

We now walked back along the terrace, stopping a footman to take from him two more cups of the steaming punch. I linked her arm in mine as we walked and she pressed herself close against me. A waft of breeze blew up around us, lavender-scented from the borders of the balustrade.

'So it was all true, your tales of murder and desperation?' Her eyes shone in the torchlight.

'I am not much one for lying.'

'I envy you. My father does not know we are here.'

I took her arm again and we walked down from the terrace to where the lawns stretched out in the moonlight, shadows from the house dancing on the grass.

'Take off your mask,' Lily said.

'If you will yours.'

'On three.' She counted and we both of us unfastened our masks. She was turned towards the light of the house, which cast upon her pale, frank face a golden glow. I was in darkness and she reached up to tilt my head that she might better discern me. 'You are the same,' she said. 'And I find I like you.' She had not taken her hand from my face, and I reached up to press my own against it. A man said something over in the bushes that circled the lawn, a woman giggled. 'My cousin Lindsay will be looking for me,' Lily said. 'He was at the university with Gray, at Cambridge. My father thinks I'm with Miss Maddox for the week.'

'Please, stay a little longer,' I said, and as if it were the only way of tarrying her, I leant forward and placed a kiss on her full, red lips. I felt them open beneath my own, felt the softness of her skin, the wetness inside her mouth as I dropped my cup of punch and placed the hand that was not clasped in hers against her back, feeling for the skin beneath her bodice and shift. After some moments of standing there, pressed together, the beat of our bodies seeming to pulse in the air and root into the ground, she drew back.

'I must go,' she said. 'But may I come and call on you?' There was a sudden urgency to her voice. 'We are invited to visit the Nesbitts in July. My father has politicking to do. I will find you when I am in Winchelsea.' She leant forward and kissed me again, then ran up the slope towards the house.

I stood for a while longer, caught in a moment that seemed so much of a piece with the dreams I'd had of it that I wondered if I might not wake in my hammock on the ship, or in my bed at home. Eventually, I made my way back up towards the light and noise, retying my mask as I went. I took a cup of punch, drank it down in a hurry, then picked up another, my mind all turned about itself. I stumbled through the throng of bodies, half-looking for Lily still, or for my brother, but all I saw were masked faces: wolves and plague doctors and Jack-in-the-Greens, all of them quite sotted with drink, the whole great hall radiating with the heat of those who danced within. I saw in the corners that already many had taken on too much: there were men lying in crumpled heaps; a woman with a trail of vomit coming from her lips; one of the footmen lay stripped of his clothes, propped against the wall and grinning empty-headedly. I saw a pair of antlers bobbing in the centre of the dancing press of bodies and followed them down the room, stepping one way and then the other to avoid the surging mass of drunken revellers.

When I came to the figure in the deer mask, I saw that it was not my brother, but Gray, and that he had removed the white ruff and cloak and now stood in a black shirt and breeches. He put an arm around me and guided me further into the hall. He said something in my ear, but the noise of the music and voices was too loud. He laughed and, his arm still tightly around me, moved us towards a large doorway. Once through, the sound of the festivities was much reduced, and I saw that we were in another hall, this one smaller than the last, from which a stately staircase wound upwards. Gray removed his mask and left it on the table at the foot of the stairs. I did likewise, at the same time collecting a drink that someone had left there. It was cold, but it was still strong and good.

'Come,' Gray said. 'I wish to show you something.' He set off up the stairs at a fast clip. Following him,

I recognised I was not quite steady on my feet, and had to stop for a moment on the first landing to gather myself. Then, Gray led me to a chamber with doors set all about it.

'Here, Goody,' he said, opening one of them. 'You have no fear of heights?' The door gave on to a narrow passageway that ran like a cloister around the inside of the upper level of the hall. From this galleried position, we could look down upon the crowds below, who seemed like swarming insects, or sprats writhing in the hold of a fishing barque. We went further along, down a set of steps, and I saw that we were now above a gaming room, a boxing ring, above the dim salon in which couples and trios still lay in convoluted embraces.

'Look at them,' Gray said, coming to stand alongside me. 'We are but animals after all. There is beauty in it, though, think you not?'

'It is like nothing I have seen before,' I said. 'I know not quite what to think.'

Gray placed his arm about my shoulders. I felt a sudden roil in my stomach, a shifting beneath me, a sense of being both too enclosed and exposed at once. Gray's arm was heavy, his voice distant. I could smell again his eau de cologne, the heavy scent of orange blossom.

'We are friends, are we not, Goody?' The bodies beneath squirmed and wrenked. I saw a man's face contort and then relax as he spasmed. The woman beneath him had her mouth tightly closed. I wondered then how many of those here were guests, and how many in the pay of the man whose hand was now travelling down my back, then to my buttocks. Suddenly he was kissing me, his breath hot and sour, his tongue forcing its way into my mouth. I felt him press himself against me, felt the thinness of his clothing, the hardness of the muscle beneath.

For a moment I kissed him back; allowed myself, who had never been kissed before, to marvel at the fact of two such embraces in a single night. I seized a handful of his hair and met his tongue with my own. I could feel in him an upswelling of lust, a power that terrified and excited me in equal measure. Then he began to tug at the front of my tunic, attempted to unlace the fastenings at my chest, and I realised I was at risk of more than a kiss. With a twist of my shoulders, I broke free from him and ran back down the gallery. I heard the heavy tread of his feet behind me; stopped for a moment as I turned a corner and could see that he was closing fast. I ran again, up the steps and along the final side of the walkway to the door that led to the stairwell.

Gray was almost upon me when I burst out through the door and into the arms of my brother, who, unmasked and smiling, had just ascended the stairs.

'I've been looking for you,' he said, his smile fading as Gray came pantingly into the chamber. 'Is aught amiss? Goody? Arthur?'

Gray gave us a sour little look. 'Nothing, friend. I have been showing young Goody my viewing gallery. Now, if you'll excuse me, I must return to my hostly duties.'

We watched in silence as he descended, then Francis ushered me through one of the other doors, along a corridor, and, lifting a window, helped me out on to a small stone balcony that overlooked the terrace below. 'I'd warrant a little air will do you good,' he said.

XI

WE STOOD THERE for a while as my breath slowed. The hour was grown late and the guests were beginning to drift away into the night. I heard carriages arriving on the far side of the house, the echo of horses' hooves and shouted farewells. Francis drew out his pipe, stuffed and lit it, then puffed for a time.

'He tried to molest you.'

I wasn't sure if it was a question or not and so gave a half-nod of my head.

'Goody, you need to show more caution. These are dangerous men. They would think nothing of hurting you.' A pause, a break in the music below, the kee-wick of a brown owl in the woods over towards Hawkhurst. 'Gray has always had a penchant for young girls.' Francis looked at me after saying this, and I sensed some deeper signification to his words.

'I can manage my own affairs, brother. You must not over-coddle me now. And next time Gray wishes to ravish me, perhaps I will let him.'

'Don't be a fool. His fine manners mask a murderer's heart. He's killed many and he'll kill more. You did not wonder at the haste with which his cousins departed the earth, allowing him a full inheritance? He's more of a fiend than Poison and Kingsmill combined, and unpredictable at that.'

'I admire him,' I said, realising that I was purposefully needling my brother. 'And he is very handsome.'

Another pause as Francis knocked out his pipe, restuffed it, lit it and puffed again. A kind of heaviness settled, and my brother's voice was very serious when he spoke. 'I will tell you something of Gray, then. And you may form your own decisions of him. As you know, he is a year or so older than me, and when I first came to Winchelsea he used to come into the Salutation every now and again, having a thirst for strong liquor and being barred from many of the taverns in Rye for one reason or another. He spoke of how he was meddling with the scullery maid at his uncle's house, and how she was now with child, and had been let go from his uncle's service. She had, Gray said, thrown herself on him, pleading that he should do his duty by her. This, of course, was quite against his way of thinking. He was about to go up to the university, he had the world before him. He told me that he'd given her a handful of coins and sent her on her way.'

I lowered myself down to sit on the cool stone of the balustrade, my back against the parapet wall. It had taken me but a moment to comprehend the import of the story that my brother was telling me. I felt all at once very weak, as if I should never be able to stand again. My voice came small from me when I spoke. 'She had the child, did she not? And then drowned herself.'

'Aye.' He stood over me, his eyes kindly. 'I am sorry.'

I realised that I was crying, but whether out of pity for my mother or horror at the recognition of the blood that ran in me, I knew not. 'We must go home,' I said, sniffing and wiping my sleeve across my face.

We made our way back down the stairs, through the dregs of the soirée, and out on to the gravel, where footmen were despatched to fetch our horses. We were silent all of the way home, picking our way slowly through the deep blue night, through the woods that hushed and crackled about us, then down to the Tillingham Bridge and over the marsh to Winchelsea. It was nearing four of the morning when we finally came in through the gates of Paradise, and the first birds were beginning to stir in the garden. I gave my brother a swift kiss on the cheek and went up to my room.

I wanted to scream, and so I did, bending over and yelling, kneeling on the floor and twining my hands in my hair. Then I was still. I thought about the blood that ran through me, product of an act of violence, marked by deceit and death. I pictured Gray's cunning, vulpine face, his calculating eyes. I rose and went to my looking glass, trying to find his face in mine. It was there: only the whisper of a resemblance, but once seen, it was unmissable. I ran to the window and screamed again, out into the night, caring not if I woke the whole town. I heard my mother's footsteps come to my door, pause for a moment, then retreat, and I was glad of her tact. I slept with that scream still ringing about me. I slept on, through the whole day and much of the next night, waking before dawn with a feeling of desolation just below my heart.

PART THREE

Winchelsea, May 1743

I

I SPENT A week in which I felt entirely untethered from myself. I went wandering in the Under-Reach over the course of those days, roaming darkly with no light to guide me, finding in the clefts and crannels of that subterranean world a kind of comfort, but also a reflection of my own benighted soul. I often howled as I roved about down there, barking and yelping into the darkness. I recognised that, while my mother – my real mother – had always been a solid figure in my mind, I had preferred a father who was nebulous, an airy villain. Now that Gray had stepped into that role, it felt I'd lost some especial connection to Ezekiel, to the man I called Father.

Then, as if emerging from those tenebrous caverns prompted a lifting in my spirits, I came up into the house one evening to find Francis waiting for me by the hall table. In candlelight he stood, and there was great kindness in his large, dark eyes. He seemed to glow just then, with all the light behind him, and looked so strong and capable that I couldn't help but stumble forward into his arms. We remained like that for some moments, my breath coming fast, his arms hard about me. Then he spoke, placing in my hands a bundle of papers, all tied up with a white ribbon.

'I have been looking for a moment to share these with you,' he said. 'They will likely persuade you to look kindlier on our enterprise, on our father. Indeed, it sorrows me that I did not show you these long ago.'

I sat myself at the table and opened the ribbon. The papers were letters, written in a childish, slanting hand. They were addressed to *My Dear Doctor* or *Dr* and signed *Charles P.* It took me a while to decipher the script, longer still to fathom the spelling, which was so haphazard and wrong-headed that I wondered at the sanity of the author, or certainly at his schooling. Then I read one of the letters, which seemed particularly well-fingered, and I understood why my brother had chosen to share them with me.

Palazzo Muti, Rome, December 31st 1738

My Dear Dr,

I thank you for your letter and your counsil, the which is always as welcom as it is needed. What you say of luck is true and right, viz. that scholars and politickers make too little of it, when in fact it is luck that plays the largest part in the meteing out of fortunes and catastrofes, victorys and defeats. We have had our fair share of bad luck, and but for ill winds and trecherous noblefolk my father would have carried the day in '15. If only all had possessed your bravery, and that of Baron Caryll. The King my father speaks to me often of your friendship in those days and it is my hope that when I launch my own attempt, you will be beside me, sword in hand.

I am writing to you in the year's last midnite, and the dreg ends of the day in which I reach my majority. I have — you will be little surprised to hear — taken too much of drink in celebrating the twin festivities, but I am aware that there are soberer days ahead. I travel to Paris on the morrow, hoping to persuade my cousin Louis to support my father's claim in deed as well as word.

My father grows weaker and more fuddled by the day. I wish you were here to treat him rather than the sycofantic and lecherus doctors with which he surrounds himself. He once better knew how to choose his freinds. Soon, he promises me, I will be regent, and will add an R to the P after my name. When that day comes, we will be reunited again, my dear Ezekiel.

I send my fondest wishes to you and your wife, to your dear and loyal children, too. I thank you for the contriburtions you make to our cause and promise you that I will repay you one day. Please continue to write me. Knowing there is still such faith, such strength of spirit in England, it gives me hope that either in the shape of my father or of me, his regent, the King Over the Water will cross the water home.

With warm affection,
Charles P.

My first sentiment – irrational perhaps, but true – was one of jealousy, doubly tinged by the fact that my father had had this surrogate son whose presence he had kept from me. I saw them in my mind – the famously handsome Prince, my father as a younger, haler man – striding beneath the walls of Gaeta, lost in the pleasure of one another's company. The Prince was seven years older than I, a decade younger than Francis, and had written several dozen letters to my father over a period of many years. I thumbed through other letters in the pile, watching how the lettering altered as I moved back in time, the spelling worsening, the sentiment less sophisticated, but nonetheless touching. I felt as if I had been looking at a dissected map with a single missing piece, and that piece had now been presented to me.

With a nod to Francis, I picked up the sheaves of paper and carried them up to my chamber. I lay on the bed for an hour or more, sinking down through the words and the years into the time my father had spent with the young Prince in Italy and Spain: the adventures and escapades, the daring rescues and night-time assaults. I recognised that my father had lived heroically, had experienced more in a few short years than many go through in the full span allotted them. While Mother had awaited him back at Winchelsea, while Francis had represented his interests among the smugglers, my father had laid siege to Neapolitan forts, crossed the mountains of Extremadura, drunk in Spanish taverns and Swiss lodges. The young Prince had worshipped my father and I saw in his admiration a reflection of my own love of the man. My jealousy transformed itself into something warmer, something which seemed to knit me closer to my father, and through him to Charles, to Francis, to the cause in which they were all so invested.

I compared this noble figure with my blood-father, with Gray, and all comparisons were injurious to the latter. It is a terrible thing, this sense of having in your veins the blood of a villain; as if a poison has set in, one that will envenom you chronically, over years, turning all that is good, bad. I saw my life as if from a sudden distance, and I knew that all that was wrong in me, all that delighted in the aberrant and perverse, was down to him, to Gray.

The first time I saw him after my brother's revelation, we were in the saloon of the Mermaid, making preparations for a run. I looked at him with particular keenness, and he turned his face up to me with a serenely insouciant look, bade me good day, and passed a jar of ale my way. There was no mention of our last encounter, and not until the very end of his life would I reveal that I knew what he was to me.

II

ALL THAT SUMMER, we ranged across the broad reach of the sea, acting now as much as pirates as smugglers. Our success on the guinea run had emboldened Gray, suggesting new means of profiting from our prowess and position. There had been some accommodation made with the smugglers of the far west, those Cornish and Devonian gangs whose activities occasionally overlapped with our own. There was also the fact of the war in Bavaria, which necessitated a large number of poorly armed Spanish, French and Neapolitan supply ships making their way to the Prussian ports.

In re-outfitting the *Albion* after the Ostend run, Gray had abandoned all pretence of the ship being a trading vessel. She now bore twelve heavy guns proudly on deck, with a further eight swivellers fore and aft. We had hired new men, the main of them privateers from Deal – a leather-skinned, scar-faced crew who cursed and spat and moved through the rigging like monkeys.

There were others who'd previously volunteered for the Mayfield Gang, or for the Seasalters of North Kent, whose operations had been much curtailed by the efficiency of the dragoons out of Chatham. The ship's armoury had been replenished, with a great stock of musketoons and blunderbusses, bayonetted fusils and grenadoes filling the gun deck. Gray had even had a Jolly Roger fashioned expressly for the Hawkhurst Gang, with falcons in the corners of the flag, each of them seeming to peck at the crossed bones.

Our principal occupation remained the transportation of contraband, which produce seemed to be coming to us in greater quantities than ever before, stoked by the escalation of the European war and news of our success at Ostend. We were well-moneyed and Gray used our gold judiciously, sourcing the best jenever from Flushing and ankers of over-proof brandy from Nantes. We loaded up crates of good black Bohen tea at Dunkerque and bales of exquisite calico and muslin at the dock in Dieppe. In a single run at the end of June, we landed a full ten thousand gallons of brandy on the beach at Pett, which was swiftly taken off into the Weald by the land-men that awaited us.

Such activities were handsomely augmented by the gold and goods we seized from the supply ships we encountered in the Channel, or from French merchant vessels making their way along the coast of Normandy. Whilst the *Albion* was being repaired, she'd also been repainted and resailed, so that her clinkered sides were now black with pitch, her sails deep red. At night she was barely visible upon the waters, and many a time we were on a ketch or a sloop before they'd seen us, sweeping out of the darkness like some nocturnal predator.

We descended upon them with our swords drawn, and with such a volley of musket fire and yelloching that there was rarely need to employ our new cannons. Occasionally, a crew would put up a half-hearted fight, and when they did we showed no quarter. And I was ever there at the van, my sword held high and a raw growl in my throat. I knew what it was to sever a man's hand, to hack into the join of his neck and shoulder, where all is muscle and bone and tendon and you need to put your boot on his chest to draw your sword back out. When I think upon it now, I picture that summer as if through a veil of blood, with dark blood pumping from a man's throat, and white, moon-reflecting blood pooled on the deck of a Genoese sloop, and the bloody voids where Poison had taken out a man's eyes with his dagger. We are always the heroes of our own stories, but it strikes me now that over that summer, and maybe after – perhaps a long while after – I became something else, something hard and desperate, something like a villain.

What of Lily? She, too, sent me a letter, one in which she set out plainly both the depth of her feelings for me and the impossibility of any further meetings between us. Her father and Albert Nesbitt were well advanced in their arrangement of marriage between her and Arnold. She would treasure our friendship always, but to see me would be to open a wound, one that she wanted healed up for good. My longing for her sometimes struck me with such violence that I could scarce draw breath, and I have no doubt that the growing viciousness with which I comported myself as a smuggler was in some manner a reflection of the fury I felt at being denied further contact with Lily.

III

WHILE WE HAD the run of the seas to ourselves, the navy being taken up with the War of Jenkins' Ear and duels with the French in Biscay, on land we had new troubles with which to contend. More than a dozen dragoons had been summoned from Hythe and stationed in the reparelled chapel at Greyfriars. Deprived of his income from the Mayfield Gang and wishing to ingratiate himself with the authorities, Albert Nesbitt placed his son in charge of a crew of well-marshalled men who had served on the Continent and been sent back to reassert the government's control over the smugglers. The war was costing the exchequer dearly and Pelham had responded by raising the taxes on tea and spiritous liquors, whilst simultaneously enacting a raft of swingeing new laws against the free-traders, to be enforced by dragoons rather than the shilpit and ineffective Revenue men.

There was now a watch post in the ruined tower of the chapel, from which the soldiers could survey the long stretch of coast from Jew's Gut to Fairlight. Arnold's men carried out regular reconnoitring rides along the shoreline, so we often looked down to see their fine grey horses outlined against the sea as they moved swiftly over the ridge of shingle that curved from the cliffs to the mouth of the Brede. They sat high in their seats, their rifles slung across their backs, their swords clanking at their sides.

This new and unwelcome vigilance meant that we could no longer land our goods willy-nilly, but rather were obliged to implement a host of new measures to secure the passage of the contraband. So it was that we hired a team of land-men to help us move the goods to the Under-Reach with the greatest speed. We furthermore had a shore-man to coordinate the approach with our spotter, Smoker, via a series of pre-arranged signs and symbols. The shore-man, who was Perin's son, had been given the duty by Gray, part out of pity for the boy's mother, but part because he knew every stone and creek of the shoreline, having had little else to do in his life thus far than wander along it.

As we made our approach into shore, Young Perin would shine a spout-light from within a cottage on the outskirts of Pett. Smoker would respond by firing a pistol charged only with powder, emitting a strange blue light. A responding blue light from Young Perin would signal that we were clear to land. The continued burning of the spout-light indicated that we should hover offshore until the sign was given. If he extinguished the spout-light, then we were to withdraw into the Channel. It was a variation on the signalling that had been used by the smugglers for centuries, whereby a candle would be lit in one of the caves in the cliffs below Fairlight. If all were clear, the candle would be allowed to burn; if the riding officers (or their ancient forebears, the owl-catchers) were abroad, the candle would be extinguished and the furze on the cliff top set ablaze to warn off the approaching smuggling vessels.

Given that Arnold's men carried out such frequent circuits of our favourite landing spots, making shore became a complicated, nervy affair. Our land-men would bury themselves in the shingle once dusk had fallen, positioning their pebble graves in the expected vicinity of our eventual alighting, although the precise spot would only be decided once Kingsmill and Smoker had surveyed the dark shore with the night-glass. Most runs, we had to endure two or three hours' hovering, furling the sails and weighing anchor three hundred yards offshore, waiting for the skittish Young Perin to signal us in.

As soon as we saw the blue light, we made in hard for the beach, weighing anchor some twenty yards offshore, just before the waves began to arch their necks. Then it was a matter of launching the tender-boats as full as we could load them and landing them on the steep shingle. At this point, our land-men would rise like phantoms from where they were buried, and we'd hurry the goods across Trecherie and into the Under-Reach, where they would be stored until such a time as we were certain that Arnold's men were out on the Jew's Gut side of the Rother, and we'd effect a sortie up to Knellstone.

It became part of the rhythm of our runs, these periods of waiting, followed by violent activity. And because I knew Arnold, because he had spoken to me of his heart, of his fear, I could not take him over-seriously, for all the respect in which his soldiers were held. I remembered Lily's words – *You're more of a man than he*, she'd said – and I knew that, should it come to it, I'd be equal to Arnold. The fact that he was likely to spend his life with Lily gave a bright hue to my imaginings of our meeting. I would kill him swiftly, sever his head, and take it to my love as a gift.

IV

THERE WAS ONE other change to the pattern of our runs in the wake of Ostend. With the Deal privateers came another member of the crew, a whore by the name of Moll Dunk. Moll was a slow-eyed, buxom girl of nineteen, and had been part of the negotiation to bring the Deal men aboard. A partition curtain was rigged up at the far end of the forecastle, and there Moll would lie in her hammock, quite placidly, while the sailors had their way with her. In those long hours while we hovered offshore, the breeze sighing in the shrouds, the waves slapping gently along the distant beach, Moll became an object of pleasurable pastime for the men. Gray appeared to feel himself above such things, but otherwise all went to lie with her in turn, the fucking meted out according to the hierarchy of the ship, with Kingsmill first, then Francis, then Poison, then the rest of the men according to their place within their own particular faction, with the Deal crew ranked above the Seasalters, then the assorted cabin boys and loblolly boys, although rarely were we becalmed long enough for the queue to reach its tail.

One night, during a long wait for the turning of the tide, all the men had finished their spells with Moll, and so I went to her, passing through the closely packed hammocks where Smoker, sated, lolled and puffed on his pipe, shooting me a salacious wink as I passed. I climbed in beside her and she felt about me for a moment before giving a laugh.

'Why, it's Mistress Goody!'

'It is. Might I lie here for a moment, just to rest?' I had seen little of Moll, but I felt kin in her, another who was a woman in a man's world, although less fortunate than I. I realised how little there was of womanly presence in my life: my mother, certainly, but she was not wholly corporeal, being now a silent, elf-like creature. There was only Lily, who still came often to my thoughts, but who seemed to recede with every passing day, as my own life's path diverged ever further from hers, and I began to despair of seeing her again.

Moll nestled herself against me, so that my head came down upon her plump shoulder. I wondered for a moment what it would be like to slip my hand into her lacy drawers, to kiss her as I had kissed Lily. But what I felt for Moll lacked the heat of my passion for Lily. Here, there was only sisterly softness. We lay together for some minutes. Her breath was low and I felt a great weariness overtake me. I had been agitable for some weeks, sensing that we were being over-daring in our actions, that Gray's decisions were made by gut and not wit, that we risked losing everything for the sake of some spangled gewgaw to adorn the tables at Seacox Heath. All of my other shipmates, even Francis, seemed caught up in the same smuggling madness, so that any time we weren't actively pursuing or pursued seemed somehow unearned. It lent a close, febrile atmosphere to the ship, and I realised, as I felt the warmth of Moll's body and how we rocked in our hammock a beat later than the roll of the ship beneath, that I was dead tired.

Thenceforth, I'd go to visit Moll whenever I was able, finding in that frowsty, sour-smelling chamber the repose that I lacked elsewhere. Although she at first seemed slow-witted, I soon saw that this was a show she put on, and that her mind was as sharp as any. She talked to me of the foibles and peculiarities of the smugglers, the ones who'd sob as they tupped her, others who'd ask to call her by some special secret name, or who'd insist she turned on her front and let them press her down into the hammock with a hard hand about her neck.

One warm night in July, as we waited in Rye Bay for Young Perin to give the signal, I told Moll the story of Gray and my dead mother, of how I felt I'd lost something in uncovering the identity of he whose blood ran within me. When I'd finished, Moll gripped my hand, declared me brave, and said she was glad to have me for a friend. 'We must stick together, us two,' she said. 'These men don't give a frig about me, and they don't about you neither, not really. You wouldn't believe the things some of them tell me. I'll watch your back if you watch mine. Are we square?'

We spat on our hands, shook, and I bade her farewell as one of the Deal men began to bellow and curse on the other side of the curtain.

V

ON THE NIGHTS that the Hawkhurst Gang had no run, we'd all of us meet together at the Mermaid, or ride up to Seacox Heath to drink and dance and roister until morning. We weren't friends, precisely, but it was simpler to behave with one another as if we were. These were the moments when I continued to feel myself as one on the outside of things, looking in, because I was a girl, but also because I came from a different world to these men, even Francis. Poison and Kingsmill appeared still to regard me with some suspicion; it was clear that I owed my position to the sponsorship of Francis and Gray. So it was that I found myself increasingly thrown together with my brother on such occasions. And he, too, appeared to seek out my company, leading me out into the garden of the Mermaid, where it was quieter and cooler. We'd sit and drink and talk until the stars were visible overhead, and sometimes Gray would come out to join us, and we'd listen to him speak of his childhood, of his plans for Seacox Heath, of his increasingly vaunting ambitions: to move into the political world, to buy up a rotten borough – Winchelsea, even – and rise and rise. Here, he'd circle his pipe in his hand, and the sparks from its bowl would lose themselves amongst the stars.

There was not another great shiveau at Seacox Heath that summer, but there always seemed to be people coming and going, and the great fire in the hall was lit even on the warmest nights, with footmen bustling around filling glasses and laying tables for supper in the small hours of the morning. Sometimes there would be girls there – Moll and her sisters and others from the Ypres Inn. Or fast young men down from London in their embroidered summer suits and lace cravats, stockings so snugly fitted about their calves that they seemed painted on to skin. There was always dancing and music and laughter, and always the figure of Gray circling about in his dark suit, as if he were the spirit of the place, and if he stopped moving, it would too.

Francis and I would take a few bottles of wine, or flagons of porter, and retreat to the balustrade at the back of the house, where we'd look out over the lawns to the purple clouds of oak woods that surrounded the estate. Or we'd wander the corridors of the enormous house, opening doors on to still rooms in which the furniture sat in packing cases, and the windows had no curtains, the washstands no basins. We would turn corners to find that the corridor ended in a precipitous drop, for the house was still in the process of being built, and a whole wing skeletoned with scaffolding. I knew that Gray spent the days with his architect, who'd moved himself and his ménage down from London to supervise the construction. Gray pored over plans and maquettes in his cabin while the ship waited to make land and the rest of us gambled or slept or had our time with Moll.

I always hoped, each time that we rode up to Hawkhurst, that Lily would be there, walking along the terrace, that she would go back on the words of her letter, would engineer an encounter between us that would solidify or progress our relations, whose next iterations I had imagined with such regularity that I longed to be abed, or in the secret places of the

Under-Reach, so I could give myself over entirely to these fantastical visions of our love. But she did not come, and all my searching for her was in vain.

It was one of these nights at Seacox Heath, after the dancing and the drinking, after a short-lived but bloody fight between Poison and one of the Deal men, after Gray, high-flown with drink, shepherded me into a corner and pressed himself against me, and Francis was once again obliged to come to my rescue, after Moll and her sisters danced a naked gigue along the centre of the hall to the sound of cup-shot huzzaing. It was after all this that my brother and I sat side by side on the balustrade and watched dawn break over the woods. I was always careful not to take too much drink at Gray's soirées, for although I had gained a stomach for it, particularly porter, my capacity was nothing compared to my brother's. He was still sipping contemplatively at a tankard of ale as the light broke over the oak woods, coming like a wave over the green-gold leaves, and just then, when the sun touched us, Francis leant over and I thought he might kiss me. I felt my mouth half-open. Instead, he said, almost in a whisper:

'Let's go for a swim.'

We made our way back through the house, down the stairway and through the hall, where Poison and Smoker were sleeping in a drunken heap on the parquetry, and the casement windows stood open, letting the fresh morning air and birdsong into the room. We walked out, along the terrace and down the steps, and without consulting, we both began to run. We stripped off our boots and stockings, feeling the coolness of the grass beneath our feet, then, still running, we stepped from our breeches, pulled off our shirts, and then Francis was splashing out into the lake, and I was too, and the water was so good and so cold, and it was as if we were children again as we swam into the cool, dark lake, half of which was still covered by shadows from the surrounding trees.

The lake was visible from the house, yet distant enough that I had no fear of revelation. We swam like otters, frolicking in water that took the breath from us, chasing and ducking one another beneath the smooth surface, opening our eyes in the green depths. The sun rose higher and the pool held its light. It was as if we were trailing our bodies in the dawn. Dragonflies and damselins danced above the water and the birdsong was a cloud of sound from the woods all about, the birds dissolving the dark.

It was only once we emerged that I looked at Francis, and saw he was looking at me, and we stood there for a moment, breathing. I felt the key to the Under-Reach hanging heavily about my neck, and could see that Francis saw it and how his eyes then followed it down between my breasts. I noticed how the water dropped from his body, from the golden stud in his ear, from the silver-tinged hair of his chest, from his well-muscled thighs and calves. I could see something alter subtly in his regard, as if he were seeing me for the first time that day. I reached down to pick up my clothes, and he came behind and gathered his own from where he had left them. I could feel the strength of him, the heat of him, as he stood there, and I wanted greatly to lean back into him just then, to feel our skins together.

'We must leave,' he said in a thick voice. 'We go to Domburg this evening, and you and I have not slept.' We dressed in silence, then made our way back up to the house.

VI

AND SO THAT night we set out to Domburg, where we were to pick up a shipment of black Bohen. Pelham's government had just raised the levy on tea to five shillings a pound, and there was great demand for uncustomed leaf from the tea shops and private parlours of London. Tea and tobacco were easy to shift and store, so long as you kept them dry. I liked to go down into the hold whenever we were carrying them and press my nose to the dry, odorous bales, imagining the glossy Indian hillsides on which the tea had grown, or Andean mountain passes green with swaying tobacco plants. Francis had told me about the brutality of life on the plantations and I understood that our wares did not harvest themselves, and that those who had gathered the crops that would make us rich were perhaps as miserable as the unfortunates that Francis had described to me those few times he had spoken of his childhood in Brazil. There was also, always, with tobacco, the shadow of the fact that, at best, a hard life in the American plantations beckoned for us were we apprehended. More likely, it was the gibbet.

The run itself was unremarkable, Domburg a Low-Country port like any other, the journey back rolling gusty. We came into Rye Bay just after midnight and drew in to shore, near where the Fairlight cliffs meet the long line of shingle beach at Pett. Smoker had taken the night-glass from Francis and scanned the coast. There was the spout-light burning in the window of the cottage up the hill from the tavern at Pett Level. Carefully, adjusting himself to the roll of the deck, Smoker filled his pistol chamber with powder, held it above his head and pulled the trigger. A crack and a ghostly blue flash, and time moved in the strange, halting way it always did. We waited for Young Perin to return the signal. Ten seconds passed, then twenty, then we all crossed to the shoreward side of the ship, looking for the blue light. No response. A minute passed, then another. I felt Francis come up alongside me and was reminded, as if recalling a dream, of the sight of him in the lake at Seacox Heath, the gleaming water falling down about him. We stood there together, eyes fixed on the yellow spout-light. Gray had come up from his cabin, took the night-glass from Smoker, put it to his eye and brought it down again.

'Take her off a little,' he said.

Kinsgmill barked an order and the jib was hanked on, hoisted and caught a burst and we drifted away from the coast, back out into the full blast of the Channel. Smoker still stood there, as always, night-glass fixed on the hut. After several more minutes had passed, he lowered the telescope, nodded at Kingsmill and took the wheel. With a little growl, Kingsmill barrelled along the deck, down the steps and towards the forecastle, towards Moll. Then Francis let out a shout. Kingsmill turned at the top of the steps.

Francis was pointing towards the shore. 'The light

is out,' he yelled over the wind. Kingsmill crossed the deck at a run, was up the poop steps and beside us. Gray stood looking through the night-glass at the dark coastline.

'There,' he said. 'A flash. You saw it, did you not?' He turned first to me, then to Francis. 'Bring her in, boys. There are duchesses awaiting their scandal-broth.'

Kingsmill growled again. 'You're sure, Arthur?' he said. 'The signal was given?'

'Certain,' Gray said. 'Now, take us in. I wish to be in my bed before dawn.'

Kingsmill went to take the wheel from Poison and we approached the beach once more. As we drew closer, the men began to bring up the bales, tar-palling canvas lashed about them. Kingsmill manoeuvred us to the break-line of the waves and there we weighed anchor. The bales were loaded into a tender-boat and lowered into the water that roiled and crashed below. I followed Francis down to ready the second tender, tying the bales tightly to the boards of the boat, then climbing down myself. The men above lowered us with the windlasses, and there was a moment of peril when first we met the churning water and a wave threatened to dash us against the flanks of the *Albion*. But then we were rowing and Francis and I were together on a bench, pulling with all our might as the small boat rode the waves into shore.

I turned my head just as the first boat made land, and I saw that spiritish scene – the land-men rising from where they were buried amid the pebbles, many of them with lanterns already lit, the lamplight ascending eerily as they shrugged free of their makeshift graves.

They rose one by one, shaking the stones from their clothes, stamping their feet and coughing. They were a mixture of local farm lads and petty criminals, some employed merely to carry the goods, others as bat-men armed with cudgels should the Revenue or some rival gang appear. I pulled a few more times on my oar, and then felt the grind and jolt as we came up on the pebbles. We leapt out into the water, heaving the boat on to the shingle and unloading the tea into the arms of the land-men. I saw that the first boat was already empty, and readying to set off again, when Francis let out a curse and turned to point.

I followed his gesture and saw, up on the first ridge of the Fairlight cliffs, an orange glow. Whipped by the wind, it kindled into a conflagration, and I could perceive the figure of a man dancing before it. With one hand he clasped his side, with the other he was waving. It looked as though he was shouting but the wind stole his words. Francis cursed again as the fire swept along the cliffs.

'It's the old signal,' he said to me. 'The gorse fire.' And just at that moment, outlined against the wild blazing on the hill behind, there appeared a host of shadowy figures, all of them mounted, guns raised. At first, seized by some strange spasm of memory and imagining, I thought them the Mayfield Gang, come for vengeance. Then they cantered down the pebbles and began to shoot, and I could see them for what they were – redcoats, Arnold's Winchelsea soldiers.

Our land-men stood quite still for a moment, looking towards me, towards Francis. Then they ran – some to the boats, others up the shingle towards the marsh.

The dragoons had dismounted and were now kneeling and taking aim with their rifles, moving forward a few paces with each discharge. Some of them had spout-lights they shone about, better to acquire their targets. I saw men fall, heard the wet sound of a bat-man hit in the neck. Francis took me by the shoulder and pulled me into the cover of the boat. We crouched behind it and loaded our pistols. Our bat-men were in disarray, most of them having abandoned their weapons and now, with the other tender set off for the *Albion*, they either surrendered or risked their lot in the waves. I saw several of the bat-men caught up in the water, the flailing of their arms as they were sucked into the backdraught of the waves. Behind them, I could make out the dark shape of the ship, the lights that flickered aboard her as the tender was winched upwards. Then she moved off, and we were abandoned.

VII

IT WAS A desperate moment. Francis and I loaded and discharged our weapons in the direction of the redcoats as swiftly as we were able, but we were outnumbered, and with each volley the carapace of boat that protected us became more fractile. The soldiers were well-drilled, their advance towards us slow and inexorable. Their lamps were trained upon us, and in the dying light of the gorse fire everything was cast in an infernal glow. I looked to Francis and saw, as he loaded his pistol, he had made a decision. His next shot was aimed not at the approaching dragoons, but rather at the flanks of the horses tethered behind them. I could not bring myself to fire upon a dumb animal, but could see that Francis's plan might bear fruit. I concentrated my fire on the centremost of the soldiers, who was kneeling, ready to discharge his rifle. With some surprise, I shot him in his temple.

Like anything, killing becomes easier with practise, and I found myself – if not untroubled – then certainly less agitated than I had previously been on ending the life of another – the soldier on the mole at Ostend, or Old Joll in Boulogne. I also had less time to contemplate the act, for now Francis had loosed another round upon the horses. Wild-eyed and rearing, they broke their reins and kicked out at one another, then went charging off in all directions, a number of them galloping along the beach towards their masters. Some of the soldiers turned to protect themselves, others attempted to continue their advance, but were knocked to the shingle like kittle-pins. Francis and I ran up the beach. The furze fire on the cliff had died down and it was quite dark under the sky, and so it was that I knew Francis only by the sound of his feet on the pebbles, and didn't see the soldier until I was quite upon him, and the collision knocked the wind from me.

It was Arnold, who had been surveying the ambush from this elevated position and now caught at me with one hand; with the other, he pressed his pistol into the flesh of my neck. It all happened more swiftly than the words can recount. Francis, who had disappeared into the darkness, carried forward by his momentum, now turned and came back towards us – I could hear the shingle skittering back down the incline. Arnold appeared to pause for a moment, perhaps hearing that there was another of us in the darkness, but I also saw in his face a different kind of hesitation, that of the man who is attempting to place a half-familiar stranger. He peered at me in the darkness, and I saw something like a smile appear on that thin, collusive mouth. I took his pistol by the barrel and moved it away from my throat, then leaned towards him and placed a kiss on those lips, feeling him stiffen in surprise. At that moment, Francis brought the haft of his own weapon down hard on Arnold's head. The look of astonishment on the soldier's face scarcely altered as he sank to the ground.

Now, though, the dragoons had gathered themselves on the beach and were heading towards us. We made our way up the final steepness of shingle under a volley of shot and then out on to the marsh, where I took the lead, surer of my way in the darkness than Francis. The ground beneath us tilted and oozed as we moved across the shifting, hungry earth. How do we come to know a place? Through familiarity, through feeling, by laying out the map in our minds over the landscape. So it was that I knew to keep to the ridge of land that ran between the stagnant pools of Pett Level and the banks of the Brede. So it was that I avoided the dreadful sucking mud, the swampy ground at the foot of Iham Hill. I led us straight to the gate in King's Cliffs that gave into the Under-Reach, and there we paused amid the ferns.

From our seclusion we could see that the soldiers had not fared as well as we had in crossing the marsh. There was a circle of lanterns around one of the pools. I perceived a perturbation in the centre of the pond, and saw one of the soldiers attempting to hold out his rifle to his mate, while others gripped on to the man's legs to stop him following his friend under. There was a deal of shouting and imprecations, but I knew that they would not see their mate again, that the marsh never gave up that which it had claimed, that Trecherie kept hard to the word of its name.

I opened the gate with the key about my neck, locked it fast behind us, and we made our way into the blackness of the Under-Reach. Again, Francis was reliant on my intimate knowledge of that subterranean world, on the long-learnt memory paths I stepped along. He held tight my hand, and I sensed some childish fear of the darkness in him, a fear that seemed to rise as we moved through Holly Rood cavern, past the boarded-up fissure in the rock that led down to the Deeps and that breathed at us as we went by – the soughing, hissing breath of ancient times. I remembered my father's stories of the elvish folk that dwelt down there, beyond the flooded caves and depthless shafts, and imagined for a moment that I heard them calling to me in high, plaintive tones, and speaking of Arthur and Avalon and Caerleon. I paused for a moment, then continued, and we were soon through the gate into the northern portion of the Under-Reach, and took the curving stone steps up to Paradise.

VIII

FRANCIS WAS UP in the grey-eyed hours, notwithstanding the lateness of our return. I heard him speaking to my mother below as I woke and I went down to join them at breakfast. My mother had been awaiting us the previous night, as she always did when we were out on a run. She had a quire of notepaper before her, and began to write out her slow and hieroglyphical script.

ALBERT NESBITT, she wrote. HERE LAST NIGHT. HIS SON, THE SOLDIER, GRAVE WOUNDED. I GAVE HIM HERBS. FRANCIS, TAKE HEED. HIDE YOURSELVES.

'We know about Arnold,' Francis said. 'We are a match for them, for anyone.'

My mother paused for another moment, then wrote. YOU ARE A PINFAITH, FRANCIS. YOU ARE BOTH OVER-TRUSTING. THERE IS TREACHERY AFOOT. REMEMBER YOUR FATHER. After this, she stood, looked at us hard, and retired into her glass-house, from whence there emanated much pounding of pestle in mortar, much clattering of vials and albarellos.

Just after ten of the morning, a message-boy appeared at the gate, asking us to come to the Mermaid post-haste. We saddled the horses and bade our goodbyes to Mother. She was still funking in her glass-house like a peevish woodland sprite. The morning was a warm one, the especial warmth of the end of summer, when the season itself appears desperate to stay.

After stabling our horses, we went straightway through the public chamber of the tavern and up to the private room. There we found Gray and Kingsmill, Poison and Smoker, and several of the Deal men, all of them already well embarked on their tankards of ale, their flagons of porter. Gray had a hectic, feverish air about him, and slurred as we took our places at the table.

'We landed the goods at Jew's Gut. Lost twelve bushels, fifteen perhaps. Nothing that should over-trouble us. Here, have porter? Wine? No?' Francis accepted a jug of ale. 'We lost five men and Young Perin is in a bad way. Gut-shot by the redcoats who sprung him.'

'How fared the soldiers?' Francis asked.

'Two dead, three more won't trouble us for many a month. Young Nesbitt has a bandaged head, but they say he'll scrape through, more's the pity.'

'So what now?' Francis set down his jug and looked squarely at Gray, and I perceived a subtle alteration in the atmosphere of the room, as if all had turned their attention on the two men.

Gray paused, weighing matters. 'No doubt greater scrutiny upon us. Already word is that two navy frigates are being sent from Lymington. More redcoats, more Revenue men, greater risk.'

'Aye,' said Francis, 'and all the while the Cornishmen will take trade that ought by rights be ours.'

'I did not say that we should cease our operations, friend,' Gray said with an edge to his voice, a sudden sense that he was more sober than he seemed. 'Only that we needs must be cautious now. And not only because the King's Men will be making us their hobby. It's said that there are French ships at Dunkerque, troops moving northwards from Paris. We will not be the only ship making use of this accommodating shore.'

Francis gave a cold smile. 'You know the treaty we agreed upon. The Hawkhurst Gang will not stand in the way of any move against the king, be that from France or Scotland. I had your word on this.'

'Quite so,' Gray said with a placatory hand. 'I care not which king's face adorns the gold I amass. My sole concern is that nothing disrupts the flow of goods in one direction, and the money to pay for them in the other.'

'Then we are well understood,' Francis said, finishing his jar. 'The land-men are now en route to London?'

'They are.'

'Then we have been lucky this time. Let us hope we do not run so close to the wind again.'

IX

WHEN WE RETURNED home, Francis requested that I dress myself in a gown and bonnet. It would be expected that I go to visit Arnold, given the care the Nesbitts had shown to us in the wake of my father's death, and the closeness that had developed between the families. I put on my best dress of cotton and taffeta, and tied the stays of my bodice, squeezing the life from me with each yank tighter. I set out alone, through the graveyard of the church with its crumbling bell tower, then down Monks' Walk to Greyfriars. I bore on my arm a basket of sweetmeats from the village shop and a vial of some ointment my mother had prepared for the wounded man.

There is a blossom that comes upon certain of the cherry trees in the autumn, and all of the orchards about Greyfriars were frothy with pinks and whites. I stopped for a moment before the house, thinking back to the party I'd attended there scarcely five months earlier, and all that had been crammed into the short time since, all that I'd learnt and lost, felt and suffered in that time. I was tired and a little maudlin-feeling, as if the summer's passing contained some deeper, sadder message: Goody, the child, might be gone, but the person who had replaced her was as yet inchoately formed, self-mistrusting and often wicked. I gave my head a little shake and stepped towards the portico. There was a carriage stationed in front of the stables that bore on its flanks a crest of three pelicans vulning themselves in their breasts.

I knocked at the door and was shown into the hallway by a liveried footman. I sat there with my basket in my lap until I heard footsteps on the winding stairs above me. I looked up to see Lily, her hair spilling from beneath a silk bergère. It took the breath from me, to have her before me, as beautiful, as vital as before.

'You are here,' she said, a little cold and alert. 'Albert Nesbitt was visiting with my uncle in Stanmer last night, when we received notice that Arnold had been assaulted. Uncle Henry insisted I come to nurse him.'

'It is good of you, Lily,' I said, shocked by the feel of her name on my tongue. 'And how is he?' I apprehended then that I cared to know the answer. Another jolt: I had been responsible for the injury of a gentle man, a good man, and it had taken me near four-and-twenty hours to feel the guilt. Francis may have dealt the blow, but I had been his co-conspirator. I remembered the kiss I'd given him in the darkness and felt the full weight of the betrayal.

'He is being brave and self-reproachful by turns. He looks tired.'

'Has he eaten?'

'Little, thus far. He will live, though, and for this he blames himself, when two of his men did not.' Now she leaned closer and spoke to me in a confidential voice. 'Were you amongst the ruffians who did this, Goody? For if you were, I will never forgive you. Arnold is a buffard and a milksop, but he is decent, and that can be said for too few of us in these injurious times.'

I saw how much she longed for me to deny my role in the assault, but I could not, and so Lily looked at me narrowly, turned and I followed her up the stairs, feeling the cold currents of disappointment in her wake. We walked along a hushed corridor with lace curtains and fine oak doors. At the end, one was open, and we entered to find Albert Nesbitt, hat in his hand, sitting beside his son's bed. Arnold was as pale as the lace pillowcases he rested upon, as vague as the winding bands about his head. He might have been dead, but for the meagrest rise and fall of his chest. Albert had nodded off and woke with a start at our entering, then leapt to his feet.

'Goody! Lily! You must excuse me. It has been a long and worrisome night.' I went over to him and he bent to kiss my hand, but I could see how much the night had told on him, and so I took him in my arms and embraced him. He began to sob, very quietly, in the hollow of my neck, and I patted him gently on the back all the while, shushing him as if he were a babe.

We sat, the three of us, by the bedside, until dusk fell and the candles were lit about us. Arnold did not stir, nor open his eyes, and we did none of us speak. A wind brewed up around seven of the clock and Lily went down to fetch soup for Albert, who looked at it disinterestedly when we brought it to him on a tray, supped a little if only to please us, then set it down.

'The doctor will come again on the morrow,' Albert said to no one. 'Then we shall know more. He was talking quite intelligibly to us this morning, you know. It were only when he fathomed that he'd lost two of the boys and had three more pensioned off with their wounds that he fell into this stupidity.'

'He is mending,' Lily said, her voice very soft. 'And he must have time for that. You have slept but little yourself, sir. I will walk Goody down to the door and instruct Maberley to accompany her home. Then you must yourself to bed. I am mistress of this house for the nonce and it will run by my rules.'

The old man gave a little chuckle, stood to bid me farewell, and once again we moved past formalities and warmly embraced. The English do not, as a rule, clasp each other in this fashion, but I could feel Albert drawing strength from me just then. I was glad that, having brought such sorrow into his life, I was able to relieve it a little.

Lily showed me down the stairs and out of the front door. We stood there in the dark. The wind was high, sending curlicues of blossom into the beam of light cast by the door. Lily leant towards me, and I thought she might kiss me again, felt my mouth drop open a little in expectation.

'Don't come here again,' she said. 'Not even if he asks for you. Not ever. You do not deserve your name, Goody, for you have done evil things. To Arnold. To me.'

'To you?' I seized her by the wrist and pulled her towards me. 'What did I ever do to you, other than love you?'

'Just that.' She drew back, surprising in her strength, her voice channelling all the anger it could into a whisper. 'You bewitched me, Goody.'

'And you me,' I said. 'So why is the fault mine?'

'My father has indicated that I am to marry Arnold. The discussion with my uncle and Mr Nesbitt last night was to settle the matter. Now this – poor Arnold – and I find that you are the culprit. You were a brief distraction, a bagatelle. There could never have been aught between us.'

I stood looking at her, feeling a sob rising in my chest. Having dreamed of this encounter for so long, here it was transposed in the most nightmarish fashion imaginable. 'You will live here, you and Arnold?'

'I know not. Perhaps. For now, I just wish to scrub you from my heart, from my life. Farewell.' With that, she turned back inside, went up the stairs, and left me standing in the cold path of the wind, blossom blowing all about me, and a great void in my heart.

X

WHEN I ARRIVED home, my emotions all troubled and turbid, Francis was waiting for me at the table in the hall. There was a tankard before him, and empty bottles. His air was high and excited, and he beckoned for me to sit, pushing a half-finished bottle of ale towards me.

'How was he?' he asked.

I paused for a moment, picturing the paleness of Arnold's face, the sense of one caught between this world and the next. 'He is gravely ill,' I said.

'Excellent,' said Francis, raising his jug as if to toast his success, then holding it in the air, waiting for me to lift the bottle on the table. 'With luck, we'll have a clear coast for weeks to come. And we must now speak of what's ahead, sister. We have much to achieve before the year is out.'

I felt a coolness settle over me. I had not supped and it was eight of the evening, but I could no longer sit with my brother just then. I stood and walked to the glass-house. My mother was hunched over her preparation table, humming quietly to herself. I came beside her, looked down at the mixing bowl in which a richly perfumed amber liquid gently bubbled, then leant to kiss her. She turned up to me then, surveying me darkly. I felt her judgement settle over me, although I had no sense as to its signification, nor the nature of her appraisal. I found myself wishing more forcefully than ever I had before that my mother could speak, or at least that I could speak to her. I recognised that her silence mirrored a deeper silence that lay between us, one that had obscured the channels of discourse between us long before Old Joll had cut her tongue from her.

I went upstairs without affording my brother a glance, betook myself to my chamber and undressed. I cleaned my teeth and brushed out my hair, and lay on my bed in the darkness. Several hours later, my brother stumbled by, tacking from one wall to the other as he sought his own sleep. Then all was silent, save the owls kee-wicking in the night, and the dim and distant roar of the sea. I thought of Lily, of Arnold, of Gray's blood that beat within me, and that was perhaps the reason for my ill deeds, my wrongfulness. I wept until there were no more tears, and slept with a great weight upon my soul.

Morning came with autumnal hesitancy through the curtains of my chamber. It was a day of low cloud and squally gusts of wind, a day in which the sea was near obscured from sight and yet loud all about the streets of the town. I came down to find Francis already descended and sorting through a bundle of papers by the light of several candles on the table in the hallway. 'Did the message-boy waken you?' he asked. I gave a shrug. 'There is news from France,' my brother said. 'Good news. Take some coffee and come sit you beside me.'

The letter, which was signed by the Duc de Belle-Isle, ran over several pages and was accompanied by a map of the Essex and Suffolk coastlines. It brought the information that King Louis was prepared to approve an invasion of South-Eastern England, an attack that was to be coordinated with a rebellion by the Scottish lords, who would march down the spine of the country to meet the French in London. The Spanish, with whom Britain was already at war, would contribute ships and troops, while France would declare an end to her neutrality in the War of the Austrian Succession with the move. Britain and France had already entered hostilities at Dettingen and Louis believed that it was now time to install a friendlier monarch across the Channel, to break the Anglo-Austrian alliance and the new British friendship with the Dutch.

A date had been set for late January for a landing at Maldon in Essex. Troops would gather at Dunkerque in the early days of the year, and at Boulogne and Dieppe and Calais, so there would be fifteen thousand men or more by the time the invasion was launched. The British were fighting wars on several fronts and had deployed soldiers to Germany and Poland, ships to the waters off the Spanish Main.

Francis looked up at me with large, lucent eyes. 'Our time is coming, sister,' he said. 'Soon life will have a quite different flavour. No more skulking, no more pettifogging with smugglers.'

'A larger stage, a worthier audience?'

'The Prince from Scotland will bring Jacobites new and old, and England will fall without a drop of blood being spilled, so deep is the love for the old ways.'

'Your faith does you credit, brother.'

'We must work hard between now and then,' he said. 'Harder than ever we worked afore. It is imperative that we show ourselves able to contribute to the cost of the invasion, that we deliver sufficient gold to our French friends that they feel sure of our continued commitment.'

'I stand ready,' I said, somewhat surprised at the strength of feeling I found in the words, in myself. Whether some seed of Jacobitism had been sown by my father in childhood, I knew not. For who can say what legacies are bestowed by the tales we hear before the shape of the world is clear to us? Certain it was that I felt through the Jacobite cause a strong connection to my father, a means of paying honour to his memory, to my love for him. Folks have been willing to die for less.

XI

IT WAS AN autumn of high seas and sudden storms, when the building-up of troops in the French seaports was ever more evident as we docked at Caen and Le Havre, at Boulogne and Dieppe, and above all at Dunkerque, whose harbour was busy with military vessels, and along whose quayside marched serried ranks of soldiers and sailors. From every low dark tavern, there came the sound of voices French and Spanish. All about the place was the coiled urgency that comes when troops gather in the foreshadow of battle. We found in these soldiers a ready source of, and demand for, our goods, so that we carried casks of British beer out with us to furnish the harbourside inns, returning with jenever and hock, or with Spanish wines that Louis' allies had brought up with them from Jerez, Oporto or from the far-off African islands where canary was made.

It happened that the night of the Bonfire Rejoicings, we were out on a run. It was a foul evening, the wind blowing sheets of rain and curtains of cloud down over the hills of the Weald, over Iham and Rye. It was hard to know where the sea did end and the land start, so dense was the rain, so violent the spume. We left port just after four of the afternoon, figuring that the soldiers would be taken up with the roustabouts and scoundrels making charivari on the streets of the towns. The wind saw us swiftly over to Calais, then swung about, clearing the sky as it did so, to set us back in Rye Bay not long past ten that night. At the last, the tide was against us, and so we were forced to linger off the sandbanks at Jew's Gut, waiting for the waters to rise sufficiently to allow us to make land on the dunes.

It was a full moon that night, and perhaps due to the inclemency of the earlier weather, the fireworks were still popping and fizzing over the roofs and marshes, great curlicues of light lacing their way across the darkness, showers of silver raining down like the slow shattering of some heavenly vessel. We stood there on deck, Francis and I, and watched the rockets, listened to their blasts, which came long enough after the light that we felt ourselves unhinged from time a little, drifting out there in the watery emptiness. I knew that our minds both turned upon the same thought – that a year had passed since the death of our father, and that we missed him yet. I found myself wishing I had possessed then the courage and strength I now owned, for surely I would have been capable of rescuing him from his captors. I recognised, though, that my fortitude was the result of Father's absence, and were he still here I would have remained a child. Francis put an arm about my shoulder just then, perhaps sensing the current of my thoughts, and it was his proximity that prevented me from falling when we struck the sandbank.

It was perhaps the fault of the moon pulling the tide more vigorously than usual, or mayhap Kingsmill was distracted by the lights over the land, but we had come in too close upon the sandbar and our keel was now caught fast. The boat's timbers complained and we listed a little before settling. I heard Kingsmill let out a curse. Gray came up from below deck and looked over the side.

'What fuckery is this?' he said, turning his glance first upon Kingsmill, then on the crew more generally. 'Are we run aground?' His question required no response. He turned and stomped back below. We would need to await high tide, which was not expected until the early hours of the morning. In the meantime, we would be stranded out here, vulnerable to apprehension by the navy, or any passing pirates who cared to board us. I saw that many of my crewmates celebrated the delay, taking themselves down to visit Moll, or to play cards in the light of a candle, spending the pelf they'd not yet received for their part in the run. I was about to sit and join them, when Francis took my arm.

'Come and stand with me, sister,' he said, 'where I stood before, all those years ago. It will be salutary, to step on the same sands I stepped in before I knew our father, when I was but a heartsick boy from Brazil.' At this, he took up a length of rope from the deck, and knotting it to the taffrail, he launched himself overboard, then shimmied down the broad bulging timbers of the boat. I went down after him, more shake-stance and hesitant, and landed on the sandbar beneath, the cold water soaking at once through my boots. It was only ankle deep, though, and the sand was firm beneath us.

'God's bores,' I said. 'It is icy, brother.'

'As it was that night,' Francis said.

We walked a little away from the ship, testing each step for soundness before shifting our weight forward. Then we were still for a time, watching the last of the fireworks burn themselves out over the marsh, imagining to ourselves the sighs and murmurs that went up from those who stood spectating in Winchelsea and Rye. I wondered if our mother was in her glass-house, and if she thought of our father. 'You seem to care little for any knowledge of my past, sister,' Francis said, and his voice was quite changed.

I looked sharply over at him. 'It is not that I wasn't interested, but rather that I did not wish to force you back into past sadness. I know that you lost a great deal.'

'And with each day that passes I lose more.' At this, my brother strode off across the sandbank. I watched him go until he was just an outline, his shadow interrupting the fretful moon on the choppy sea, his figure illuminated briefly each minute by the searching beam of the Dunge Ness lighthouse. I went over to join him, feeling even in the shallowness of the water the tugs and eddies of the currents. I put my hand on his shoulder and was surprised to find that he was sobbing. I looked back at the ship, where a few low lights burned in the portholes, then over to the land. No more fireworks, just the hilltop beacons of Rye and Winchelsea, the isolated inns and cottages of the Marsh, then, for an instant, the lighthouse beam upon us.

'I cannot begin to comprehend the sorrow in your heart, brother,' I said. 'Because I know that the death of our father is just one of many such deaths, that his absence must stand in the stead of other absences for you. Your father and mother. The real ones, I mean.'

'I knew them not,' Francis said, now turning towards me. I could feel that the waters were beginning to rise – where they had before come only to my ankles, the calves of my breeches were now wet. 'Or I remember them not. That voyage across the ocean wiped the slate of my mind clean. Now I can only think of Father, the man who took me in as a whelp and built me a life.'

When we got back to the ship, she was still grounded, and so we hauled ourselves up the rope and on to the listing foredeck, where Kingsmill awaited us, a jocund look in his eyes. 'You fools think you're Jesus Christ on that water? Or does Francis prefer the company of his sister to that of young Moll?' Here he clapped me about the shoulder, hard enough that I should know that he was not speaking entirely in jest. 'We have another hour, perhaps two, afore we're afloat again. Now go you Francis down and take your pleasure. I have done so already and she is as wet and warm as a Molucca girl tonight.' He held and kept my eye as he said this, and I felt suddenly the coldness of the wind.

XII

FRANCIS WENT DOWN as Kingsmill had commanded, and I followed with him, our feet squelching in our boots, the feeling of being grounded a strange one when we navigated the little corridors, pitching ourselves to accommodate the lean of the ship. We came to an opening just by the doors of the lazarette, where Smoker and two others sat in the dim light of a candle and played Jucker.

'Come, Francis,' Smoker said. 'Let us deal you in a round. You owe me two guineas already. Another won't hurt so bad, and may make those you owe come quicker.'

Francis looked at me, then back to the game. 'You go on, Goody,' he said to me. 'I know Moll enjoys the company of a fellow maid. Tell her I'll be with her ere long.' He lowered himself down cross-legged like a Brahmin and I could hear the sound of their laughter and raillery as I made my way to the forecastle. I opened the door and stepped within.

It was very quiet there amid the hammocks, and very dark, and I carried no candle. 'Moll,' I said in a low voice, and, hearing no response, I felt my way in the darkness to where the sheet was rigged up across the narrow end of the cabin. I pulled it back, said her name again, and found that the hammock was empty. She was, I presumed, in the head, sponging out of her the accumulated mettle of all the sailors and ship's boys, the cook and the deckhand. I removed my father's sword, my damp boots, my breeches with their sodden cuffs, and settled myself back into her hammock, naked from the waist down. I let myself swing from side to side – a strange feeling for the ship to be so still, so silent about me. Occasionally, there came to me shouts and laughter from the card players down the corridor. Otherwise I might have been drifting in the emptiness of space, or in my mother's young womb. I fell swiftly, deeply asleep.

I was wakened after what may have been a few minutes or an hour, feeling as if the ship had shifted slightly on the sandbank beneath. I heard someone moving slowly down the cabin towards me. *Moll*, I thought, but hesitated before speaking her name. Whoever it was carried no light, and I could hear the boards beneath them creak with each new step. The darkness was complete, the sense of being untethered from the world almost overwhelming. I heard the rustle of the curtain being drawn back and then the sense of a heavy body, the breath of large lungs.

'Moll,' a voice said.

It was Francis, brother mine.

Now and then our bodies seem to take the helm, to drive our wasteful past into an essential future, our presumptions into dust, our death into comedy, our truth into darkness. I had been aware, in the occluded, animal part of my brain, of a change in my feelings towards my brother, ever since the morning that we swam together at Seacox Heath and I sensed his eyes upon me. Now I felt a great urge to have his body against mine. It occurred to me – not in the moment, but later, looking back – that this hunger in me for the corrupt, the forbidden, was Gray's doing; it was the dark half of me speaking through my actions.

So this is what I did: I uttered no words, but rather reached up towards my brother and pulled him down on to me. He had taken drink with Smoker and the card players: I could smell it as he came down into the hammock, causing it to rock dangerously, almost landing us both upon the floor. He began to kiss me, first upon my forehead, then my cheeks, then in the hollow of my neck. He reached down and placed a finger inside me and for a moment the whole world was whittled down to that finger, to the points of intersection between us.

I felt the moment like a harp string in the air, although Francis said nothing, only withdrew his finger and pulled back for a moment. I heard the rub of cloth against skin. I could feel my heart everywhere: in my chest, in my head, in my eyes. Then my brother came close again. He placed a hand beneath me and moved me down towards him, then pushed himself into me, very gently. At that moment, the tide rose enough to lift the ship from the sandbar, and we were swaying in the hammock with the rocking of the ship, and suddenly there were cries from above, and cursing, and all the time Francis moved inside me, and it hurt a little but that which was not pain was the most intense and exquisite pleasure and I had to bite my lip to stop from calling out.

Then a closer noise – the door of the cabin opening. Francis thrust twice more, and with the last he let out a small sound, somewhere between a cry and a sigh. The person who had entered the room carried a lamp, and I saw Francis give me a wild and fearful look before, in the half-light that came around the edges of the curtain, he pulled up his britches and was gone. I heard him greet Moll – for it was she – with a grunt. A few seconds later the cabin door slammed behind him.

When Moll drew back the curtain, I was still lying back, a little stunned, a little sore, a trickle of blood and what I presumed was Francis's nature weeping out of me. Moll narrowed her eyes. 'Are you taking trade from me, friend?' Then she smiled and, placing her candle on the floor, leant to embrace me. 'You're a woman now,' she said. 'Let's get you cleaned. They're aiming to land, so you'd best be collecting yourself.' She took a handkerchief from the folds of her dress, mopped first at my face, where I realised I'd been crying, and then between my legs. I stood, a little unsteadily at first, and Moll handed me my breeches, my boots. She brought out a looking glass and I adjusted my hair. Then, with a heart that lurched first one way, then the other, so that I scarce knew whether I might burst into tears or song, I went to rejoin the men on deck.

XIII

MY BROTHER AND I never spoke again of what happened that night in Moll's bunk, although he was not able to catch my eye when I came up on deck, nor did he speak more than a few words to me as we rode home after the drop. He went up to his chamber as soon as we returned to Paradise, while I sat at the hall table a long while, musing on the turn my life had taken. I counted my emotions: shame, foremost, but with it a kind of giddiness; regret, but not enough to wish the act undone; curiosity, as to how my brother would be with me. Again, it struck me that my first three amatory encounters had been with a woman, with my father and with my brother, and that this must speak to some tainted part of me, to a flaw deep within.

The next morning, my mother and I were already at table when Francis came down. He was merry and talkative – his old self. He opened the letters, one of which was from Albert Nesbitt, inviting us to spend

Christmas with him and Arnold, who was now much recovered and would soon be taking up again his official duties. Our mother smiled and nodded, while Francis shot me a shrewd look. The next letter was from Baron Caryll, inviting Francis to come to mass at West Grinstead the coming Sunday.

There was another letter, which Francis perused for some minutes before raising his head and looking over to me. 'It is from the Prince,' he said. 'From Rome. He will be in Paris for Christmas, then ride north for Dunkerque. He wishes to meet us there on the tenth of January.' He had the look of a small boy about him just then, one in receipt of a kind word from a teacher. 'We are to convey to him the funds we have raised, so that he might contribute to the salarying of the troops.' He leaned back. 'The Prince wishes to pay his own way as far as possible, so as to express his independence from his cousin Louis.'

'So we make a run to Dunkerque?'

'Indeed. We must keep this to ourselves, though,' he said. 'Secrecy is everything now, when the moment is so close at hand. Not a word to Gray. We'll take the ferryman's wherry. He has been well looked after these past years. He owes us a gratuity or two. She is not at her happiest in high seas, but she'll see us to France and back.'

XIV

BEFORE DUNKERQUE, THOUGH, there was Christmas. I sat on that bright, snowy morning between my mother and Francis in the coolness of St Thomas's. During the singing I looked across the aisle to where Albert stood, peering down through his pince-nez at his hymnal, his chin on his chest, his jowls all gathered up around his neck. Beside him was Arnold, who carried a stick to walk and had a slack and vacant air. He looked upwards as he sang, as if attempting to recall something, and the movement of his mouth appeared to bear but little relation to the words of the carols. Beside him stood Lily St Leger and her father, the Member for Winchelsea. She was demurely dressed in a sober mantua of dark blue wool, her laces high, her features unreadable.

After the service, we walked together through the snow down to Greyfriars, and I took Arnold's arm. He walked with deliberation, careful on the icy cobbles. We soon fell behind the others. Albert, wrapped in furs, was walking with my mother, while Francis, Lily and the Member for Winchelsea discoursed upon some political matter. I saw that Lily, despite herself, was caught up in the confabulation and, outraged at a provocation of Francis's, batted at him with her muff.

'I understand you came to visit me in the days after my accident,' Arnold said in his new, laborious voice. 'I wished to thank you for it. We need friends in times like this. I have no doubt that your presence played some part in returning my wandering mind to me.'

'Lily deserves more of the credit than I.'

'Indeed. She is an angel. I feel quite embarrassed to think what the past months have been like for her. She has read to me a great deal, and says that her time at Greyfriars has been more of an education than anything she received from her governesses.'

'Will she now depart?'

'She leaves with her father on the morrow. The house will seem quite empty without her there. But, God willing, she will return in a more formal sense before long.'

'You have news, Arnold?'

'Not quite yet. But we are hopeful, very hopeful.'

We came to the gates at the entrance to Greyfriars. Lenten roses were coming up through the snow at the feet of the beech trees that lined the driveway. I saw that there was a group of uniformed men stamping and clapping their shoulders before the front door of the house. Arnold raised his arm in greeting. 'The lads have been to worship at St Giles's, feeling it more suited to their brand of faith. I have asked them to join us for the Christmas meal. We are back to our full quotient at the barracks.' Now his voice dropped. 'There is word of a French invasion. I was at Hythe three days since and they are billeting men in the stables and sties. A thousand dragoons, all ready to send Marshall Saxe back.'

Inside, we sat ourselves around the long table and there was a moment of silence before Albert said grace and the goose was brought in. The soldiers were just boys, I saw, and must have missed their families. I sat between Arnold and a young fellow named Oliver Price, and I asked the lad about his home in Rochester, about the traditions that were followed in his household. When he spoke of his sister, tears came suddenly to his eyes and he looked away.

The day outside dimmed and we three women repaired to the salon while port was brought for the men in the dining room. My mother placed herself at the window, looking out into the gloaming. Snow had begun to fall again and we all of us stood and watched the movement of the flakes in the light thrown from the house. Lily took me by the arm and led me to a corner, where she drew a small parcel from the shelf.

'I wanted you to have this,' she said. 'Seeing that you ignore my wishes and return to this house, I can at least provide a counterbalance to the coarseness of your other influences.'

I looked at her, trying to read her expression, but her face was still closed to me. I opened the package and found inside a fine edition of Milton's *Paradise Lost*. It was adorned with engravings and prefaced by Dryden. It was beautiful.

'I thought to get you a Bible, but I knew you would not read it,' she said. 'I saw you in the church today.' She cast a glance over towards my mother and continued in a lower voice. 'I have said nothing of your dual life to Arnold. I know that you are not bad, but I know also that you have done bad things. I do not judge you, Goody, but I wish you to know that there is another life, one which is honourable and decent. The path you have chosen is not the only path. I will not give you up, but if we are to see each other, it must be as friends, and you must convince me that you are moving away from those blackguards.'

We were silent for a while. Gusts of ribaldry came to us from the dining room. I could make out Francis's particular laugh, which was loud and infectious, and brought a smile to my face. I felt a sudden sense of inequity that we had been excluded from the room, Lily and I, who were every bit as bright and entertaining as the others in there. And my mother too, for all that she was unable to contribute to the quippery. I looked over at her now; she was watching the snow.

'Is your mother dead?' I asked Lily.

'You are never afraid to state what is on your mind,' she replied. 'No, she is not dead, merely beside herself. She became ill when I was but a child, and my father had her detained in a private institution in Hampshire. We go to visit her once every year.' She was silent for a moment. 'She seems not so mad to me,' Lily said. 'Or rather, no madder than I should be, were I abandoned in a place like that.'

Friendship is an edifice built by the gradual accretion of confidences. I knew that Lily was angry at my role in Arnold's accident, knew that our relations would always have a complex undergrowth, but I also knew that it took her some courage to confess to me her mother's misfortune. I said nothing, only reached over and squeezed her hand.

It was not until it was near suppertime that Francis, much the worse for drink, opened the door and, taking a moment to bring us into focus, spoke our names. 'Come join us, you three. Come drink in the new and out the old. We have been too long without you.'

Much later, we made our way home through the snow-muffled streets. I had taken too much of the port, and I found my feet slipping from beneath me as I stepped down the driveway. Francis held my mother by the arm and let out a hiccough now and then. Albert had granted us a lamp, and the light of it cast a happy glow as we moved slowly through the silent town. There is a particular quietness that comes over a place at Christmastide, when all are within and surrounded by their families, and it feels like a transgression and an indulgence to be about.

When we came home, my mother went straight up to her room, while Francis and I stayed at the hall table and took some more drink. My brother had several bottles of good Flemish ale, and then brought out an old flask of the apple brandy the Normans call calvados, which we drank down in stinging gulps, laughing as we did so and toasting the King Over the Water and shouting out, *Revirescit!* Then, when the candles had burnt low and the owls owned the night outside, and the snow fell so thickly that it changed the quality of the air about us, and made the panes of Mother's glasshouse creak and complain, Francis came and sat in the chair beside me.

'Goody,' he said, and his voice was thick and deep. It was not until I moved my head towards him that I recognised how drunken I was, and it was not until he pressed his lips against mine that I realised how much I did want my brother. He took my hand in his and led me up the stairs, and we went into his chamber, and the pleasure and the pain and the wrongs of it all are not to be set down here.

XV

THERE CAME A morning when Francis opened a letter at the breakfast table and I saw his face change with the reading of it. It was January, and the snow had not ceased its falling. The garden was bright with frost, the limbs of the orchard trees reaching up to a sky white like bone. 'He is moving north,' Francis said, and I needed to know no more than that. It was time for us to leave for France. I went up to attire myself in my black tunic and hose.

So it was that night, under the clear winter moon, we took ourselves down through the snow to the ferry, where the ferryman was waiting for us, the wherry rigged with dark sails. It was cold but clear, a fair south-westerly blowing itself along the coast. We had the horses with us, each of them loaded down with a coffer of gold bullion. There were further sacks and purses of cash and coinage, and a collection of charts and maps showing the placement of coastguards and army garrisons on the Essex shore. We loaded our cargo into the old, flat-bottomed boat, and pushed back from the dock. I looked up as we pulled out from the bank, through the leafless branches, each of them garlanded with stars.

Francis took us out into the channel of the Brede, steering his way past dead reeds. We came to the snow-covered spit that marked the river's mouth and were soon running in the clear night-time ocean. Every now and again, Francis would ask me to trim a sheet, or to give out more sail, and I'd do so; otherwise, I watched the passing of lights on the coast, and kept a more wary eye on the faint horizon, aware the goods that kept us sitting low in the water would interest any passing customs-man.

We had not been sailing long when I saw the great beam of the Dunge Ness lighthouse and, bobbing in the water ahead of us, the dim glow of sails. I took up my brother's night-glass and looked more closely ahead. We were off the spit, just where the shingle of the promontory gives way to marsh, and I saw it, the very nightmare: fifteen or twenty ships ahead of us, and we should soon be amongst them.

'Brother!' I said in a fierce whisper.

'Aye,' he replied. 'I had expected as much.' We took a hard tack to the south and, once we had retreated some distance, Francis handed me the tiller and took up the night-glass himself. 'Norris's fleet, out of Portsmouth,' he said. 'They are readying for the French attempt. It's a good sign they're here. It means they are not off Maldon.'

We made our way carefully around the fleet and saw no other craft until we came into the reach of Dunkerque harbour, where several large ketches and a sloop-of-war were moored just offshore. The wind was stronger now, gusting in bursts that sent us fast into the port, where we pulled up alongside a French man-o-war whose sailors watched us dock with insolent appraisal.

We stacked the chests and sacks on the trolley, then set off up the quayside. Sailors sat in huddles, smoking their pipes or playing craps or telling stories, while in the darkness behind, urchins crouched and regarded us, shivering in the wind that swept down the dock. The Prince was staying at the Château de Steen, a mile outside of the town towards Gravelines. We found ourselves a cab to convey us and, leaving the rumourous port behind, set off into the night.

The château rose like a cliff from the surrounding countryside – a moated castle with lights burning from its embrasures, torches glowing on its turrets. We pulled over the drawbridge and into the courtyard and unloaded our precious cargo. Francis paid the man, and he whipped his horses and the cart went clattering back across the cobbles.

There was the sound of footsteps and, as our cab-man departed, two well-dressed gentlemen came into view. They looked at first startled to see us, then, perceiving Francis, the taller one let out a bark of greeting. 'Have you brought us gold, friend?' He wrapped my brother in an embrace and then bent to inspect me. He was an angular, heronish man, his limbs thin as branches. Francis presented me and introduced the man as Hugh, Lord Sempill. The other gentleman, who was younger, and very handsome with the angular cheeks of a Slav, named himself as the Chevalier de Johnstone in a smooth and educated voice. He was no more than five-and-twenty and wore a sword of highly polished silver at his belt.

A group of servants was summoned up and so it was that we entered the great hall of the château with the gold we had to offer to the Stuart cause borne along-side us. There was much laughter and cheering as we came in, and as pipers and fiddlers played, Lord Sempill danced about us, calling out that Francis was arrived and with him his sister Goody, and we brought gold and good cheer from England. There were torches burning on the walls and a great fire in the hearth, and all was cast in a warm glow. We were led forward to the main table, where cuts of meat were laid out, and there stood many flasks and flagons of wine and ale. And there, at the centre of it all, sat the Prince.

The Young Pretender was much as I had heard him described – a well-proportioned, handsome man with fair hair. His smile, when it came, took in all of his face, particularly the eyes. From the moment of meeting him, I felt a great upswelling of confidence in the Jacobite cause. Francis lowered himself on to his knees and, somewhat overcome by the moment, I did likewise.

'Rise,' the Prince said, 'and come sup with us. I wish to hear of Kent and Sussex, and of my friend the Baron at Grinstead. I would that you would both speak to me of my old friend Ezekiel, that I may mourn him the better for knowing what befell him. But here, some claret.' The Prince's accent was a gallimaufry of his Continental childhood, his Polish mother, and his Scottish forebears. He sounded like no one I have met before or since.

Is there not always an old man beside a prince? As we sat ourselves at the table, the Prince presented us to his: a fat man in military uniform named John Sullivan, who had been at the university in Dublin with my father, and spoke with an Irish accent.

'I was at Gaeta with Ezekiel and the young Prince,' Sullivan said. 'We were brave, then, as we shall be brave in the weeks to come.' His voice, which had been soft, suddenly hardened. 'Are you a scholar, Goody, like your father?'

'I can speak as well as him, and fight as well, too,' I told him. 'Not all of the former keepers of this gold donated it to the cause by choice.'

'Ah, a brigand,' he said with a twinkle. 'We will need our share of those. I have long admired your brother Francis's skill with the pistol. He has made a great contribution to our prospects. He will be well rewarded when the day is won.'

Lord Sempill and the young Chevalier came to join us, and there were other noblemen, Scottish bonnet lairds and Irish chieftains. I sat back a little from the group and observed them, perceiving how easily the Prince held his drink, how well-costumed he was, with a coat of rose-coloured velvet embroidered and lined in velvet tissue. He wore a gold ribbon in his hair and had large, brown eyes that shone in the light of the torches and the candles on the table. His face was powdered pale and his lips large and feminine. There was something magnetic and compelling about his company, and it was clear to me why so many had followed him, why a nation might be prepared to rise up in his name.

The gold was taken off by Lord Sempill to be stored in the castle vaults, while Sullivan and the Prince cleared a space on the table, upon which they unfurled a large and intricate map of Britain, the Channel and the northern coast of France. All about the map, but in particular concentration in the north of England, in Scotland and in Wales, there were pinned small cockades fashioned of white fabric. I looked and saw one in Winchelsea, another several in the country about Rye, and then a more prominent cockade at West Grinstead. I recognised that these trinkets were symbolical of those who would stand with the Prince Pretender come the counter-revolution. Looking up the country and over to Ireland, or in the hills of Scotland, I felt stirring within me tremors of a great excitation. I had never truly believed the Jacobite cause might credibly achieve its aims. But here, before me, was a map that said the young Prince could call upon followers the length and breadth of the land.

'I hear dragoons are being marshalled in Kent and Sussex,' Sullivan said. 'It seems our plans are still not widely known. Have ye heard aught, Francis?'

'Whispers,' my brother replied. 'I was at Grinstead the other day and was told of much speculation. It is thought that we will land at Camber and make our way up the Rother. There are apparently a thousand men stationed at Hythe, with a thousand more expected in the coming week. Norris's fleet is at Dunge Ness, which proves to us that there are indeed agents in Paris and Rome, and that they are not so close to us to know the truth of our intent.'

'Then all is well,' the Prince said. 'We mistrusted those whom it was right to mistrust, and our faith in our friends was justified.'

We sat up much longer, and soon several of the men were asleep with drink, while others bellowed out 'When the King Comes Home Again' and 'The White Cockade', banging their chests and clapping one another on the back, and cheering *Vivat!* and *Revirescit!* between verses. Francis, Sullivan and the Prince spoke in low voices which I could but little follow. They pointed often to the map, concentrating themselves first on Essex, then the Highlands, then the Welsh Marches. Finally, the Prince seemed pleased with what had been decided and he rose to his feet, as steady as if he had been drinking but water all night.

'Friends,' he said, and there was immediate silence,

and several of those who had been sleeping now stirred. 'Rest now, all of you. Keep the Honest Cause in your hearts and know that God is with us. We will restore the line of ancient and rightful monarchs to England, and all who have suffered hardships in my name will live as princes in the days to come. Good night and God's blessings on every one of you.'

The Prince embraced Sullivan and Francis as he left. When he was going past me, he placed a hand on my shoulder and, in a low voice, said, 'It is well to have you with us, Goody.' I felt a shudder go through me at his touch, as if there was some magnetism in those gentle fingers.

When he was gone, many merely turned and slept where they lay, but Francis and I, taking with us a bottle of claret and a small lamp, went in silent agreement into the darkness of the castle. We walked up winding stone stairs and through echoing cloisters where our breath hung in the air. We found battlements that looked down over the moat and a courtyard that seemed suspended high above the surrounding land. There were turrets and keeps, a castellated gorge tower and giddy walkways over unseen baileys below. We made our way out on to the island of the barbican, and heard geese squabbling in the moat, wind in leafless trees, the distant surge of the sea.

Finally, and again without either of us saying a word, we came to a high corridor whose heavy doors were all closed save one. Inside that door was a chamber, a curtained bed all made up with fine linen and a heavy counterpane. We fell out of our clothes and into the bed, and when I woke in the small hours of the morning, I could feel only the heat and closeness of Francis all about me, could smell only his scent, and I was happy as I had never been happy before.

XVI

'THE WEATHER LOOKS not fair,' the Prince said. 'Stay a while with us, why don't you? We will hunt and return to six cases of claret just arrived from Bordeaux. You can then cross with us and see me installed upon the throne by the week's end.'

We were standing in the courtyard of the château as grooms and stable boys led the horses out into the January air. The Prince wore a red tartan embroidered with gold, a blue sash over his chest. I liked the idea of riding out with him, of coming back to another night of plotting and singing, and then, of course, of lying in the darkness with my brother.

Francis, though, was for heading homewards. On the morrow the French fleet, under the charge of the Comte de Roquefeuil, was bound for Maldon. They would be accompanying transport ships with fifteen thousand troops on board, more than all the soldiers currently stationed in England. The Prince and Marshall Saxe would jointly lead them through the Blackwater Marshes and then down to London, and it was thought that the country would fall with nary a gout of blood shed.

'We must go, my liege,' Francis said with a bow. 'There is much yet to achieve with the Association of Gentlemen. When you ride into London three or four days hence, I wish to be there with those who have done so much to make this moment possible. God speed, sire.'

The Prince insisted we take his own carriage into the port. He stood surrounded by his attendants, and they let up a cheer and threw their hats in the air as we departed.

The Prince had been right about the weather. It was but three of the clock when we arrived at the port, but the sky was overcast and black. A vicious wind shrieked in the rigging of the ships moored in the harbour, while further out, past the mole that marked the entrance to the port, we could see sloops at anchor, bobbing and rolling amid white-capped waves. On the mole, sailors and townspeople stood and watched the weather gathering over the ocean.

'A boisterous crossing,' Francis said, his voice raised over the wind.

'You're not thinking of taking the wherry out into this?' I would have been troubled to set out into such weather in the *Albion*, let alone in our fractile vessel.

'We must return. I have sailed in worse and lived. They say there may be eviler storms yet to come.'

'And the French fleet?

'Nimble, but under-armed. Foul weather will keep the English in port and speed our cause.'

So it was that we took our pitiful boat out into the high water. As we passed the mole, there went up from the gentlemen gathered there a cheer that was part disbelief. Out amid the waves, I leapt from one side of the ship to the other to counter the pitch and roll. Within ten minutes we were both drenched, and I was exhausted with all the jumping about and tying-in of lines, all the mental and physical acuity that was required of me. Francis appeared calm, even when a large wave reared up with the special purpose of emptying itself over our craft and ourselves. For a moment I wondered if I had been washed into the sea. Then we climbed again, and the bilge drains did their work, but we were a sorry pair, my brother and I. My cap had been washed from my head, my jacket drenched and heavy. In the valley of the next wave, I bent to empty my boots of the water they had collected.

At last, from the peak of a wave, we saw the light of Dunge Ness, far off to the north-west. Francis altered our course, knowing well that Norris would have taken the fleet into the lee of the spit, and would not go after a mere wherry in weather such as this, even should we be spotted. As it was we passed the light at a clip, the wind swinging round to the east. I had no notion of how long we had been out on the water. Everything was heavy upon me – my sodden jacket, my father's key about my neck, his sword at my waist. I diddered and chattered my teeth, clapped myself about the shoulders, pulled from Francis's flask of grog when he offered it to me, but still I could not get warm. By the time we saw Rye glowing mistily in the rain, I fear that I was sobbing.

Once in the bay, the force of the wind abated and the sea grew less wild. We went past the mouth of the Rother, then, in the darkness, and using the lights of Winchelsea as a guide, Francis steered us towards the smaller opening that marked the place where the Brede disgorged itself into the sea. I let the jib out as we came in, then got myself down in the boat, trusting in Francis's preternatural ability to navigate the channels of the river even in the dark. I heard the slap and grumble of waves breaking on the shingle, then a slight diminution in the sound, and I realised he was sailing as much by ear as by eye. He headed us towards the place where the waves were not breaking, for that was the entrance to the Brede.

I was thinking ahead to my bed and being warm again, when I saw the figures standing on the spit at the river's mouth. *Redcoats*, I thought. I said my brother's name, then again, but saw he'd already caught sight of the men, two on horseback, more standing, their lamps half-hidden by spouts. 'Pull in the jib,' Francis said, very calm. I did as he urged, and saw that he was pushing the tiller full hard away from him. 'Now lean out.' Again, I did as he said, and I thought for a moment that we would clear the shore, would head back out into the bitter night, waves that had seemed so fierce now to prove our saviours.

It was not to be. The wherry was an unnimble craft and the circle in which we turned was not near tight enough to escape the shore. We found ourselves grounded on the spit, and already the men on horseback were upon us, their rifles aimed at our heads. The men on foot came down the shingle towards us, and all of them bristled with arms. Whether it was the spout-lights shone in our eyes, or perchance I was stupid with the cold, but still it shocked me when I heard one of the men speak, and it was Gray. I felt a desperate flush of relief.

'Francis, Goody, 'tis late to be out, is it not? Particularly when there are so many Revenue men about. And soldiers.'

My brother had taken the wherry's anchor and buried it in the pebbles. He turned and gave the hawser a great heave until the boat was quite out of the water. I saw him look up at Gray, mizzle pearling on his eyelashes. 'You are not our keeper, Arthur,' he said. 'And I see more guns than appear friendly here. You were awaiting us, or some other craft?'

'We were awaiting you.' A silence descended at these words. Some of the men had removed the spouts from their lamps, while others wore their faces masked or blackened or in skeps. The misty rain drifted about them. I was suddenly recalled to the night with my father, of the treachery of once-dear friends, the loss and the pain that came with it. I saw Poison with his great blunder-buss held before him, Kingsmill with a kerchief pulled up over his mouth, and Smoker, whom I knew from his frame rather than his face, as he wore a pale bee-skep on his head. 'Now the question is what to do with you.'

'We have no quarrel with you, Arthur,' Francis said, and he gave a chuckle that scarce hid his nervishness.

I saw Gray put a match to his pipe, then puff a moment. 'And yet we have quarrel with you. With you both.' Here he took a torch and held it up towards us. 'We always agreed to overlook your Popish conspiring, unless it made too severe an imposition on our dealings. Now the Marsh swarms with government, and the Winchelsea barracks are overspilling with men, and there is not a whore in Hythe with whom a dragoon does not sleep. Norris and his fleet sit in the Bay. It becomes impossible for us to carry out a run without descending half of His Majesty's soldiery upon us.'

Francis smiled, spreading his arms. 'This is but a

temporary burden for us to bear. There are momentous times ahead, friend, and you know you will benefit when the new order is established.'

'I have lived long enough to know change takes more than a few years and a few French mercenaries to achieve. Jacobites were carping when you and I were in our cradles. In the meantime, we lose opportunity. And since the Deal men have come aboard' – here he nodded at some of those standing beside the horses – 'and risked their necks for us, the share must be divided between a greater number than before.'

'And so you will dispose of us? Who have been through so much with you?'

'Aye, alas.' Gray shook his head and spat a little tobacco from his mouth.

'I am sorry,' my brother said, and with astonishing swiftness he leapt forward at Gray, knocking him to the ground. The two men began to wrestle on the shingle, rolling down towards the sea and away from the light. I reached to draw my sword, but then Francis cried, 'Goody, run!' and there was something about hearing my name that rousted me then. I plunged between the horses and down into the marsh.

XVII

I TURNED JUST before I stepped off the bank of shingle and saw that Poison and Smoker were coming after me. The latter had taken off his skep and held a dagger in his hand, while Poison hefted his fire piece over his shoulder and carried a lamp. At first the two horses seemed to be joining them in pursuit, but their riders could not persuade them out into the damp and shifting ground. I ran with my memory as my only guide, shutting my eyes and feeling for footholds, counting the bounds and leaps until I reached a familiar piece of solid ground, or jagged left to skirt around a claggy pool. I turned again and saw that Smoker and Poison had been met by another, his face masked, who appeared to know the marsh as well as I did, issuing them with instructions as they ran. I saw the blackness of Iham Hill ahead of me and redoubled my efforts, peeling off my heavy coat as I ran, gripping my sword by its scabbard so it should not impede me. Despite my exertions, though, I could tell that my pursuers were gaining.

I passed the bend of the Brede that wound close below the hill, near where I had seen Gabriel drown Jim Lawrence, and, as I began the climb up to the gate into the Under-Reach, I could feel the closeness of those who hunted me, could hear their squelched steps, their breath in the air and the soft, precise instructions of their guide. I reached for the key about my neck, letting go of my scabbard and near stumbling over it as I hurried to thrust aside the brown fronds of bracken that grew about the gate. My fingers remained numbed from their exposure and I willed them to close about the key. My first attempt to direct it into the lock failed, my second the same. Only when I forced myself to draw in a deep breath, and clasped my right hand with the left, did I manage to drive the key home. I turned it and, with a slow and grinding noise, the resistance gave.

I staggered into the entrance tunnel just as my pursuers began to climb the path to the gate, being not ten or twelve feet behind me.

I had not time to withdraw the key, nor to lock the gate, and so I swung it shut and made my way into the dark maw of the Under-Reach. I was near panicked, flailing about in my mind for escape. I knew that the gate to the northern tunnels was locked shut, having secured it myself on the completion of our last run. I knew there were only so many places to hide in the three caverns that made up the southern portion of the warren. I passed through St Bartholomew's cellar. I came into the second of the large caves, the Holly Rood cellar, just as the lights of the three men became visible behind me. I heard a shout and the pounding of feet and, acting swifter than my thoughts were able to follow, I drew my father's sword, crossed swiftly to the boarded-up entrance to the mines and placed the blade behind one of the boards. I gave an almighty pull on the hilt.

The board creaked and gave and, as the footsteps of the men were almost upon me, I clambered through the gap and fell head-forward into a pool of grimy water. I stood, reached to retrieve the sword, fixed it in the scabbard at my waist and lurched into the dripping tunnel. My path was lit for a few steps by the torch of my pursuers, who were now hacking at the other boards and making fair headway from the sound of it. The tunnel turned and I was plunged again in total darkness, now without the benefit of having foreknowledge of the terrain. The path began to slope downwards and all the time the water at my feet grew deeper. I could hear the men behind splashing as they came after. Finally, I took a step forward and my foot found no purchase. I plunged into the water and discovered that the tunnel had become a stream that disappeared into a culvert beneath the rock. I felt the entrance with my fingers and found that barely a sliver of air remained at the top, scarce enough to accommodate my lips, let alone my head. I remembered my father's stories of the Deeps and a flooded passageway and his own father finding him waist-deep within it. Light played upon the water and I saw Smoker, his knife bitten between his teeth, a lamp in his hand, scurrying towards me.

I took a deep breath, then another, and I plunged beneath the water, kicking my feet out behind and pulling myself along on the smooth-worn rock. The flow of the water had not seemed fast when I entered and yet it gathered pace as I went, and I perceived that the tunnel was turning downwards, taking me deeper under the earth. I opened my eyes and saw strange visions there in the water: dancing sprites and nereids, constellations of stars and obscure glyphic inscriptions. There was a time when I felt the desperate need to breathe, and then the burning tightness in my lungs ceased and there was only the frantic rush of the water, the luminosity of the drifting creatures and their eldritch world.

Then, just as I seemed to be falling so deeply into that visionary existence that it felt as if I might be lost within it forever, I found myself spat out of the mouth of the tunnel, falling now not through water, but through air. There was time to take a huge and gasping breath before I again found myself submerged. This time, though, I recognised that I had landed in a lake or pool, deep enough that it was cold, and no matter that I had fallen some distance, I touched no bottom. I struggled to the surface and pulled myself through the water until I reached the edge, where I succeeded in heaving myself up on to the rocks.

XVIII

ON EXITING THE pool, I took survey of my person. Nothing was broken, I felt sure, although much was bruised. My shirt had been torn ragged by the passage through the underground stream, my boots were nowhere to be seen and I was without a light, deep in the belly of Iham Hill. I should have despaired at this point, but I was very young and hope came easily to me back then. Also, I felt a strange perceiving in me. I closed my eyes and found that it was brighter like this, that I could still make out the eerie shapes and flashing apparitions I had seen in the tunnel. They seemed to be gathering in one direction, these phantasms, and so, having no better choice to make, I followed them.

I venture that you have never known real dark. For even in the blackest night there remains a penumbral half-light about things, a sense that these trees and rocks about you were once bathed in the rays of the sun and will be again. In the Deeps there was none of this, no shadows nor dim glow that hovers in the corner of the eyes, no gradations of darkness. Here, the blackness was absolute and consuming, an uttermost dark, inconceivable. Sound in such blankness was magnified, so that I could hear the rushing of the torrent into the pool as if the water were all about me. I could judge the size of the cavern by the way the noise hit the walls, could even sense that to my left it opened out, while to my right, in the direction of the falling water, there was a narrowing.

I walked with my arms held out before me. I moved swiftly at first, for although I was near-certain that Smoker would not follow me, and that neither Poison nor the masked stranger would be able to fit themselves into the runnel, I knew the sooner I moved, the more chance I had of saving myself. I suffered a different sort of cold now, for though the mines themselves were warm enough, being far from the frigid earth above, the cold had settled into my bones and for all I stamped and shook myself, it did not depart.

The spectral figures behind my eyes proved themselves but little help as I made my way through the darkness. A shelf of rock protruded from the side of the cavern, positioned in such a fashion that my arms did not encounter it, but my head did. I was not moving with great speed and so it was more painful than deranging, but I began to feel my way along the wall, crouched low beneath the overhanging rock. It took me a long time, although time, like all else, is mistempered by the dark, but finally I felt the movement of air on my shoulders, on my cheek. My fingers found an opening in the wall of the cave and I made my way slowly through it and into a tunnel.

The roof of the passage was scarce taller than me, the sides narrow enough that I could touch them with my hands as I went. The path turned neither left nor right, but, dishearteningly, it seemed to slope more down than up. The sound of the torrent receded as I went deeper into the mines, to be replaced by the slow drip of water, the shuffling of my bare feet, the rasp of my breath and the pulse in my head. I counted my steps up to a hundred, then began again. At one point, the tunnel came to a fork. I chose left and was rewarded with an upward slope that swiftly resolved itself downward once more. I was tired and lay for a moment. As I felt sleep begin to settle over me, I bethought myself how long I had been underground and was able to find no answer. I was thirsty. I ran my fingers along the damp wall of the tunnel, then brought them to my lips. The taste of it was stale and a little salty, but it slaked enough to allow me to sleep.

I was woken by a sound. At first I persuaded myself that it had been but the legacy of some forgotten dream. Then I heard it again. It was not to be mistaken – the pad of footsteps, far-off but coming closer, echoing towards me down the tunnel. Next I perceived, again faintly, a subtle lessening of the darkness from the direction in which I had come. It would be too much to call it light, but I recognised that someone was coming towards me, and that I must move.

I gave up all efforts to protect myself from the surrounding rock, and barrelled down the tunnel from one side to the other. I unsheathed my sword from my belt and held it out before me, hoping that it might serve to warn me of any approaching collision. I was aware that I was making a great deal of noise and that my pursuer would redouble their efforts now they knew themselves to be on the right course, but I was gripped with a desperation that superseded rational thought. I let out a beastly howl into the darkness, whether to fright my pursuer or embolden myself, I knew not.

As I have said once already, sometimes I know a thing before it happens. I slowed myself to a walk. I felt a change in the atmosphere about me, and was just about to step forward, when my toe met an object on the floor. I lowered myself on to my knees and felt about before me. I realised there was a plank on the ground, and that it extended over some sort of chasm or fissure. Had I not tripped on the lip of the plank I would, in all likelihood, have fallen into whatever abysmal depths lay beneath. I scrabbled around for a rock to drop into the void. It was a long moment before I heard a distant clatter beneath. Then the footsteps again: approaching, relentless.

I had no way of knowing how long the plank was, nor how sturdy, but given that turning back would take me straight into the path of my pursuer, I steeled myself to press on. I decided to settle on the plank and effect my crossing by edging forwards on my bum. My first movement was too energetic and the plank shifted dangerously beneath me. Then I moved more carefully and timed my shifts forward with the swinging of my legs. I attempted to judge the length of the plank by how much it buckled beneath me, but with each move forward it seemed to bend more, until it surely could not hold. It creaked, but did not break, and I shuffled again and it seemed that perhaps the give was less pronounced, that I might have passed the halfway point.

I turned to look back and saw again just the dimmest glow in the mouth of the tunnel, a darkness less absolute than it should be. The footsteps were rhythmic and inexorable, and I knew I must move fast if I was to traverse the plank before I was apprehended. I readied myself to heft forward again, when I chanced to look down. There, in the darkness beneath me, I saw the pinpricks of a hundred tiny eyes, shining not from any light projected towards them but rather out of some strange alchemy of their own. The eyes were yellow in hue and almond-shaped, and from them was emitted a sense of such evil that it seemed to reach out and grab me by the throat. I fell sidewards as all balance, all composure, left me. The whole plank rotated so that I hung beneath it, and it was as if the creatures below were urging me down amongst them.

I clung to the plank with every last bit of strength left to me and, hanging bat-like beneath, continued to inch along it. I finally felt my head hit rock behind me and, hitching first a leg, then an arm, around the plank, I propelled myself atop it and on to the firmness of solid earth. The light in the tunnel on the opposite side of the chasm – no more than eight feet in width – was brighter now. Not waiting to see the face of my pursuer, I kicked the plank off the edge and into the ravine and made my way forward into the darkness.

XIX

MY ESCAPE FROM the Deeps was undramatic. After further wandering, I became aware of the sound of the sea ahead of me, then the softening of the darkness and a pool of blue light far off. Finally I was in a cave, stepping between dimly luminous rock pools, then out into the terrible brightness of the morning. I stood for a time with my hand over my eyes, taking this punishment for having seen so clearly in the dark. Through my fingers I saw the sun was low in the east still – not past eight of the morning – and that I stood on the beach at Fairlight Cove. Above me were the cliffs from which my father had plunged more than a year since. This time, though, the tide was far out, the sand marching away in ruffled lines to the distant breakers. A cool wind whipped along the shore and I looked down to see that I was shoeless, my feet blue with cold, my shirt torn and stained with grime and blood. My hair was matted and my hands were scratched and raw. I was alive, though, and this fact stunned me for a moment. I wondered then of my brother and began to take measure of this latest whemmelling of all that I thought I knew of the world.

I walked out to where the sea met the sand and, heedless of the cold or the chance of being espied from the cliffs, I made my way through the rising light, watching seabirds flitter in sharp arrows above the water, the fishing boats in the bay and the plumes of smoke that rose from the rooftops of Rye and Winchelsea. I kept out in that deserted space, feeling the lap of the low waves on my bare blue feet, until I came to the mouth of the Brede. The river carved a channel through the sand here and I followed it up to the shingle, where the wherry still lay, listing, its anchor buried in the stones. I could see where my brother and Gray had wrestled in the pebbles, could see the hoof prints of the horses where they'd stepped hesitantly on to the shifting marsh.

I took a quick survey of the land about. Three women walked along the Rye Road, baskets held at their hips. A single horseman was visible coming up the road to Winchelsea from Ore. I knew I should not be seen, dishabilled as I was. I forced myself to run across the marsh, as much to warm myself as to evade detection. I went up the path to the gate and saw that it was closed firm and that the key was no longer in the lock. I clambered further up King's Cliffs, ducking as I ran, then skirted the edge of Greyfriars' cherry orchard, keeping a close eye on the watchtower that Arnold had had constructed in the belfry of the old abbey. Either there was no look-out, or they were surveying further off, for none called after me. I kept to the hedgerows and ditches, pressing myself into the stone wall at the bottom of the Hundred Place when a carriage came by. Finally I was on Rectory Lane and, abandoning subterfuge in favour of speed, I winged up the road and into the gate to Paradise.

I walked up the path to the front door, which was unlocked, and stepped inside. There was no fire lit in the hall, nor in the parlour, and my mother was not in her glass-house. I called out for her, climbing the stairs to look in my parents' chamber, which I rarely did, and which always brought to mind my father in his nightshirt. The bed appeared not to have been slept in. I thought with something like wonder that mayhap I was alone in the world, perchance I had lost my mother and brother as well as my father, and the horror of it felt like it would o'erwhelm my senses. I tamped down the thoughts, recognising that there would be time for mourning, time for revenge should that be needed, but there were more immediate requirements to be addressed.

I was aware that with the warming of my feet and hands, pain was creeping into them both. My feet were no longer blue but the white of one long-dead, as if they had never known blood. I went down into the parlour and made up and lit the fire, then, when I had rubbed more feeling into my limbs, I went to fetch the bath pan and kettle and heated some water. I took off what was left of my clothing, looking with wonder at the bruises and welts on my shoulders, the gashes and abrasions on my legs and feet.

I stood in the bathtub and poured great steaming gouts of water over me, and it was perhaps the splash and slosh of the water that masked the sound of the door opening. I was about to send down another gush of water when I caught a movement at the edge of my vision. I turned, clutching the jug to my chest. My mother stood in the doorway, a stricken look on her face, her arms out towards me. She moaned a little, then came and placed her hands on my face. I had yet to regard myself in a glass, but it seemed that the events of the night showed themselves in my countenance. She let out another low sound, then went back to the door, beckoning for me to follow her.

I wrapped myself in my bath sheet and crossed the hall to my father's study. My mother sat herself at the desk and, pinching together her features in concentration, began the slow process of marking out her words. It was all I could do not to read over her shoulder, but so laborious was her lettering that I forced myself to stand by the window wrapped in my sheet, looking out into the January sunshine. Hellebores nodded in clusters on the lawn, while the first of the snowdrops gleamed in the rose beds.

My mother cleared her throat and I turned. She held up the paper before her.

IT WAS I FOLLOWING YOU IN THE DEEPS LAST NIGHT. YOU WOULD NOT AWAIT ME.

I shook my head at her. 'It can't have been. How did you get there? How did you find me?'

She scratched again at the paper. I waited.

I KNOW THINGS YOU DO NOT KNOW. I CAN BE PLACES YOU CANNOT BE.

I went over to stand by her. My voice was quieter now. I lowered myself so we were at the same level. 'Please, then, can you not use this power of yours to locate Francis? Tell me, mother, where is he? Where is my brother?' And as I spoke it, I began to cry. My mother looked at me and I saw all I needed to see within her dark eyes. I felt as if the threads of my world were all unravelling at once. I sank to my knees, thence to the floor, to my dear father's Turkey carpet, where I curled myself up and keened like a beaten dog. I know not why I was so persuaded by my mother, nor why her eyes seemed to convey to me something that I knew deeply within me. Whatever the cause, I let the bath sheet fall from me and rolled and sobbed and cursed until I was spent.

Only then did my mother come over to where I lay, naked and wretched on the floor. She stooped and placed a fold of paper into my hand. She then laid her hands over my stomach and her lips moved in what may have been a spell or a prayer. Then she turned and went. Through my tears, I read the note she had writ for me.

YOU CARRY HIS CHILD.

XX

NEXT DAY, I rolled my father's large oak chest before the door that led down to the Under-Reach – which seemed suddenly to have become a point of weakness for us, rather than of security. I then went out looking for Francis. Both that morning and for so many that followed, I put on my best dress and my shawl and I flung myself out to the edges of the marsh, seeking some sign of my brother. I looked for Gray or for Kingsmill, or any other member of the Hawkhurst Gang, but they seemed to have vanished from the earth, all of them. It was a damp and gustsome spring and I walked out in all weathers as my belly grew and my heart sank. I looked for my brother in the inns and taverns of the town, and it came so that I'd take a drink whenever I could, hoping that some barkeep would remember seeing a handsome Moor, or would speak of Gray or Smoker or Poison. I was certainly attempting to find Francis, but it strikes me now that

I was also trying to flee the burning house of my mind, for I had gone mad with the loss of him.

I became convinced that it had been Young Perin guiding my pursuers across the marsh that night, given that none other knew the ways and wiles of the shifting ground as well as he. I went several times to Perin's house out on the rainy flats above New Romney, but it was dark and empty, the doors standing open to the wind, a few hungry-looking cats hissing and spitting in the undergrowth, and the sense that none had ever lived in so inhospitable a place. The whole marsh felt that way, given that all the soldiery was now departed and it was mercilessly cold. There was no invasion, nor any hope of one, and all the news was bad.

The storm that had near whelmed Francis and me that night had struck the French fleet just as it was leaving Dunkerque the next day. Hundreds of men were drowned; the Prince escaped with his life but little else; Marshall Saxe and the Comte de Roquefeuil had quarrelled and were refusing to serve in the same cause again. The invasion had thus had all of the impetus sucked from it and the Prince now brooded in Paris. The old Baron Caryll, hearing the news, had suffered an apoplexy and died, while Pelham's government began to hunt down the Association of Gentlemen, arresting the Earl of Barrymore and Sir Robert Abdy and holding them in the Tower.

So I sat that spring and summer long in the corner-nooks of lonely taverns, sipping ale or mead and thinking of how low my fortunes had sunk, having promised so much. I returned late to my home, where my mother waited up for me, her face growing more drawn and sorrowful with every passing week. Arnold came to call upon me several times, but I could not face him and scrawled him notes pleading indisposition. I knew that the townspeople had begun to point at me – the wandering, wild-eyed girl increasingly unable to hide the signs of her gravidity. I took to leaving Winchelsea early in the morning, before anyone was awake, and coming back in darkness, the beer sloshing within me. Sometimes I'd take Hero and ride up to look at the blackened windows of Seacox Heath, which appeared to have been finished and abandoned by its murderous owner. I'd stop in Hawkhurst or Sandhurst for a drink on the way back, and people would look at me, scandalised. Occasionally folk would attempt to speak with me on the road, or while I drank, and I'd feign idiocy, or speak a few words of Flemish, and they'd swiftly leave me be.

I could not readily conceive of the creature that was growing inside me; I felt in no way connected to it, or happy to be carrying the relic of my brother. I did not want some mewling simulacrum of Francis, I wanted my brother himself. I hated what the child inside me was doing to my body, the way my hips flared out, my belly now large enough to balance an ale mug upon. I had always been tall, but now I was broad, hefty, a big woman, and I liked it not. Even my tunic and breeches – those kindly travesties that permitted me to step outside the strictures of womanhood – no longer fit me. I was reduced to wearing a great sack-like dress which I hefted immodestly above my knees in order to mount Hero.

Finally the summer passed and my groaning-time

approached. Something was awry in my innards, my womb-liver leaking out of me in dark gushes, so that I was forced to wear my monthly rags in my undergarments. On one of the last days of my wandering, I was out near Jew's Gut, in a filthy tavern where only a humpbacked innkeep and two sotted patrons endured the draughty saloon with its rats scuttering behind the wall-boards. I had tied Hero to a rail in the yard and I was looking through the window at him, at his sad, patient face, and the rain that fell about him, when I felt a dampness beneath me. I stood, upending my ale jar, and turned to see that there was pooled upon the seat of my stool a dub of blood, dripping darkly on to the sawdust beneath. Picking up the trail of my skirts, I saw that I had dyed them quite black with gore. Heedless of the spectating barkeep and the swivel-eyed drunkards, I placed a hand up my skirts. When I drew it out, I saw with fascination that it was coated in blood, while on my fingers there were the darker streaks of the muggets and numbles that had come out of me. I put my hand down again and tried to force back up that which was attempting to escape me. With my other hand, I placed a coin on the bar and then, still holding the stuffing up me, went out to get atop Hero and home.

When I staggered in the door of Paradise, it was as if my mother had been waiting for just such a moment. She laid me down in the parlour before the fire, stripping my sodden skirts from me, before bustling off into her glass-house. I looked down at myself, at my blood-streaked legs, my great egg of a belly heaving under the fastness of my breath, and I wished to die, thinking to myself that if my bleeding-out didn't finish me, then I would throw myself into the Brede, as my true mother had some eighteen years previously, my own child tucked snugly within me so I could be sure that it did not escape. My mother returned with warm water and sponges, which she used to clean me, and a spoonful of her green paste that she fed me. She then pressed a poultice of wood sage and goldenrod against my quiver, and caused me to drink a little of a bitter liquid. Soon, I slept, and when I woke my mother was beside me. It was dark outside and the flames played upon her small, pinched face.

XXI

I REMAINED STRETCHED out in the parlour for the month that followed, my mother placidly beside me. The blood continued to flow from my quaint, alternating between the gush of vivid red liquor and the darker, clotted run-out of my womb-cake. My mother, who tended me ceaselessly during this time, prepared a dressing made of ergot, which is a mould that grows on certain breads, and of the mashed fruits of the laurel tree. It did reek most horribly, but I applied it to myself each morning and night, and I am certain it was this that saved both me and my child.

None came to visit us then, not Arnold, not any of the Association of Gentlemen, and save for when my mother went out marketing, we merely sat and awaited the coming of the child. The fire burnt, the year rose and dwindled, and I grew massive. The skin of my belly was stretched so tight and thin that it felt as if I could almost reach through it and touch the baby that beat its fists and kicked its legs on the other side of this blue-white wall.

It came around again to the Bonfire Rejoicings, and whether it was the remembrance of what had passed upon that day in previous years, or the excitation of the drumming and the rockets outside our window, but I began to feel things quickening just after nine of the clock that night. I had no expectation of what lay ahead, having never been schooled in such matters, and so was unprepared when the first throes of discomfort arrived, spreading up from the depths of me. There was a sudden rush of pale pink fluid which my mother sopped up with towels. The waves of pain came more quickly, though it was no sort of pain I had ever encountered before, seeming both contiguous with my body and greater than it, as if it emanated from some secret source deep within me and spread out to occupy all of the house, the town, the countryside about. It was just as the last rockets were fading in the darkness above the house that I rose and began to pace the room.

I have no sense of the time it took, nor when it was that I left the parlour and went first to the hall, then to the cool dampness of the glass-house, alternately crouching and bellowing, feeling myself more animal than ever I had before. I felt belly-bound and costive, as if I needed to take a strong emetic or a long shit, and yet there was no movement in my loins and it seemed the only way I could let anything out of me was through sound. So I yelled and yelled and clung on to chairs or the bannister, or my mother's mixing table, or swung like a monkey from the door lintel. My mother was always with me, but never so close as to irk, for the last thing I wanted at that moment was to be touched or in any way forced out of the deep internal place to which I had gone.

It was in the small of the morning that the process entered a new phase. The throes had evened out to one every three minutes or so, and had been that way for some hours, when I found myself in the glass-house, hunched in the darkness under the work-bench, my arms crossed on the floor and my head buried within the fold of them, my haunches raised up in the air. I felt a new kind of dampness seeping out of the raw back of me, and recognised that the child was coming. The yell that emerged from me now was longer and louder and higher than any that had come before, and finally my mother was right with me, and I felt her small, adept hands pull me round so that I was on my back and facing her. I met her eye and I saw great certainty, great strength there. The child, though, would not arrive, push as I would. The pain came quicker and harder, so that it was all I could do to gasp between the waves of it, and there was no fading of the agony as there had been before, but rather a constant and exhausting perduration of suffering. This went on for an hour or more, and then there was only despair, and I began to sob and cry out to my mother to do something – anything – to stop it.

The baby came just as dawn broke. I was on my hands and knees, numbed to the pain, broken in mind as much as body. And there, all of a sudden, was the baby, a boy with winter light coming down upon him. My mother cupped him like an offering in her hands. He was smeared with blood and merd, his skin an unlikely yellow colour, and he wore a near-full head of hair on him. He began to scream from his yellow little face, and my mother again held him up. I recognised that she wished me to take him. I did so, but not willingly. He did not stop screaming, but rather now it felt that his anger was directed at me.

My mother fetched more hot water and began to wash us off. I looked down and saw on the earthen floor of the glass-house that the remains of my womb-cake had passed and were now seeping into the dirt. I must have voided myself several times during those final hours as the stink was high and noxious in there amongst the plants and potions. My mother helped me carry the baby up to my chamber, where we climbed together into bed: the child, my mother and me. She placed him at my breast and he began to suck, and a certain glutted feeling about my chest eased. But very swiftly I was asleep, and I slept through the day and night and into the next, my mind spooling off into magnificent dreams, in none of which was I a mother. Perhaps it was then, while I walked with Francis on the decks of dream ships, a pistol gripped in my hands, or wrestled with redcoats on Pett Level, or bounded on Hero across the marsh, that I missed the chance to love my son.

For, when my mother brought him in, late on the second morning of his life, I found I did not wish him near me. I begged my mother to take him away, and he began to scream. Then, when my mother did not depart, I screamed myself, so that my child and I emptied our lungs at one another. Finally, they went, and when my mother came back an hour later, the child was not with her. I did not ask after him, but thanked her for the food she brought, and told her that the baby should be named Ezekiel. What she fed him on I knew not, how she comforted him in the night, or ensured that he was safe when she went marketing, I cared not. I remained in my chamber for the rest of that week, and the following week, and the week that followed that, and soon it was Christmas and I had not seen my child in near two months, and by the time spring arrived and I was ready to take to my feet once more, I scarce remembered I had a son, and everything that once lived within me was dead.

XXII

I RESUMED MY wandering that spring. I had lost the whelp-weight I'd gained and more, and now dressed myself in black as one who mourned, though part of what sorrowed me was alive – I heard him calling in the night from my mother's chamber. I became convinced that they'd thrown Francis in the sea after killing him, and thought how the waters of Rye Bay had claimed three of those closest to me: my blood-mother, my adoptive father, my brother. I imagined stepping through the waves and walking out into the wide emptiness of the ocean, going down along the seabed until the water seaweeded my hair and I stood amid the ruins of Old Wynchelsea, looking through the petrified stumps of the sunken forest of Dymsdale, to see the dearest ones of my heart going happily about their business. I took to spending more and more time at the beach, either on Hero or on foot, looking out into the waters, hoping for a sign.

It was in early June that I found him. There was a spring tide that lifted the sea halfway up the dunes at Camber, then sent it far out, so that the sand seemed to march for miles and the water shimmered, dreamlike, in the distance. I galloped Hero right out to the tide-line, and there, amid the worm casts and crab tracks, I saw a skull half-buried. It may sound like mere evidence of my distractedness that I knew it for Francis at once, but I was sure it was he, recognised the line of his jaw, the way the salt-scrubbed bones of his teeth seemed almost to smile up at me. I placed the skull carefully in my bag and returned home.

My mother was in her glass-house when I got back, and at once I took the skull from the bag and held it up to her. She closed her eyes, then opened them again and gave a sad nod. We buried the skull in the garden, between two bullace trees, and I felt a measure of relief at having laid some part of my brother to rest. My mother burnt a posy of herbs atop the grave, moving her lips in the silent cantation of some antic prayer as she did so. I remembered the words she wrote after tracking me through the Deeps, and thought to myself that my mother had powers greater than ever I'd credited. I stood beside her solemnly, certain that whatever she spoke would ease my brother's passage to a place of peace.

The next day, a letter arrived. The man that delivered

it to us was tall and fair-haired and wore a white cockade in his hat. He spoke a few words with the suggestion of a Scottish lilt and did not rest long at the door. The envelope was addressed to Francis and bore a seal in blue wax upon the reverse. I opened it at the hall table, my fingers clumsy in their haste. I looked first at the signature, which was that of John Sullivan, the Prince's chief military advisor. I then read his words:

Dear Francis,

We have not heard news of you for some months; I trust that all goes well in the south. Here in France, there is much excitation. Since Marshall Saxe trounced the Pragmatic Army at Fontenoy there is a warlike feeling all about, as if drums were beating on the streets of Paris and Fontainebleau. There are regular parades in the street and one hears as much the name of King James and Prince Charles as that of Louis and Maurice de Saxe. The Prince has charmed the Court and won many friends; all speak of his gaiety and vigour. It seems that now the French gaze turns once again to England. We intend to come down the country from our friends in the north, before meeting the Marshall in London. It is time to act, friend, and we may finally forget the fiasco of last year. We depart for the Western Isles on the 15th July. Come and join us there and bring as many brave and loyal men as you can lay hands upon. Bring your sister! It is real this time, Francis — I can near taste victory already. I wish you could see the passion with which Charles addresses the cause. He is glowing with the light of it. I have entrusted

this message to a dear and doughty friend. He will not
rest for some days yet and has many sleeping giants to
rouse. Go well, Francis. Until we meet at Eriskay!
  Yours,
  Sullivan

There are decisions which are the fruit of logical reflection, and those that come upon us unbidden and
surpriseful, fully formed in their perfection. The news
of a fresh attempt at an uprising shot a thrill through
me. I had spent more than a year living a meagre,
circumscribed existence, moving from the monotony
of my confinement to the sheep paths of the Marsh.
Here was an invitation to join once again with the
Prince, with the Stuart cause, to fulfil the dearest aspi-
rations of my father and my brother. I rose from the
table and went in search of my mother.

She was in the garden, sitting in a sunlit corner
against the high walls, looking over the heap of turned
earth where we'd buried Francis. The child was
sleeping in its basket at her feet. She saw me coming
towards her and I had the sensation that she knew
what was in my mind before I spoke. I told her of
the letter from Sullivan and of my wish to go north.
I said that I would stop first at West Grinstead to
inform John Caryll, who was now the Baron, of the
plans that were afoot, although I had little doubt he
was more in the know than I. We would travel to
the Western Isles together, the Baron and I, and
whichever members of the Association of Gentlemen
wished to join us.

Just then, perhaps because my voice had increased

in volume, the baby woke and began to bawl. My mother at once reached down to him, but I got to him first and picked him up in his swathing-bands. Whether it was the sun in his face or the sense of being lofted in new arms, he stopped his plaining and blinked at me with large, dark eyes. Whilst it had not of course been possible for me to avoid my child altogether in the seven months since his birth, I had managed largely to ignore him through a mixture of ingenuity and frequent absences. So it was that I looked upon him now as if for the first time, seeing how round and healthful were his cheeks, how bonny the tufts of black hair that sprouted from the top of his head. Little Ezekiel smiled at me and I would be lying if I said that I felt nothing then.

Something slowly and painfully began to unfold within me just at that moment. He said a word – *Ma*, or *Ba* – and then giggled at the sound of it, his laugh all on the in-breath. I passed him back to my mother as if he were scalding hot. My mother drew out a strange gourd, about whose neck she had affixed what I recognised after a moment to be a dried cow's teat. The baby suckled hungrily and I left them there, in the late morning sun, not knowing how long it would be until I would be with them again

Later, I stood in the scullery and took a pair of shears to my hair, which was already shorter than was fashionable, and required little to reduce it to a few tufts that might be easily hidden beneath a wig. I dressed myself anew in black tunic and hose, one of Francis's greatcoats and my father's wig. I fixed a pair of pistols

to my belt and a hat to my head, and packed myself
a portmanteau of undershirts and provisions, throwing
in also the copy of *Paradise Lost* that Lily had given to
me. I hefted the bag on to my shoulder and surveyed
myself in the glass by the door. The childbed had
changed me – my hips were wider, my chest larger. I
was not wholly convincing as a boy, but nor was I
identifiably a woman.

You may think it monstrous, or incredible, that I
should leave my child like this, a mere eight months
after birthing him. But I had scarce seen the boy, and
I believe I was mad just then, mad with grief, with
anger, with the loss of so much that was dear to me
– not least of which my childhood, for I was now a
woman, and did not wish to be. I was not ready for
the child, and fleeing served the double purpose of
honouring my father – for I would be fighting for the
Prince he did love so much – and escaping the burdens
of motherhood that had been thrust upon me with
terrible haste. So it was I left my mother and Little
Ezekiel, and I was not happy to do so, but the sadness
I felt seemed of a piece with all the other sadnesses in
my life just then.

I left a purse of gold on the table in the hall and
then went to the glass-house window to cast a last look
out at my mother, my child, through the branches of
the orchard trees. On the mixing table, as if she had
prepared it especially, sat a stoppered beaker of the
green paste. I slipped it into my travelling case, then
went outside to saddle Hero. We made our way slowly
down the hill to the ferry, and it was as if there were
two ropes attached to me: one pulling me onward to

adventure, one calling me home. The ferryman rowed us across and I looked up at Winchelsea, at her crumbling walls and ruined gates and canted rooftops, and I wondered when I would next walk her streets again, when I would next see my mother, my child.

BOOK TWO

From the Memoirs of the Chevalier de Johnstone

Foreword

I HAVE BEEN moved by a friend to go back to the recollections that I presented to no little acclaim some years hence. I did by necessity overpass a part of that story, fearing that any attempt to include the history of my wandering heart would reflect poorly on my own propriety and, by reflection, on that of my Prince. Now, with the revolt little more than a melancholy recollection, and given that there has been expressed some interest in my great friend, William Stuart, I set down here my remembrances of him. The nine months that we were as brothers to one another were the dearest of my life and I know that when the veil finally drops upon my own journeysome time on this Earth, 'twill be the cherished face of young William that is foremost in my mind.

I will briefly summarise my own position at the time of which I write: I was but six-and-twenty when the revolt took place, but had already travelled a deal abroad, my aunt, Lady Jane Douglas, having sent me to represent her interests at the Court of St Petersburg. I went by the name of Johnstone of Moffatt, but was called the Chevalier by the Highlanders, on account of my having served with the Prince in France. I had done some military service in Muscovy also, and fought three duels, yet there was still in me during the '45 that youthful spirit which believes itself invulnerable to the swords and guns of the enemy. I was headstrong at the outset, not to say foolhardy; a vain wee fop, too proud of my breeks and silks to come to any good. By the end, though, by that bitter and calamitous end, I had been fashioned into something else: a man.

The revolt made a man of me, 'tis true, and it was in search of the high certainty I felt whene'er I lifted my sword in the name of the King Over the Water that I scoured the battlefields of France and Flanders in the roving years that followed. There was, however, a deeper and more troubling absence that propelled me o'er blasted heathland and blood-soaked moors: the love and loss of the one that was dear to me in the braw and barry days of the uprising: William.

I begin my tale at Derby, for it was there that I first encountered William, who was to become my bosom friend, my helpmeet, in the months that followed.

EXETER HOUSE, DERBY, DECEMBER 1745

WHEN FIRST I set my eyes on William, it was in the rising light of an early December morning. He had come to the Prince's lodgings, a mansion in Full Street. As one attached to the Prince's retinue, I was charged that day with receiving whichsoever guests should attend His Highness. So it was I saw arrive a man of above middling height who tethered his fine grey horse in the courtyard and stood before the door in a woollen greatcoat, a three-cornered hat upon his head. It was his face, though, that drew my notice when I opened to him.

I hope in years to come that the pox will go the way of the sweating sickness – that some physician or herbalist will find a curative; or that it will be settled that it is grave air or impure water that carries the disease and can therefore be eluded by practice of habit. William's visage was covered in the most bolned and blotchy swellings, each of them near bursting with pus. I don't doubt but that I grimaced upon seeing him, for it was a sight very gruesome to behold; but then, remembering myself, I asked him to come in out of the dreich weather.

We were served beer and bread by the scullery maid, the Prince being still abed and over our breakfast, William presented himself. He told me that he was distaff kin of Ezekiel and Francis Brown, both of whom had been most helpful to the cause in years past. I was much aggrieved to learn that Francis had followed his father into the grave. William's face took on a very noble and tragical air when he spoke of his family, and I could see what a bonny lad he would have been before the pox emblemished him. I recognised that I had overcounted his years when first I saw him, and that he was not much more than a boy, albeit a large and buirdly one.

William recounted to me how he had set off at once on hearing of the Prince's intention to land on Eriskay in July. The scheme, he said, was to stop at the home of the Baron Caryll – that dear and faithful servant of the cause – and there to collect others with whom to journey north. Alas, on arriving at West Grinstead, he had found the house deserted, with a terrible miasmatic stench hanging about the place. When he pressed further inside, he discovered bodies heaped atop one another, flies moving in great, gobbling swarms, the sweet and putrid smell of dead flesh. It was the black pox, and had taken the inhabitants of the house and its servants; the dogs and horses, too. William was about to leave when he heard a thin sound from upstairs. He climbed over the several bodies laid out in the upper corridors and came to the room of John, Baron Caryll, who was abed, alive, but grievous sick.

William nursed the Baron for a month, through the great sweating fits and their accompanying phantastry, the buboes and the bursting sores, before, with a great and dreadful shriek, that dear man finally gave up his life. William buried him out under the old mulberry tree in the garden, in which I recall, five years hence, feasting with the Baron until our fingers were black. It was then that William came down with the disease himself, as is so often the way with one who cares for another, and made his peace with death, lying in the same bed in which his friend the Baron had rendered up his spirit. Then, miraculously, in the last days of the autumn, when the first snows fell, he discovered that he was better. This was when he continued north, much depleted in health and spirits, to find his King.

I have no shame in recounting that I wept upon hearing this tale; in part it was because I had known the Baron well, and how decent and fervent was his commitment to Jacobitism. In part also it was the figure of this young man before me, whose devotion was so plain in its earnestness, and who had arrived just as the fire of the revolution, which had hitherto burnt so brightly, was being extinguished. We finished our victuals and I suggested that we go for a turn around the camp, given that the Prince rose late and liked not to be disturbed in the first hour of his waking. (I confess that I did also shrink from the prospect of presenting His Highness, who set high stock on fair-seeming faces, with such a stigmatical creature so early in the day, notwithstanding my new friend's obvious loyalty.)

We made our way through frost-silvered streets to the River Derwent. It was still early of the morning and yet the lights of the various manufactories of the town were all ablaze, smoke fairting from their chimneys. The towers of these places of enterprise outreached even the spire of the cathedral. We heard the army before we saw them: the high, sad note of bagpipes drifting through the air, the occasional yell and counter, the whinny of horses.

Our encampment was in a field nearby the Derwent. I helped William over a stile and we wandered in amongst the tents; several men were washing in the half-frozen river, having broken through the ice, and I made note of this to my friend – confirmation of the fabled hardiness of the Prince's soldiers. I called out to several of them in their own brogue, and they replied in kind. It is a fine thing, the Highland tongue, as hard and musical as the folk that speak it.

We walked between the tents of the cavalry, where the horses were tethered and cropped the frozen grass. The Highlanders slept not in tents but out in the open, with only their plaids to cover them, and the few that were still abed lay beside their broadswords as a man might lie with his wife. Others were gathered about the fire, spooning gruel from clay porringers. They were indeed fearsome figures, Viking-like with their great beards and wild eyes, their kilts and purses, dirks and low-heeled shoes. I could see that my friend was impressed, as was I when first I came to fight alongside my Highland kin and was awed by the size and strength of them.

We dandered then a little further by the river, as the sun climbed into a wintry sky, and the land about us let out its dank breaths. I told William of the course of our campaign so far, of the fall of Carlisle with scarce a shot fired, the raising of a Manchester Regiment who enlisted to fight alongside the 'yellow-haired laddie', and then, laughingly, of the fording of the Mersey, where the Prince was up to his waist in the river but raised no complaint, and then the march upon Derby, where the local Yeomanry had seen a herd of cattle making their way through the morning mist and, mistaking them for Highlanders, had fled.

As we turned back towards the town, I told William, in more confidential tones, that he had arrived just as the success of the counter-revolution had begun to curdle. Divisions had opened within the Prince's Council, with the Duke of Perth and Lord Nairn arguing for a swift attack on London, with the aim of securing the throne for Charles before the year was out, while others, led by Lord George Murray, coun-selled caution, reckoning that a force of six thousand men could never hope to overcome the massed ranks of Hanoverians in the capital.

When we got back to Exeter House, I conveyed William to a parlour at the rear, where, before windows that looked out over the river and the business of the camp, the Prince sat. He turned his pale face up and I saw William take in how beautiful His Highness was – and that was the word for it; not a bonnier boy was e'er born.

''Tis William Stuart, Sire,' I told him. 'Friend of the Carylls, and kin of Francis and Ezekiel Brown.' The Prince's face brightened.

'You have a likely surname, sir,' he said in that odd accent that steered from Rome to Warsaw via the Royal Mile. He looked about, those large brown eyes darting. 'And Francis? Is he here?'

William made his deferences and then told His Highness of the dire fate that had befallen Francis; I saw the Prince's eyes grow moist. Charles then said many pretty words about the service rendered to the cause by Francis and Ezekiel Brown, and that since God's will was that the Stuart line should be restored, all those who died in pursuit of it would be favoured in heaven. The Prince had a way of speaking that suggested he knew well that folk would be noting down what he said, then or later, and expected his words to live for centuries in verse.

It had begun to snow lightly outside and now the Prince departed with his *chef de camp*, an Irishman by the name of Sullivan, for a meeting of the lairds, in which it would be decided whether to press on for London and glory, or to follow Lord George Murray back to Scotland. William and I sat in the gloomy salon for near two hours, and it seemed that both of us dozed. When we woke, the fire had burnt low, and it was cold in the room, and standing above us was the dejected, snow-flecked Prince, the doughty Sullivan by his side, and I scarce needed to ask the outcome of the council, so much was disappointment inscribed on both their faces. The Prince gave me a sad smile and withdrew to his chambers, while Sullivan, with a curse, told me to prepare for our departure.

CULLODEN MOOR, APRIL 1746

WE MARCHED NORTH in baleful weather. Those who had huzzahed us on our way now mocked our retreat. We scarce let out a cheer when we came into Scotland, and while we won a piffling victory over Hangman Hawley at Falkirk, it was the last roar of a dying beast. The Prince came down with a grippe when we festivated Hogmanay at Glasgow's College Green, then disappeared into the bedchamber of one Clementina Wilkinshaw, which lady was named for the Prince's own Polish mother. Many of the Highlanders, who had not been paid for a month nor fed for several days, took the opportunity to return home with the spoils of victory. The lack of direction in the following days left us short more than a thousand of our bravest warriors. I could see that the gallant William, who was a fixture at my side on his fine grey horse, was trying his utmost not to fall prey to dejection, but it was a bitter time indeed, with the men starving, the lairds squabbling and e'en the horses hollow-chested and dead-tired.

There was still, 'tis true, some hope. It was thought that if we were able to get to the far side of the River Nairn, we might wait out the winter in the Highlands and then re-gather, raising a new army with which to drive the English out of Scotland. We undertook to move ever-northwards, seeking to get beyond the Spey, then the Nairn, to where the Highlands begin in earnest, and where Inverness stood as a bastion of supplies and men. And yet we were harried all the way by Cumberland, and the Prince had his mind set on a final great battle. So it was, with our backs to the lofty mountains, that we turned to fight, on a moor called locally Drummossie, but which became known by the name of the house to which Charles repaired once it was clear that we would flee no further: Culloden.

On the 14th of April, in the hall of Culloden House, which belonged to Duncan Forbes, the traitorous laird who was now on the march with Cumberland, animus within the council chamber erupted into fury. There was a most ill-tempered debate between Murray and Sullivan, with the former stamping his feet and cursing and at one point refusing the Prince permission to speak. Murray was in favour of a retreat into the mountains, from which raids could be carried out against the English occupiers. Charles, though, as he always did when other avenues of justification were denied him, declared that it was God's will that he should be King, and God's will that they fight on that wind-blasted moor. After much disputation it was decided that a third option would be pursued: the following day marked Cumberland's twenty-fifth birthday. The Hanoverian troops who were stationed at Nairn would, our spies told us, be distributed two gallons of brandy a regiment and would be roaring or snoring that night. Murray planned out a subtile approach under cover of darkness.

A little after eight the next evening, we left our encampment, which was arranged on the lawns in front of the old stone house. It was fearful dark, with clouds over the moon and a cruel wind carrying in it memories of the winter we'd lived through. We took no horses, but went by foot, and all the while Sullivan and Charles spoke about the night victory they'd won at Prestonpans, and how swiftly and awfully they would fall upon their foe. Murray marched at the head with several of the other lairds and the most doughty of the Cameron and MacDonald clans, leading us across the rugged hills and through rocky valleys in order to elude the government outposts that had been established on the road. William marched alongside me, his scabbed yet noble face a little leaner for the weeks of fasting and fighting, his mouth set in a thin determined line.

It was not until this march, I think, that Charles recognised how woefully mistreated the general mass of his men had been, nor how close they were to expiration. For while Murray and the van marched ahead, the Lowlanders and conscripts who made up the body of the ranks began to flag and fall. It seemed that the quartermaster had refused them sustenance at Inverness, and many had not slept more than an hour a night for several days. I watched perhaps a dozen of those about me tumble face-first into the heather and feared that we had been ambushed; when I came close by them, I saw that they were not dead but sleeping, so exhausted that neither call nor shake nor, on occasion, the jab of a bayonet could bring them awake.

Others were so maddened by famine that they roved off into the hills in search of anything they might sup upon, with some going so far as to chew the coarse grass and heather like so many sheep. We marched without lights, and many of the men, having worn through their boots, had bound up their feet in sacking cloth, and so it was impossible to see or hear where these deserters wandered off to. Nor were we able to fire upon them to bring them back to us. All this time, the van marched ahead, and it was soon evident that we had lost them in the night. The darkness gulfed around us. Hours passed and we marched slower and slower, and no one spoke, and any jollity that had existed at the beginning of the night had passed, and with it all hope. Sullivan insisted that he go ahead and halt the van, which by a miracle he did succeed to do, but by the time we were upon them, the first faint light of dawn lay along the eastern skyline.

It seemed that the van had halted of their own accord, for Murray had recognised that they were only arrived at Culraick, and that Nairn still lay an hour's march hence. It had taken us too long to make our advance, and we would come upon Cumberland's camp in full daylight. What's more, when we were able to take stock of our number, we found that we missed near eight hundred men, and that the Prince was not with us. At this last revelation, Sullivan raced off in search of our leader, fearing that he had been apprehended or had fallen into a quarry or cave. Murray and the lairds refused to march a step further, and so it was that we turned and trudged woefully back in the misty daybreak, lamenting the midgies, the cruel terrain, and the God who had forsaken us.

I did not know this until after the battle, when Sullivan told me at Ruthven, but the Prince had indeed found himself lost, and had pressed on with the men until near five of the morning, when they were espied by the enemy in the dim dawn light, and fled. There was a brief pursuit before the redcoats turned back, better to prepare for a more definite assault upon our troops. The Prince and his soldiery returned to Culloden House soaked, starved and tavering in their exhaustion. It were as if the Prince had, during that fateful march, comprehended truths about his men that had thus far been denied to him: that they were not only tired and hungry; they were dying from want of food and sleep. He commanded that instant for three of the company horses to be butchered and roasted on a fire before the house, although again the beasts were so straggling and tendon-thin that they scarce fed a single man. William and I discovered some bread and whisky in the kitchens of Culloden House, which we distributed to Highlanders whose eyes were red and wild, their woollen bonnets and plaids sodden, their cheeks hollow with want.

The rain came in great long draughts across the heather, while in the distance beams of sunlight fell down on the mountains, as if beckoning those Highlanders which remained upwards, to safety. Men were everywhere asleep – the officers across the floors and bannisters of the house, draped like dolls upon the furniture, heaped willy-nilly up the stairs; the Highlanders were huddled in their plaids in the rain, or stretched out as if dead, heedless of the mizzle.

Then came the announcement that Cumberland's army was on the march, and the sound of pipes and drums was struck up, enough to rouse all but the deepest sleepers, whom Sullivan strode about pronging with his bayonet. There was a moment of disputation as the troops took their places in the field, for Murray had commanded his Camerons and Athollmen to occupy the right flank, a position typically reserved for the MacDonalds, who were obliged to take up the inferior left flank. It was, in any case, a far from ideal situation that we had assumed, with two great dykes either side squeezing us as if into the neck of a jug. What's more, there was a large patch of boggy ground to the fore of us, such that even should we achieve some success, any advance would be hampered.

Finally, we were all arranged looking down across the moor to the north-east, from whence the enemy would appear. William and I were seconded to Lord Balmerino's brigade, and were thus behind the MacDonalds and John Roy Stewart's men. We led our horses to the ridge behind the troops, then took our places beside the stern-faced nobleman. William sat proudly atop his Hero, sword clutched in one hand, musket in the other, a feather tucked jauntily into his hat. I looked along the line and it was clear that our numbers had dropped precipitously since Falkirk. There were two lines only, with the Irish Piquets, the Royal Ecossais and the Lowlanders forming a nominal reserve. We had only fifty cavalrymen, with another dozen horses held behind the ridge to provide officers with a means of escape should the day go against us. Our drummers and pipers had fallen silent, and there were no birds singing there on the wild and wind-harried heath, so we heard the rat-tat of the enemy's drums long before we saw our foe.

Then they were all before us, and it was the most dreadful sight: an army that filled the horizon, the foot soldiers in three lines half-a-mile wide, with cannons and mortars interspersing, and two regiments of mounted dragoons on either wing. Our pipers and drummers struck up, but there was a fearful, hesitant quality to their playing, and the wind seemed to whip away the high notes of the pipes, the drizzle dampened the thud of the drums. I figured that their numbers were twice our own or more. I could see the breath of their horses in the air, could feel the thump of their drums in my bones. Their men let out a series of loud huzzahs.

A blast of wind swept down across the moor, and I saw the Prince ride along the front of the line. His words came to me only haltingly, but I could tell that the men were roused by the sight of him. 'Only those who are afraid can doubt our victory,' he said, and it was all I could do not to laugh, but I saw a great change come over the Highlanders about and before me. Whatever might be said of the Prince and his doomed campaign, he had a near-supernatural ability to climb inside the hearts of the Highlanders. He said something that I didn't follow, but which elicited a great cheer from the front line. 'The soldiers in the Elector's army know that I am their King,' he went on. Another cheer. 'They will not dare to fight us. God is on our side!' He raised his sword, the loudest cheer of all sounded, and his horse reared up a little. This is how I will choose to remember him: near lunatic in his valour, with the rain sweeping all about him and men who an hour before had been as good as dead from famine and fatigue now ready to lay down their lives for him.

The Prince went to take up his place alongside Sullivan and Murray, and all the drums stopped, and there was a long moment of time as we regarded the enemy, and they us. Then the cannonade began, and the world was ne'er the same after. It was all noise, all smoke, all confusion on our side. The balls came at us in close succession, such that I could see them moving along the line, tearing through men and horses alike, sending up plumes of blood where they first made impact, then carrying on, crunching through bone and gristle and gore. The mortars whistled over, and where they landed the explosions appeared to suck men into them, as if hell itself had opened in the earth, only to spew them back out in bloody disgust. Every detonation felt like the rolling of a die, and I know not how fate or luck kept me whole. You could not imagine so many dead in so short a time, and our own guns were silent in response.

Cumberland's foot soldiers now marched forward, exchanging their ball for grapeshot. It was astonishing to see how long our ranks held, how even with the wrenching and rending of the grapeshot, which dispersed among us evilly and picked out its victims with a liberal indifference, the Highlanders kept their places, even to taunt and jeer at the enemy. But in time they fell all about me, and soon it seemed more were dead or loudly dying than had ever lived. At least the cannonballs had made a swift end of those they struck; the grapeshot tore into muscles, into the haunches of horses, embedding itself in all the soft places of man and beast. Sullivan told me later that we lost near a thousand men in the first fifteen minutes of the battle.

Finally, the MacDonalds, under the charge of the Elector's cavalry, broke their lines. They went at the enemy with a great shout of *Claymore!*, shaking their swords above their heads as was their wont, but they had not counted on the dragoons who had hidden themselves in the cover of the walls of the estate, and now came out firing. Those who did not fall, fled. The signal was given for us to move forward to fill their place, and I began to load and discharge my musket with automatic facility, aiming at the line of redcoats ahead of me, aware all the time how useless resistance was against such numbers.

I recognised then how battle is about the struggle in each of us between the love of life and the wish to avoid disgrace. It seemed strange to me in that moment, watching almost dispassionately as the redcoats came ever onwards, that mere shame could be enough to send us thus to our graves. Then the line of dragoons before me knelt and fired, and I saw William hit in the shoulder by grapeshot, and when I turned to succour him I felt my own horse quiver beneath me, then collapse, and everything was mud and blood and darkness.

When I came to, the first thing in my mind was to seek out William, who was lying beneath the corpse of his beloved Hero, his face most dreadful pale and no sign of life coming from him. I used what strength there was left to me to shift the beast from atop him, then, under the continued fire of the dragoons and in no little pain myself, I hefted him over my shoulder and stumbled in the direction that so many of our troops had taken: along the Moor Road, towards Inverness. In short, I fled.

Before too long I came upon a horse which had unseated its rider. I lifted William's dear prone body over the saddle and was able then to make a smarter pace. I will not dwell on the sorry tale of our flight to Ruthven. Cumberland sent his men after us, dragoons armed with pikes and Lochaber axes, and many of those fleeing and wounded were cut down on the road to the barracks, at Tomatin, or Garten, or Aviemore. We saw men dead or dying on the road, their groans and supplications coming to us from heaps of bloodstained plaid. A great and overwhelming sorrow was in my heart all the time, for I believed that my Prince was dead, the cause was dead and, erelong, my bosom friend would also join the massed ranks of Jacobite dead.

CORRIEYAIRACK, SUMMER 1746

FIRST LET ME tell you of the dire days at Ruthven, where those of us who still had breath after the slaughter gathered to take stock. William was recovered in body, at least. I had cleaned and closed up his wounds, though I could do less for his sorrow at the loss of his horse. He had travelled many miles with Hero, he told me, and there was never a man as loyal as his horse. The Prince, we heard tell, was alive, and on his way to join us. On this the full weight of our hopes rested.

The two of us spent much time those first few frantic days enjoining Lord Murray to lead the Athollmen and Camerons up into the Highlands, where we might re-gather over the course of the summer before attacking the occupier when the snows came. Already the clans were descending on the barracks in great numbers, and it was clear that in a matter of weeks we would be numerous enough to offer fierce resistance to the Elector and his forces. Such was the steepness of the mountains here, so perilous certain passes and fells, that no army would attempt to fight us on home ground, above all to attack Highlanders in a place where they are said to be capable of summoning the strength of the very mountains themselves in their defence.

The Prince, though, who limped into the barracks a few days after us, was spirit-broken by the events at Culloden, raging first against the Highlanders who had deserted him, then against the French who had failed to support him, then against his quartermasters who had provided four-pound shot for his three-pound cannon. He was resolved to flee, and to flee alone, or rather with the few men he still held dear to him, who were in the main Irish. One morning we woke, and they were all gone, and with them any hope of the Just Cause.

That same day we all of us departed: the Highlanders

to the heathery heights; the lairds to their lochs and lands; William and I into the nearer bens and braes, from whence I thought we might make contact with several of my companions who dwelt in the valleys about. It was a fine afternoon, a fresh wind gusting over the clover beneath us, clouds above the highest peaks to the west, the movement of deer along the ridges.

We climbed up the great Munro known as the Corrieyairack, whose famous pass the Prince had traversed, full of hope, those many months earlier, and over which he had left in much reduced circum- stances that very morning. It was one of the most well-used gateways into the Highlands, being on the cobbled path known as General Wade's Road, which had been constructed after the previous insurrection and linked the Great Glen in the north to Strath Spey in the south.

We spent the night in a small declivity on the slopes of the mountain, and it was wonderful to lie there in the warmth of my plaid, the night air moving over me, the grass soughing and the water from the burns babbling. My friend William curled himself beside me and I could hear the slow breath of him as he slept. I fancied I felt the mountain stirring beneath us, the strength and permanence of all that rock. I was wakeful for much of the night, although it was not an agitated sleeplessness, but rather that I did not wish to miss a moment of the stars, the cool breath of the wind, the calling of certain nocturnal birds that flew closely over us. Then there was the explosion of dawn and the sight of a stag very nearby, sniffing the air and raising his antlers to greet the morning. I could see the downy fuzz on his prongs, the heat of his breath in the air, the cleverness of his dark eyes. William woke, and looked up at the stag, and smiled his bonny smile.

Over a breakfast of oats cooked on a small fire, I told William of my childhood friend Edward Grant, who lived at a place named Rothiemurchus, some thirty miles distant. We should, I believed, find welcome there from Edward's father, John Grant, who was in great sympathy with the Jacobite cause. We set off just after eight of the clock, taking a path down the southern slope of the great mountain and then following the course of the swift-flowing Spey through fields and spinneys, past tumbledown cottages and crofters' huts. Several times we met with local folk who told us of the viciousness of Cumberland's men, who were roaming about the hills seeking the Prince and any of the rebels that they might apprehend. There was no mercy granted to any prisoner, with soldiers shot or hanged on the spot, while officers and the nobility were led to Inverness or Edinburgh to be executed. Already, we were told, the Lord Balmerino and the Duke of Perth had been taken in flight and would be led to the scaffold erelong. Our way was halting and circuitous, and we spent the night in a barn near Aviemore before undertaking the final stretch of our march.

The sun was just coming up as we drew up at Doune, the great house of Rothiemurchus, weary but glad to have made our journey without encountering the enemy. This was a place I had been most contented as a boy, roaming in the woods all about with Edward, although the two of us had grown distant in recent years, my friend being converted to the Hanoverian cause. Now we made our way up the long drive, past a series of old and crabbed trees, and then we were before the house, which was all lit up by the sun as if to welcome us.

The house sits at the foot of a high hill known as the Dun, which was an ancient fort and burial mound, the trees upon it planted in a deliberate and vatical pattern by the druids who had consecrated the place centuries earlier. It was said that the soldiers buried within the barrow, which took the shape of an upended boat, would rise and defend the Grants of Rothiemurchus should ever the need arise.

We made our way between low box hedges to the principal door of the white-fronted house, which looked out over coppices of birch to the Spey. After a time a serving girl half-opened to us, then offered us nervously inside. We stood in the cool, dim entrance hall until the creaking of the stairs announced the arrival of our host. There appeared John Grant, who had become an old man since last I saw him. He was still in his nightshirt, with a flowing beard and a crazy mop of white hair. He came straightway to me and embraced me, and then stood back to take me in. I saw a wealth of sympathetic feeling in those ancient eyes. I then presented William to old Mr Grant, who gripped him by the hand and pulled him into a clutch of similar tenderness. 'Now, boys,' the old man said in that well-remembered voice, 'I wish to hear all about the battle, and all that you can tell me of the Prince.' We went through to a dining hall where a fire had been lit despite the clemency of the weather outside. We told him of the rout at Culloden, of the Prince's flight, of our own escape. Tears sprung to those intelligent blue eyes. The serving girl brought us kippers, hot coffee and sweetmeats, and soon the hardships of recent days were put aside. I had begun to look forward greatly to resting awhile at Doune, when John Grant spoke.

'It grieves me much to say it, boys, but we mun spirit you somewhere more secretive before the day is out,' he said. 'I heard last night from Edward that General Hawley himself will come tomorrow at first light with a group of men of the 8th. They will be resting several days with me and I needs must play the host before sending them on their way. I like it not and am mutinous at having such a man for a guest, but I am too old to fight and so must on occasion endure the company of blackguards. Edward is on the rise in Edinburgh and I must sacrifice my mores for his politicking.'

So it was we packed bags with provisions for two weeks, and a rod that we might fish ourselves supper. It was just after three that we set out, with John Grant wrapped in a black cloak and leaning on a walking stick with a stag's head carved at its handle. He was still sprightly, and it was all we could do to keep pace with him as he headed up the steep-sided brae ahead of us. The heather grew high here and buzzed merrily with bees. There was a rocky outcrop that the old man leapt, goat-like, upon, and stood at the top, his cloak blowing about him.

We followed him up this final crest and found ourselves on a high eminence overlooking a long, clear loch. I remembered it as a place where Edward and I had played merrily as bairns. Pine trees lined the shores and in the centre stood an island with a crumbling ruin upon it. John Grant gestured towards it with his stick. 'The Wolf's Castle,' he said. 'From when this was a lawless place and the route passing to the east of us was the Thieves' Road. The Wolf of Badenoch had it built to defend his lands up here, in the ancient days of the Roberts.' The castle was much dilapidated, with willow and alder growing all about it, and several bushes and trees having established their roots in the very walls.

'It is beautiful,' I said, to myself as much as to anyone else. 'The Loch an Eilein.' John Grant made a sound and struck out down the hill, in the expectation that we would follow.

We stood in the pine woods on the shore, looking out towards the island. John Grant turned to us with a narrow smile. 'Mark my steps, boys,' he said, and strode out into the water. Or rather I should say that he walked upon the water, for even as he progressed towards the island, he sank no further, and only his boots and the hem of his cape were wettened. He stopped halfway over the channel and turned towards us. 'Come,' he called out. 'It is nay so hard as it looks.'

I turned to William with a grin. 'This is his habitual performance,' I said, 'with which to fright the soft Sassenach. A sunken causeway lies just beneath. Step carefully and you'll come to no harm.' I now followed the old man across the water. The path was not straight, but rather took a series of dog-legs as it neared the island. At one point I near lost my footing and tumbled into the loch, but I regained balance and was finally upon dry land. My boots were damp, as were the hems of my hose, but I knew well that the castle would make a fine hiding place for us, fugitives that we were. The ruined building had only three sides to it, and no roof to speak of, but there was a small beach where we might bathe, fresh water all about us in the loch, and the closeness of John Grant should we need for aught.

It is hard for me to write to you of the summer William and I spent together there. Our battered bodies healed swiftly, helped by the strength of the sun, the silence of the loch at night, the clearness of the water. The very first evening we were alone on the island, my friend spoke me the truth of his life, and it may seem strange to you, reader, but I was not much astonished, having perhaps had some suspicion that beneath the pox scars and gallantness lay a softer, gentler heart. There was a fire burning in the pit we'd dug, and the moon glimmered large in the water, and William told me the tale of his will-gill life, his twin natures. We sat that night in the dimming light of the fire, and he told me of growing up a girl in Winchelsea, of the Mayfield Gang and the Hawkhurst Gang. He told me of the loss of his beloved father, and his brother, and of the child he'd birthed. And I hope I listened well, only nodding now and then, or poking at the fire with a stick. When he had finished speaking, we were both much affected, and I felt my cheeks wet with tears.

'What am I to call you now, friend?' I asked him, for I still saw him as the doughty soldier who had fought beside me. It is strange, but love is propagated in the wild and secretive parts of us, and I knew only that I loved him, would love him as much were he an ass or an otter.

'You may call me as you like,' he replied. 'Goody or Will, it is the same to me.'

I then did take my friend in my arms and embraced him deeply, and we slept side by side and woke to the sound of fish eagles high in the dawn sky above us.

With the truth out, there was a new intimacy between us, and it was as if we were brother and sister, although with none of the fractiousness that so often taints the love of siblings. I had kept a journal since I was a boy and I took to reading from it to Will. I read to him of the Russian Steppes and my meetings with Tartar chieftains, of the wintry glory of Saint Petersburg, the magnificence of Königsberg. I read of a Prussian nobleman and an Irish serving girl, and how each had broke my heart. We both wept a great deal, and we swore sacred oaths of fealty and love to one another. Will had a copy of *Paradise Lost*, much-thumbed, and he read to me from it, so that the day was measured out in deep thoughts and fine poetry, as well as in the glory of nature. We talked of literature, of the novels we had read, of Shakespeare and Milton, and I recognised that books sparked the same joy in him that they did in me, for reading is an expression of fondness for life. It is love of life in the shape of words, not words in the shape of a life.

The summer passed. We spent it reading, talking, frolicking in the water. We were like Adam and Eve in the garden, and had no shame in undressing to bathe in the loch together. We would swim from one end of the lake to the other, the swallows winging down around us, the capercaillie calling their strange song in the hills above, as of wet twigs burning in a fire. We stayed submerged for hours on end, feeling ourselves stronger and haler with every day that passed. It grew so that I was not repulsed by the condition of Will's skin; indeed I would, on occasion, press my fingers into the pocks and weals that went from his wrists to his chest, thence to the white delineations left by the winding cloths with which he had bound up his breasts. We dressed ourselves increasingly in the meagrest of clothing and on the hottest days we wore nothing at all, climbing up on to the ruins and diving down into the cool clear water again and again, as children might.

We saw no other person about, and it was as if the world was all our own. I went every week or so to see John Grant, or the old man would come down to the castle himself bearing a basket of provisions, a selection of books and a few scraps of news. He'd look at Will with a kind of half-glance, as if trying to work out what secret he carried about him, attired in garments which might have been those of lass or lad, and with his hair growing out in a fashion that let it fall down about his face to hide his scarring. John was wise enough to make no mention of my friend's appearance, though, and concentrated instead upon the dire reports he received from those few rebels who had escaped capture. The Prince had reached the Western Isles, he said, and none had betrayed him. All the while Cumberland rampaged about the country, killing or ensnaring any he suspected of being sympathetic to the rebellion. The lairds had fled or faced the gallows, and the Highlanders had retreated to the far northern glens, where the Elector's army dared not venture. Old Grant looked wracked with sorrow, and I wished to offer him some small gesture of hope, but could not. Each time we watched until his hooded black figure disappeared over the crest of the hill, and on the days of his visits we were more sombre than usual.

All the while autumn was approaching, and I tried to clasp hold of time as it slipped by, to slow or stop its passing. I knew, though, that we could not remain on the island, for this was not a home for winter. I suggested to Will that we go a-roving together, seeking our fortunes in Muscovy or the Levant. Or that we went to Paris or Rome, there to await the return of the Prince and rally for another attempt on the throne. I could see, though, that my friend was much torn. Other matters weighed upon his heart, with his son, Little Ezekiel, foremost of these. He would journey homewards, he told me, and when I suggested that I go with him, he wandered over to the water and stood there, staring out for a long while. He had scores to settle, he said, as if to the lake, and he needed to be alone to settle them. Afterwards, when enough blood had been spilled, maybe then we might journey again together.

I will not tell you of our farewell that night, of how the great yellow moon itself seemed to conspire in our woe. We lit a fire in the hollow in the ruins and wrapped a plaid about us and swore friendship and loyalty and much else beside. I told him that we would have many adventures yet together, I saw great battles and wild victories, long voyages to lands beyond the edges of the map. I told him that no other would ever be as dear to me as he was, that my heart was his. I was keening without recognising the fact, and Will wept with me, our tears mixing on the dirt floor of our castle home.

The next morning I woke very early to watch mist rise from the surface of the loch. I swear that the Loch an Eilein that morning was more precious and beautiful than ever it was before, all the more so for the nearness of leaving. I thought about making one final effort to persuade him to come with me, but I knew the direction in which his heart was set. As it was, he woke and stretched, and we broke our fast for the last time together, and his hands shook a little as he doled out my portion. We walked for a last time over the sunken causeway, and back over the hill to Doune, where Old Grant had prepared a fine pair of horses for us. The old laird stood before the house and waved us off through the birch woods as we made our way down to the Spey. He looked to have aged greatly over the course of the summer we were there, and I asked the gods of the barrow to guard over him when we were gone.

We followed the river back towards its mountain source, thinking that Will should take General Wade's Road over the Corrieyairack Pass, being there less likely to be apprehended. I, in the meantime, would head north, to the wild islands, there hoping to secure a ship for France.

Once, on the outskirts of the village of Laggan, we saw a detachment of redcoats roughly searching through barns and crofters' huts, looking for rebels or loot. We took a long path around the place and then were into the familiar valley through which the road cut its long cobbled path. We climbed up towards the heights of the Corrieyairack, and it was as if all the world about us knew the pain of the separation that lay ahead.

Finally we came to the highest point of the pass, and it was evening now, and I found that I was sobbing again. Will did not dismount, nor did he address a word to me, but rather reached across and gave two swift pats to my horse's neck and then, with one hand raised up in salutation, he began the long descent into the darkened valley. I watched for him as long as I could, tears running down my cheeks, my heart urging me to go down after him at a gallop. In the end, when even the light of the pale moon that rose behind me revealed no figure on the path below, I urged my horse fiercely up the rocky slope to the summit of the great mountain. By luck I discovered the declivity in which Will and I had hidden ourselves all those months before, and I lay myself down on the heather and gave myself over to grief.

BOOK THREE

*The Battle of Goudhurst, as told by One who
was There, namely Arnold Nesbitt Esq.*

I

I AM NO author, having been from childhood awkward with words, but I wished to set out the events of the past several years so that in the future historians more gifted than I might know what came to pass in this small and unexceptional Wealden village, and how, with the assistance of a brave and gifted leader, a group of regular men, namely farmers, squires, physicians &c. did defeat the feared ruffians and brigands of the Hawkhurst Gang.

First a little of myself. My father, Albert Nesbitt, was a proud and vaunting man whose ambition finally outstripped his gift for persuasion. He had made his fortune in the law and had resolved to spend it pursuing a political career which would advance his name among the genteel people of the country. He was on terms with many of the most powerful in the land, and dined often with the Prime Minister, lords, baronets &c. He was a good man but he was not very wise, and I fear that the rudeness of his origins was wont to reassert itself when he had taken drink. So it was that he became embroiled in an altercation with a cabal of noblemen, bringing a suit against St Leger and other gentlefolk. My father drew upon all of his many contacts from the City and Gray's Inn, but he was up against the establishment, and suddenly those members of the gentry who had been pleased to sup with him began to snub him.

My father was ruined and had to sell the great house at Winchelsea to pay his debts. I had been serving in the dragoons & stationed at Hythe, but I returned to support my father through these last days of his process. To further complicate matters, I had some time before become affianced to the Honourable Elizabeth St Leger, who had been my close friend for some time and was the daughter of the aforementioned nobleman. We had intended to marry that coming autumntide, namely the September of 1746, but given her father's role in my own father's downfall, and the much-reduced prospects of my own career (I'd had to give up my commission, my landau &c.), I wrote to her and terminated our agreement.

The house auction is engineered to confer the utmost humiliation upon those involved in it, so as to ensure that it remains the last resort for those facing the work-house. My father was broken by the exigencies of his legal battle and so sat in the empty drawing room in his favourite armchair, staring ahead, while I and those of the servants that had remained arranged our possessions out on the driveway. I stood and watched as the Jurats and their wives, and all the common people of the town, came & poked & commented upon the wares of the house, noting the lack of taste exhibited in the choice of furnishings and ball gowns which had been my late mother's, but which would now be cut into pieces and reworked into cushion covers by the wives of the town.

Late in the afternoon of that glum day, when all but a few chairs and the second-best table service had been purchased, I was about to go in and enquire after my father's condition, fearing that this final indignity might push him over into madness, when a figure appeared in the gloaming at the end of the driveway. When she came closer, I saw that it was Elizabeth St Leger: the good woman had come to offer succour. We went inside and took tea together, and she said to me that the fact of my father's ruin made no matter to her, and that she loved me still, and many pretty things besides. In defiance of her father's wishes, we decided to marry in a quiet ceremony at Goudhurst, where her aunt, the sister of the Member for Winchelsea, lived, and, notwithstanding her brother's imprecations, had offered us a farmhouse on her estate where we might live in comfort, if not in splendour. I found that this picture of my life (as a farmer & the father of a brood of country children) suited me very well and we went in happily together to announce the news to my father.

Greyfriars was purchased by Mayor Parnell for a price that was much inferior to that which we had hoped to achieve. It seemed that in vengeance for his daughter's disobedience, St Leger had influenced the situation such that no other offers were made for the house, a fact which drove my father into a further black rage. When the bills were all paid off there were scarcely sufficient funds to provide for the coach to convey our last remaining goods to Goudhurst. My father was increasingly sombre & silent, and I began to fear that he had lost the ravel of his mind.

II

Two DREADFUL THINGS happened in the last days we had at Winchelsea. Firstly, there was a widow of our acquaintance, a Frenchwoman named Brown. She had been most unfortunate, having lost both husband and adoptive son to the pirates known as the Hawkhurst Gang, which fiends did also snip out her tongue so she might not betray them, and furthermore having her daughter, who was named Goody, disappear as if into the air. Before Goody went, she had a child, a fact which caused no little scandal given that Goody was not yet married and the baby being clearly the fruit of an illicit union with her adoptive brother, Francis, who was black-skinned. My father had always been very kind to this woman, and even given the notorious nature of these most recent happenings in her life and our own stricken state, continued to take tea with her every week, and doted on the child, who was admittedly very bonny and good-natured.

One night towards the end of August of that year, 1746, there came a banging at the door. I went down in my nightrobe to find the Widow Brown there holding her grandchild, a wild and terror-stricken look upon her face. She was not able to speak, but rather pulled me out by my sleeve and down the driveway until I could see the town beyond the Hundred Place where a red glow lit the sky. I consigned the distressed woman and the watchful child to Elizabeth, pulled on a duffel coat and set out for Paradise, which was the name of her home.

It was well that the walls of this place were high and of strong brick, for without them it is likely that the fire would have spread to the entirety of the town. The house had been burnt near to the ground, and while the night watch and several neighbours were there with buckets of water attempting to contain the blaze, their actions were meaningless in the face of such a devastating conflagration. I stood and watched as the fine old house collapsed in on itself and the flames were passed from the building to the trees of the orchard, from there to the grasses & shrubbery that grew in such profusion in that garden. The glass-house in which the Widow had prepared infusions, she being a kind of herbalist, collapsed with a great noise of breaking glass.

In the morning, the Widow and I returned to Paradise to see if anything were salvageable in the ruins. The stone steps that led down to the cellars still stood, and there were a few melded bits of metal and heaped bricks gently smouldering. It seemed as if some of the goods of the house had been carried off, either before or during the fire, for the Widow fussled around in the smoking ruins for some time, sobbing rather as she did so, but to no avail. We returned to Greyfriars and I was sensible of the fact that I too was about to lose my own home and felt a large degree of sympathy for the old woman.

The second tragedy occurred the day we departed for Goudhurst, which was the first of September. The widow and her grandchild had amalgamated themselves into our domestic pattern. My father, having always been much taken by the old woman, seemed cheered by her presence, even supping a little with us and taking a glass of wine after his dinner. Elizabeth doted on the child, playing a game in which she scurried about on her knees and the boy came crawling after, feeding him his gruel at breakfast and taking him out on to the lawns to be sunned in the afternoon. Her goodness is something I find hard to describe, hard even to observe on occasion, as if an angel's light shone about her.

The coach – unicorn-dressed to save costs – drew up before the house and we began the melancholy task of loading it up with the few objects of furniture, tableware, linens &c. that remained to us. I had made it a scruple to ensure that the few servants who had stayed were paid unto the last, and the housemaid, Rose, painted a most dejected figure as she bade us farewell. Finally, the coach was laden with all the goods we possessed. I offered a final adieu to the place I had called home since as a child I had come here, lifted on the cloud of my father's new fortune. The apple trees were in heavy fruit, the cherries, unharvested, lay in wasp-harried piles upon the grass. The ruined abbey which I had rehabilitated into a barracks now stood empty, with all of my men departed to suppress the civil war in the north and chase down those Jacobites which remained. But I was not one given to lamentation or regretting that which cannot be changed, so I helped the Widow Brown into the coach, where she arranged herself about a washstand, and passed the baby up to Elizabeth, who likewise had inserted herself into the overcrowded interior. My father and I rode outside, facing rearwards.

The coach began its laboured departure; Rose, the groom and houseboy all stood in the slanting sunlight, watching us go, waving their handkerchiefs. I was not at first aware that my father was unwell, so taken up was I with sealing in my mind the various scenes we passed by: the tall pines of Rectory Lane, the smouldering ruins of Paradise, the crumbling walls of the town and the Land Gate. Only when we came down towards the ferry did I look over and see my father was producing a kind of froth from his mouth, his eyes rolling up into his head, his face very red & apoplectic.

I called for the coachman to stop, and half-carried my father to the ground, where I extended him on the grassy verge of the lane and the Widow Brown came and sat beside him. She was holding his hand when he died, a fact that I believe would have given him pleasure. His passing did not look painful and, to a degree, I was pleased that he had not had to suffer the ignominy of beginning a new life in much reduced circumstances, dependent on the kindness of others, a burden where only a short while previously he had been such a proud and prevailing man.

The problem remained of what to do with his body, which we finally resolved to insert into the compartment of the coach, whereby Elizabeth passed the child to Widow Brown and came to sit beside me on the exterior. One other commendable thing about Elizabeth: she knows when to speak and when to remain silent. All that journey to Goudhurst, which, given the steepness of the Wealden hills and the slowness of our reduced equipage, took more than three hours, she merely sat beside me and held my hand in hers, but it was such great comfort to me to have her there.

III

GOUDHURST IS A small, pretty town on the road to Tunbridge Wells and Seven Oaks, built on the crest of a hill. My first task after arriving at the farmhouse that we had been lent by Elizabeth's Aunt Adelia was to find a room in which to lay out the body of my father. He was heavy in death and it required the coachman to grip him by the ankles as I carried him beneath his arms. Then I went up to the church, St Mary the Virgin, which was large, square and Norman in construction, with extended wings, castellated ramparts and ancient gravestones jostling higgle-piggle in the walled yard.

The priest, Isaac Finch by name, was not to be found, but there was a kind of sacristan or rector there in a plain black robe, who introduced himself as Silas Moore and pointed me in the direction of the rectory, which lay not two dozen yards from the south-east corner of the yard. I thanked the man and followed the path across the graveyard to the gate.

It took a long while for the priest to open his door. When he did, he parted it just the merest inch, and I could see that he carried a pistol in one hand. He asked my business and I introduced myself as a new parishioner. He ushered me in with a nervous glance up and down the lane before he shut the door.

The reason for the Reverend Finch's peculiar demeanour was soon made clear. Once he had ascertained that I was no threat, he became most welcoming, offering me a glass of whatever strong liquor he had been consuming. I declined and he then showed me to a chair in a cosy parlour and unburdened himself to me. It seemed that the Hawkhurst Gang, now free to run riot wherever they pleased, had established in these Wealden villages – Goudhurst, Sissinghurst, Hawkhurst, Sandhurst – a terrible & bloody fiefdom, with those blackguards that I had sought to conquer when I wore the King's red jacket now lords of these quiet and God-respecting places.

Finch told me of the women defiled, the men left broken and bruised or worse, the hay barns burnt and the livestock stolen or slaughtered. He told me of an old man, Octavius Webb, who'd stepped in to prevent his granddaughter being carried off by one of the brigands, a large and violent brute they called Poison. Octavius Webb was four-and-sixty when he died, beaten about the head & the body with a club before being buried head-first in a fox hole. It was like a plague upon the town, Reverend Finch said, and many had fled to the safety of London or Canterbury, boarding up their homes when they left. The redcoats had made a number of unsuccessful sorties against the smugglers, who knew the terrain better than the soldiery, and vanished into the air when the dragoons descended. 'We are losing hope,' the priest told me.

I then recounted to him my own misfortune, & my familiarity with the viciousness of the Hawkhurst Gang. I liked this priest, who was so clearly regretting taking up office in a place that must have seemed from afar like the most gentle & gracious living, but was in fact a kind of hell. I believe he liked me too, for he agreed straightway to bury my father that coming Friday, and to join the hands of me and my Elizabeth the following Saturday, figuring that a week was sufficient time for us to mourn the once-great Albert Nesbitt, scourge of the Inner Temple. He attempted again to pour me a glass of spiritous liquor, & then being assured that I did not partake of alcohol, he offered me a sincere welcome and saw me out into the night. I heard the several bolts on the door shut fast behind me.

IV

THERE WERE NO mourners for my father save Elizabeth, the Widow Brown and myself. We had left the child with Elizabeth's Aunt Adelia, who had taken a great liking to the boy. It was an inclement day and the rain swirled about us as we lowered the old man into his grave, and I thought of how much life had been in him until recently. But then he found himself on the side of the law that offers nothing but mockery to those who look to it for succour, the side that seeks to overturn the perquisites of power but is always doomed to fail. I recognised in the ruins of his life how much of my father was left unresolved, mysterious, but perhaps this is always the case with the death of those close to us.

The day of my nuptials dawned bright & mild, and it was possible in that balmy morning to forget the uneasiness that hung like a cloud over the town. Elizabeth was dressed most prettily in a white gown and, in defiance of custom, we went together to the Starre & Crowne tavern for a hearty breakfast, before walking the short distance to the church. The tavern was almost empty, the morning sun slanting in through the windows, the sound of a kitchen boy singing in the yard outside. I found that I kept looking across at the woman who, in spite of the objections of her family, and the privations to which my reduced fortunes would subject her, appeared to love me. I dreamed to myself of the children we would have, of evenings before the roar of a fire when I would read to them all from some improving book. We live in times in which money appears to be all and yet we were happy, Elizabeth & I, and we had near nothing to our name.

Several minutes before eleven, the bells began to ring out and we made our way over to the church. The Widow Brown and Aunt Adelia were already there, with Little Ezekiel dressed bonnily in a sailor suit. Being as Elizabeth's father had refused to grant his permission for the match, and seeing as there was no other male to complete the necessary duties, Silas Moore, the church-warden, was enlisted to give Elizabeth away. He was on the far side of fifty, his wig ill-arranged on his pate, but he was a kindly man and took Elizabeth from me with a smile, before reaching to lift a crown of cowslips on to her head. The bells stopped ringing, the organ struck up, and I hurried to my place before the altar.

I recount this scene not for its place in my personal history – although it was of course a moment of great pride to me when the Reverend Finch joined us in marriage – but rather for what came after. Isaac Finch was just concluding his blessing when there was the sound of raised voices from without the church. Then a rattling was heard at the door & a group of the illest-looking blackguards I'd ever set eyes upon came barrelling in. They were clearly sotted with drink, and one of them, who was near to a giant in size, carried a terrible blunderbuss over his shoulder. They were dirty, long-haired, shiftless types, with rings in their ears & daggers at their belts. One looked more like a rat or weasel than any man I'd seen: puffing on a pipe, his lips twitching and his eyes flicking this way and that. Near the back of the group stood a dark-suited man with a rakish hat covering his long hair. This, I presumed, was Arthur Gray. It was clear that not one of them had been abed that previous night, and were come here direct from one of the famous roisters at Gray's mansion. They made their way down the aisle, with the ratty one humming Handel's *Hornpipe* in a mocking fashion. I saw a look of great horror appear on the face of Widow Brown, and by instinct I went to interpose myself between Elizabeth and the men, feeling a terrible admixture of fear & bravery & affront-edness, as if such misfortune, coming fast upon so many other calamities, were a sign of a malign fate determined to o'erwhelm me.

The Reverend Finch began to make a series of mild imprecations towards the men, while Silas Moore looked thunderously at them. They came straightway towards my dear Elizabeth, though, and I fear that I was not able to protect my wife, for with a blow of his fist, the great man laid me out cold, and I was taken back into that grim dreamworld that I had inhab-ited when I was attacked in my previous life and Elizabeth had come to tend me.

Elizabeth and I never spoke of what happened next, and I cannot bear to ask her. All I know is that, despite the shrieks and most valiant essays of her aunt and the heroic interjections of Silas Moore, my wife of not yet ten minutes was carried off into the vestry and mistreated in the most vile and lamentable fashion. When I came to, she was sitting with her aunt in the lady chapel, speaking in a low voice. I went over to her and she looked up at me with her sorrowful eyes, and it was all I could do not to rush out after the scoundrels that moment.

We went back to the house and Elizabeth was shut away with the Widow Brown for several hours. That good woman had a collection of medicaments & unguents that I presumed were being employed to salve whatever injuries my wife had suffered. I sat and played with the child for a while, although my mind was much distracted and I was on the verge several times of going in to speak with them, but did not, feeling myself far on the outside of what had happened to Elizabeth. Finally she emerged, followed by the Widow, and I judged that a certain compact had formed between them. I took her in my arms then, and while she did not push me away, neither did she yield to my embrace, remaining straight & silent until I drew away from her.

V

THE REST OF the day was spent beneath a terrible shadow and it did not feel as if we stepped out of it for the entirety of that long & joyless winter. Elizabeth was taciturn and appeared preoccupied with her thoughts. She no longer played with the baby with the same joviality, but rather spent her days in the sitting room of our little house, staring at a book without ever seeming to turn a page. I had told her that I did not wish her to go abroad without my accompanying her and that I would henceforth be armed at all times when I was with her. She said nothing, but merely stared up at me again with those large eyes, and I felt my heart crack at the sight of it. I lay awake at night for long hours, imagining setting off with my pistols down to Rye to search out the three smugglers and have my satisfaction of them. Or inveigling my way into one of Arthur Gray's orgies at Seacox Heath and shooting as many of them dead as I might manage before being taken. I knew, though, that I had other obligations that I must fulfil, and that Little Ezekiel and the Widow Brown, as well as my dear Elizabeth, would be better served by my presence with them.

It became clear that my wife was with child, and I need not set down here the reasoning by which I knew that the infant was not my own. I wished desperately that she might confide in me, and essayed on several occasions to speak with her about what must have been a grievous concern to her, but she answered me not, only looking at me and giving a smile that showed nothing of her heart in it. We spent our evenings in silence before retreating to our separate bedrooms, & I came to know that loneliness can be increased by the presence of another when you wish to be close to them but are proscribed from being so.

It seemed that Aunt Adelia was not willing to support us indefinitely, and so it was incumbent upon me to seek some sort of employ. I had no talents, being neither farmer nor craftsman nor notary, & so it was that I found myself, thanks to the good offices of Reverend Finch, teaching in the little village school that stands across the way from the church, just before the dog-leg that the road takes before dashing down the hill to Lamberhurst.

It was a pleasant school, with a fire always burning merrily in the grate, and the children were eager to please, if not always of the highest intellect. I further supplemented my wages by acting as tutor to some of the scions of the grander houses of the village, and it was here that I met a certain Charles Kent, a bluff, red-whiskered man whose three sons were all equally jovial & incomplex. I was not happy to be away from home with such brigands riding about, particularly with my wife in her condition, but I instructed the Widow Brown in the use of my pistol, which I did then leave with her.

I began to look forward in particular to my visits to Charles Kent's house, and recognised that this was in part because he reminded me of my own father, even though he was perhaps only five-and-fifty years of age. His boys – Edward, George and another Charles – were what boys ought to be, namely frank, cheerful and always abroad seeking adventure, from whence they would return with shining eyes, scraped knees and tall tales. I declare I did learn as much of them as they of me, for they knew all the names of the plants and birds, could identify the stars and distinguish the trees by their bark. Their father, whilst nominally a farmer, was of a natural historical bent & had written papers on fungi for the Royal Society. He had schooled his boys well & they clearly loved him.

The mother I did not meet, she being an invalid and unable to leave her bed. The house, which was called Pattenden, was large & timber-framed with a cat-slide roof and a view over woodland. I taught the boys in a schoolroom on the first floor, a bright place with many fine books and a superior pair of globes, terrestrial and celestial. Edward was to start at Eton ere long and was the most well-learned of the three, being almost twelve years of age. George was ten, and the younger Charles just seven. I taught them Latin and Greek and some mathematics, these being the subjects at which I was most adept. Pattenden became a place of blessed relief from the atmosphere at home, a place I could laugh and forget for a while the many tribulations of my recent life. It was also at Pattenden that I first heard of William Stuart & the Goudhurst Band.

VI

I HAD STAYED late in the schoolroom with the boys. We were reading the *Iliad* and had come to the battle of Hector and Achilles, and the four of us took turns to read those immortal lines. I found a facility in Greek and Latin that I did not have in my own language, an ability to think in terms grander and more poetical. It was near seven of the clock when we finished, with the distraught Priam returning to Troy with his son's body. I saw that young Charles was weeping a little, but I feigned not to notice. I had been half-aware of some going & coming in the house below, the sound of carriages & voices, the opening & closing of the front door. As I descended the stairwell I saw that Charles Kent stood in the centre of the entrance hall surrounded by a group of men, several of whom I recognised from the streets of the town. Silas Moore was there, & Richard Mortlock, the Mayor of Goudhurst.

'Come and join us,' Charles said, holding out a glass of canary towards me. I took it rather hesitantly, never entirely at ease in company, nor pleased with spiritous liquor, and aware that I was already late for my returning. Now Charles went to stand at the far end of the hall and a general silence descended.

'Thank you for coming, gentlemen,' he said to us. 'You will be aware of the reason we are convened, namely the requirement to find some remedy for the scourge that has fallen upon our town. The Hawkhurst Gang have stolen my cattle, they have abused my sister most viciously over at Etchingham, there is not a one of us today that has not faced some indignity at their hand. It is time that we let these brigands know that Kentish Men are not so easily cowed.' Here he struck his glass down hard on the cellaret beside him and a rumble of approval went round the room. I looked up to the stairs where his boys were sat, pride and approbation shining from them as they leant eagerly forward.

'We are lucky enough,' Charles continued, 'to have a new resident of the town whose skills may prove extremely useful in this endeavour. May I present to you Lance Corporal William Stuart, a veteran of the wars in the north, and well-versed in military activity.' Here he gestured to a figure standing a little away from the lamplight. I received the impression of someone tall but well-proportioned, a wide-brimmed hat pulled low over his eyes. He wore a long dark cloak and silver-buckled shoes. He stepped forward now and, without looking up, raised a hand in greeting. The light caught his face for a moment, and I saw that he was most horribly pox-marked, his skin peaked and cratered with angry weals. He stepped back into the shadows, but it was clear that his presence had created a frisson among the men there.

'With your approval, gentlemen,' Charles went on, 'I suggest that we hold regular meetings here each Monday and Thursday evening, with the aim of forming a militia capable of repelling these blackguards. I would ask you to bring all the weaponry in your possession, whether that be antique muskets from your grandfathers' wars, or fowling pieces, or decorative cutlashes. All who are with me, say "Aye".' Here a great shout went up, and I found myself joining in, not wishing to appear browbeaten before so many of the town's great men. 'We will call ourselves the Goudhurst Band!' Charles cried, and again a bellow of assent came that shook the glasses on the tables.

Afterwards, Charles introduced me to several of those I had yet to encounter, including the town's physician, Dr Churchland, and the landlord of the Starre & Crowne, a Mr Sykes, and many other worthies and figures of local note, &c. I apprehended that William Stuart, whom I had been most eager to interrogate, had disappeared already, but I reckoned on having other opportunities to discourse with him. We raised one more glass to the Goudhurst Band, in which salutation young Edward was permitted to descend and participate, and then I took myself off home, with the good wishes of my new companions ringing in my ears.

VII

I DID NOT tell Elizabeth about the events of that evening. She was so much distracted and sombre that I did not wish her to have more cause for worry. I told her only that Charles Kent had asked me to work longer hours with Edward in anticipation of his going up to school, a mistruth which did not seem so overly far from the real state of things.

At this time, on several occasions I came into the sitting room to find Elizabeth pressed close against the glass of the window that looks up the hill behind the house. There is a wood there, and once I was certain that I saw a figure moving amid the trees. I asked my wife if she was expecting a visitor or if there was some particular object of interest in the woods, and that I might perchance accompany her there to inspect it, but she merely turned to me with her face vacant and placid, and told me that there would be no need, that she had all that she required in our home.

I kept watch for William Stuart when I was about in the town, but although I saw many faces familiar from that evening, I did not set eyes upon him when making my journey from our home to the schoolhouse, or to those other local families whose education had been entrusted to me. I awaited the next meeting of the Band with great anticipation, readying myself to demonstrate a bravery that I felt quite distant from. I had told no one in Goudhurst save the priest of my own military background, nor of the terrible attack that had left me near-dead. I feared greatly that the assault had made a coward of me, as if I were always awaiting the fall of a bludgeon.

The first meeting of the Goudhurst Band took place on a Monday evening in November. I had wrapped my pistols and my musket from my dragoon days in sackcloth and took them with me to the schoolhouse.

I had left a single pistol in the dresser beside my bed. All that day I was infected with a peculiar energy, and I found myself several times losing the trail of my sentence, or drifting off and only being reminded of where I was by the larking of one of the younger boys. Finally, it was time to walk out to Pattenden, where I was scheduled to instruct the three younger Kents for an hour before the meeting began at seven sharp.

As it was, both the boys and I wanted to speak of one subject only: namely how & when we would take on the Hawkhurst Gang & which especial secrets of warfare the Lance Corporal would convey to us. I confessed to the boys my own brief military past and they quizzed me a great deal about my encounters with the smugglers. When I told them I had been near murdered by one of them, Edward got up to run & tell his father. Charles Kent came hurrying to the schoolroom, where he insisted on me telling once more the story of my ill-fated soldiering.

Then the men began to arrive in their carriages, and a fine, if antique, assortment of firearms was deposited on the table at the centre of the hall. The main part were wide-mouthed fowling pieces, although there were also a few muskets & pistols. Silas Moore brought along a most vicious-looking halberd, whose blade he had whetted silver-sharp. Then William Stuart, still shadowy under the brim of his parson's hat, began to speak in a voice that was low & gravellish. He led us out into the dark evening, where the turning circle of the house was illuminated with lamps, and where we were commanded to shoulder our weapons and march, then to feign discharging in volley after volley, with one group always to be firing while the other recharged their weapons. It was fairly basic drill, but even so, several of the men stumbled in the execution of their orders. We went through our paces until it grew quite cold, then repaired inside to drink a glass of canary (I gave mine to Edward). All the while the Lance Corporal spoke informatively about the charge and the flying wedge, about when to employ shot and when bayonet, about how to use our enemy's confidence against them. He was a persuasive speaker and I dare say every other man in the room left that day, and the many that followed, as I did: buoyed up by a sudden hope.

VIII

THAT WINTER OF 1746 saw the Hawkhurst Gang carrying out an increasingly violent and organised assault on the villages of the Weald. The raids came more frequently and were ever more brutal in nature. Several of the younger men of the village, of a family named Grundy, attempted to prevent the raiding of their pig farm, and were set upon and beaten so badly that one, the youngest, died on the spot, while another expired a week later. Three gentlewomen of Staplehurst, daughters of the magistrate there, were carried off by the Gang, and were never seen again. I heard of one poor soul, by the name of Jarvis Lambert, who had caused some offence to Arthur Gray over a business dealing, and was chased down where he lived in Horsmonden. The Hawkhurst Gang apprehended him as he watched a cricket match on the village green. It speaks to the horror that these men inspired that they bludgeoned poor Lambert to death in front of the massed ranks of cricketers and not one man stepped in to intervene. The Gang then travelled to Lambert's house in the village and set about his wife and daughter. The wife escaped, but the daughter, who was said to be a fine and spirited girl, rejected their advances and fought most violently against them until they murdered her and misused her even in death.

There is not a child I taught that had not seen some member of his family injured, that did not glance over his shoulder when walking home in the darkness, that slept without the spectre of some villain rising up at the window in a bee-skep mask and assailing him. I saw what fear does to a place, the way it infects the very buildings and renders the most mundane of actions scareful. People slinked about the streets by day and stayed at home at night. I had occasion now & again to ride out to Lamberhurst or Cranbrook & found that there too, the residents lived as if at a time of pestilence, & that merely the sight of a stranger on a strange horse was enough to cause the townspeople to close their shutters & fast-bolt their doors.

I saw on several occasions the mysterious figure on the hillside behind the house, and perceived again that my wife appeared to be leaning towards the window. I thought of going out to confront him, but he seemed only to appear in inclement weather or at dusk, and I felt – I know not how – that he was a benign presence, a force that worked against the prevailing fearfulness of the town, rather than adding to it. My wife remained near-silent, though her belly now spoke of the events of the previous autumn, and she took to wearing large and billowing shifts, the better to hide her gravidity. The Widow Brown and Little Ezekiel lived their own self-contained lives, equally quiet and watchful; Aunt Adelia stopped in to take the boy from time to time, but otherwise there was no interruption to the stale & soundless atmosphere of the house, and I was always glad to escape to the blitheness of the schoolhouse or to Pattenden, where the good nature of Charles Kent and his boys always gave my heart a great lift.

One evening in February, I was out collecting logs from the barn. The light was falling fast and it was as if the world were illuminated from below with white snowdrops, yellow crocuses and the first of the daffodils. As I turned, my arms full of logs, I saw the figure on the hill, much closer now. Even in the dimness I recognised the hat, the cloak. I dropped the logs and raised a hand in greeting. William Stuart raised his own arm and then turned and walked away up the field towards the wood. I watched him disappear into the trees. I had not thought overmuch of this peculiar, damaged man, of the specifics of his own life. I wondered if he had family at home and what he might see in the lighted windows of my own house: a wife, solitary & languishing; an old woman and a boy on the cusp between baby and child, now walking, now mouthing words, now feeding himself spoonfuls of gruel. And what would he think of me? Unheroic, spindly and effete. I saw him again in the coming days, but farther off, in the reach of the trees, drifting in and out of the shadows and darker than any of them.

Our training in military arts continued and more joined

our association as word spread of the Goudhurst Band. Silas Moore revealed himself a gifted shot and was granted the most sophisticated of the rifles. Charles Kent had long been adept with a fowling piece and was anyway a hale and doughty man, well-able to take on the mantle of soldier. The town butcher, a Mr Jevons, joined us, as did Esau Beswick the blacksmith, and several farmhands from Charles's farm: good, hearty boys with names like Dick and Seth who did not speak much but revealed great steeliness in their disposition, a willingness to carry on drilling when others were near-dead with tiredness.

Although the Reverend Finch did not participate in the militia, thinking perhaps that it was not the place for a man of the cloth, he permitted the usage of the church as the armoury for our enterprise, it being thought that Pattenden was too distant from the heart of the town to serve this purpose. Silas Moore let us down into the crypt of the church, which was damp & low, and then revealed to us the tunnels that led off under the streets of Goudhurst to the principal houses of the town, these being a relic of the days of King Henry's persecution of the monks, when Goudhurst was a haven for the recusants. I knew of the tunnels that spread beneath my former home, Winchelsea, and wondered if every town in the area carried beneath it some kind of warren, as if the history of violence above ground had necessitated these dowers beneath.

The crypt became a bristling gun store, with a whet-stone for bayonets and several barrels of gunpowder. We repaired there one evening in March; all the Goudhurst Band, now numbering four-and-twenty, pressed into that musty room. By candlelight we gathered and passed glasses between us. Then Charles Kent declared that we were ready to fight, and William said that we were all soldiers, and there was a hurrahing & ballyhooing that might have been heard at Seacox Heath. Richard Mortlock finished off by giving a most elegant and sentimental speech commending each of us for our selfless devotion to our town, mentioning me and William by name as military men who had come as outsiders, but without whom the enterprise would never have reached its current situation. I felt much flustered to be mentioned in the same breath as William and attempted to force the flush from my cheeks. It was agreed that the church bell should not be rung save to indicate an attack, and that we would send messages to our neighbouring villages that they should light a beacon in the event of an assault by the gang. We now needed only to wait for the smugglers to move against us, and we left the crypt and fanned out into the night with courage and good humour in our hearts.

IX

WITH THE LENGTHENING of the light in the evenings, I had taken to going for walks with the Kent children for the final hour of our lessons, rather than keep them in the schoolroom. I recognised that this was often the way with young boys – that they would take in more knowledge while exercising their limbs than when trapped within the stultifying walls of the classroom. As we walked I spoke to the boys of Juvenal and Hesiod, and read them a little of the *Works and Days*, while they told me the names of the birds that began to arrive from warmer climes: devlins and martlets, huck-mucks and hay-jacks. Edward would stoop to identify a pale orchid in the grass, while the young Charles, who was a dreamer, would announce the stars as they emerged in the evening sky. We would always come back to the bright windows of Pattenden and their father standing kindly at the threshold awaiting us. I had relaxed somewhat my mistrust of alcohol, and so would on occasion take a glass of claret with him and talk of the Goudhurst Band, telling him all I knew of the smugglers, of their individual personalities & histories. I'd walk back home with lighter feet, elevated by the trust & interest he demonstrated in me, & would meet my wife's silence, the reproach in her eyes, the increasing stretch of her stomach, with greater equanimity & patience than was usual.

It was a forenoon past the middle of April, a Wednesday of warm light and birdsong. The boys and I had walked further than usual, down to where the River Teise winds lazily through the valley. We had seen a kingfisher and we were happy because of it. The birdsong was like a wild torrent of sound about us, so we did not hear the men until we rounded the corner and found them there, letting their horses stoop to drink in the river.

My insides shrank within me when I saw them. I felt at once fear and my duty to protect the boys, but more than anything I felt anger. There were four of them, two of whom I recognised – the large brute from my wedding day and his rat-faced companion, who was again puffing on a pipe. The other two villains were

cut of the same cloth, namely vicious-looking desper-
ados with knives at their belts and muskets on their
shoulders. I reached for the pistol that I kept as a matter
of habit in the pocket of my jacket, but the large man
was too swift for me, levelling his blunderbuss at my
head and grunting, which seemed to indicate that I
should deposit my weapon on the ground.

'Get behind me, boys,' I said, in a steadier voice than
I thought would come out of me. 'No harm shall come
to you.' I tossed the pistol down in the grass and, just
at that moment, using the motion of my hand for
disguisement, I thrust myself forward at the gigantic
figure, pushing the barrel of his gun aside and propel-
ling him into his companions. 'Run!' I said to the boys,
as I attempted to prevent any of the gang recovering
their footing swiftly enough to apprehend my charges.
I saw that the lads obeyed my command and were soon
haring up the hillside towards the town. Then one of
the smugglers – the ratty cur who had conspired in
the molestation of Elizabeth – rose and slashed at me
with his knife. There was a tearing sound, and it was
well that I knew not my Hesiod by heart, for the book
at my breast certainly saved my life. I stumbled back-
wards and now the large man was afoot again, his
disproportioned musket pointed straight at me.

'After them,' the ratty fellow said to his underlings.
'They will be worth something to us.' With that, the
two other smugglers mounted their horses and went
up the hill after the boys. The ratty-looking blackguard
relit his pipe and brought his face very close to mine,
while reaching behind me to fasten my hands with a
piece of rope.

'I recognise you,' he said, leering. 'Are you not Nesbitt, who was at Winchelsea? And did you not get married at Goudhurst a year hence?' I saw the larger man's face slowly shape itself into apperception. I remained silent. 'Oh, we will have some fun with you,' the ratty one went on, and, now that the boys were gone, and my weapon taken off me, fear became predominant in my emotions, for I recognised that for a smuggler to apprehend a member of the King's service, even one who had now resigned his station, was a great boon for them, and that I would be lucky to escape with my life. Then a further blow: I saw, coming down the hill in the lowering light of the evening, the pair of brigands who'd gone after the boys. They were on horseback still, but one of them carried a rope that was fastened to the wrists of young Charles, who was bawling, his face streaked with snot & blood, stumbling every few steps as he struggled to keep up with his captors.

'The other two got off,' one of them said, spitting to underline the matter. 'Scarpered into the woods, didn't they? But we snagged this one well and proper. Gave him a right good hiding, to boot.'

I saw the ratty fellow think for a moment, chewing on his pipe, then he let out a laugh. 'One's better than three, especially with an officer all trussed up. I reckon this calls for a drink of summat.'

He unloaded a bottle of grog from one of the saddlebags and they passed it from one to the other, amusing themselves all the while by aiming a series of kicks and epithets at me and poor young Charles, who had not ceased wailing, no matter that I did my best to soothe him and to let him know that I would protect him. They had bound us tightly and the great brute, who I marked was more silent and yet more ferocious than his fellows, twisted young Charles by the ear until the flesh of the lobe tore and bled most profusely. At this vile act I made my anger known in the most vehement terms, until the giant turned his ugly attentions upon me and battered me about the face and body until I was near-insensible. It was then, at first distantly, that I heard the sound of the bells of St Mary the Virgin tolling out down the valley and I had to shake my head to ensure that it was not a happy dream. For I knew it meant that the other two boys had reached the town, and that the Goudhurst Band was, God willing, on the way.

X

THE FOUR SMUGGLERS did not at first pay much heed to the ringing of the bell, but I saw that they were preparing to return to Rye, this being the centre of their activities. The giant picked up Charles by his collar and hefted him on to the back of his horse, which was a great, shaggy thing, much resembling its owner, some eighteen hands in height. My own bonds were fastened to the pommel of the ratty-looking man's saddle, and we set off down the valley at a fast pace, such that I had to maintain something between a walk and a run just to keep up.

The light was falling fast and I knew that before long we should be lost amid the shadows. I was perspiring a

great deal, and had to concentrate on my feet in order
not to fall, so it was a shock to me when I looked up
and perceived that our path was blocked by a group of
men, some mounted, some not, all brandishing a most
deadly display of arms. One of them stepped forward and
when I saw it was William Stuart, with his wide-brimmed
hat and undertaker's cloak, my heart leapt in my chest.

William stood with his musket raised, the barrel
cycling from one smuggler to the next. 'Unhand them,'
he said. 'Or we'll truss the lot of you up here.'

'And who the h--- are you?' demanded the ratty fellow.

'We are the Goudhurst Band.' At William's words, I
saw several of his comrades straighten their backs.

'Smugglers?' Incredulity in the ratty fellow's voice.
'This is our turf. You're crack-headed if you think a
few dozen milksops like you can take the Hawkhurst
Gang. The King's Men themselves couldn't defeat us.'
His pipe had gone out and he very studiously lit it,
while the large man brought his blunderbuss round to
level it at William's head.

William at this point tilted his hat back, so that his
pock-scarred face was showing in the low light of
evening. 'Poison, Smoker,' he said, and it took me a
moment to realise that he was naming the smugglers.
I saw the ratty man – Smoker – shoot a quick glance
of unease to his comrade. 'You would do well to go
back to Seacox Heath,' William continued. 'Tell your
masters that their hour draws near. Now get on with
you, afore we send you to them in pieces.'

There was a moment in which the smugglers and the
soldier stood regarding each other, and then, as if coming
to a sudden decision, the giant – Poison – dismounted

and lifted young Charles from across the back of the horse. He untied him and the boy went running to his father and brothers, the latter of whom stood radiant with the victory they had achieved. Then Smoker took a knife and cut the ropes at my wrists. I made a more dignified journey over the short distance to join my friends.

We then parted a little to allow the smugglers to pass between us, with many a jibe and mocking gesture from our ranks to theirs as they went by. Then, in near-dark, we took the road up to Goudhurst, and the boys told me in breathless voices how they had gone straight to Silas Moore, who had rung the bell, and how the men had gathered, and Edward told of where we were, and where the men might be taking us.

When we reached the town, many of the wives and daughters of the place were out to greet us, although not, alas, my Elizabeth, and they cheered and applauded most prettily as we went by. We repaired to the Starre & Crowne, where the landlord stood us jars of ale and mead and Charles's farmhands brought out a fiddle & pipe and began to play. It was very late when I came home and the house was silent, but I went to bed and slept more deeply than I had for many a night.

XI

In the town, there was a new hope in the air after the events by the river. Isaac Finch stood tall at the lectern that Sunday as he addressed his sermon, which was on the subject of Christian heroism. I saw Charles Kent give Edward's arm a little squeeze. William Stuart was not a churchgoer, as neither was the Widow Brown, who had kept the baby at home, but most everyone else was there, it being that sort of town, where folk went more out of neighbourliness than piety. 'And what we have learnt from this,' Finch concluded, enjoying his performance a little more than was seemly, or so it appeared to me, 'is that righteousness will always triumph over evil. I am proud of my flock this day, proud that the good men of Goudhurst succeeded where the massed forces of the soldiery failed.' I thought the priest was overdoing the significance of our victory. It was, after all, just four men we had seen off, and I was certain that the Hawkhurst Gang would not allow such a slight to pass without some form of retribution.

I cast a look sidewise at my wife, who was now great with child. She had taken on a kind of glow in those final months of her pregnancy, so that there was no shift bagsome enough to hide her, and her cheeks were always flushed, her breath fast. I had told her nothing of the events of the previous Thursday. We discussed little save the daily necessities of running a house, the health of the child or the cows that I had begun to farm in a half-hearted fashion. It was as if a great wall had gone up about her, and without it lay all the gaiety and courage she had evinced before. I knew that she regretted tying herself to me in wedlock, and I wished I could think up some easy way to release her. It was as my mind was dwelling upon these melancholy thoughts that there came a great noise from the entrance of the church, following which the doors were thrown open and several men came striding into the room. Behind them, carrying a heavy musket and wearing a sword at his waist, was George Kingsmill, one of the leaders of the Hawkhurst Gang, whom I recognised from having perceived him several times at the Mermaid Inn at Rye. Kingsmill himself had been born in Goudhurst, and although his family was now departed, his name maintained a sinister currency in this place.

To give him his due, Isaac Finch made at least a show of protesting the ingress of these ruffians into his church this time. 'Gentleman,' he said in his high voice, which did seem to quiver more than was usual, even for him, 'you are in a house of worship. Please, step outside. I must insist . . .' It was rather more than he had done the day of my wedding, but Kingsmill seemed not to hear him, coming to stand at the front of the nave and addressing himself to the congregation in a massive voice. His words have been well-recorded in the history books, for all their profaneness, but I will mark them here all the same.

'I have been at the murder of forty of His Majesty's finest officers and soldiers, and I'll be d----- if I'll have my men harried by a mob of farmhands and sops. You made a d--- error taking on the Hawkhurst Gang with your trifling band of gads and sods. I swear I'll broil four of your hearts for my luncheon this coming Thursday, and wash it down with four pints of your blood. Goudhurst will be a town of ghosts and shadows by the time we're done with it, you mark well my words.' With that he gave a terrible grimace and proceeded back down the aisle, his face fixed in a leer. The rest of them filed out into the brightness of the day, leaving a vast silence in their wake. It took a long time for anyone to say anything and it was Charles Kent who broke the quiet, pulling at his whiskers as he spoke.

'Friends,' he said, 'it seems to me that our choice is clear. We can disband our little militia, flee our village, give up much that is dear to us, or we can stay and fight.' He looked about with brave, desperate eyes, & I spoke before I had time to regret it, despite my shyness in such public forums, & notwithstanding the fact that Kingsmill's words had struck great fear into me.

'I'll fight with you, Charles,' I said, and went to stand beside him. Then Silas Moore joined us, and Mayor Mortlock and Mr Jevons the butcher and many others, including several who had not yet shown themselves at the meetings of the Goudhurst Band. Edward even stepped forward and his father ruffled his hair, and of course George and young Charles sought to subscribe themselves too. It was decided that we should send for William Stuart and convene a council at the Starre & Crowne to make plans for our defence.

XII

THE NEXT DAYS were spent in great business of preparation. William was named our General & immediately identified the church as the likeliest site for our defence, it being well-sited on the highest eminence of the village, with a view of all possible advances. The younger men were tasked with fortifying the church-yard, blocking up the entrance gate & stile with a mixture of mud and broken gravestones (the latter being heaped in one corner of the yard). These same grave-stones (and, I regret, several that were of newer vintage) were arranged into a series of barricades that our men could cache themselves behind in order to fire upon the enemy. Esau Beswick, the blacksmith, lit fires around the yard and set about casting ball and shot, and there was such a great deal to achieve that we had no time to feel frighted.

Then it was Wednesday, and William Stuart declared that all of the women and children of the town must be conveyed to the neighbouring villages. It was not necessary to explain this decision; all of us knew what would happen were we to be outfought by the Hawkhurst Gang. The loss of our own lives would be but little compared to the suffering that our wives and daughters would endure. I did, of course, ask that Elizabeth depart; she responded that she was her own woman and could make such decisions for herself. I had not the courage to countermand her. On the Wednesday night, I did succeed in persuading Widow Brown to take young Ezekiel down the valley to Aunt Adelia's house, where I entreated her to barricade the doors and retreat to the cellar come morning. Then we installed ourselves within the church and waited for dawn.

At around four of the morning on that fateful Thursday, William Stuart fired a shot into the air and asked that everyone take up their positions. I was to go with William, Charles Kent and Mayor Mortlock to the battlements of the church. Others were arranged about the churchyard. William gave a brief and unsentimental speech in which he imprecated each of us to complete the tasks we had been allocated, and to trust in the ability of good military tactics to overcome brute force. He charged us to be brave but not foolhardy, to be merciful but not soft-hearted. Then it was time to wait.

Dawn was a line that became a swathe of colour in the east, that in turn became the sun. It was cold enough to see our breath. Just past six, there was a sound, very distant, of raised voices. Then they were closer, and we heard hoofs on hard earth. I spent the time counting. There were twelve of us up on the ramparts, a further sixteen arranged behind the gravestone barricades. Twenty-eight men. I noticed, though, that I did not see Silas Moore. Our fires still burned here and there about the churchyard, and their smoke drifted across the grass and graves, and I thought perhaps Moore was disguised by this smoke. Birdsong was loud in the trees all about the church, the birds being unaware of the moment, the way that time was sharpening to a point.

Just then, I heard a noise from behind, from the winding stone staircase that led up from the vestry to the battlements. I turned with my musket drawn, as did William, and I was horrified to see Elizabeth there, a look of hard determination on her face, her great belly thrust out before her. 'I am come to help,' she said. 'I wish a part in the downfall of these villains.' I saw William and Charles Kent look towards me here, and perhaps a stronger husband would have found words to send her back down to hide amongst the robes and surplices. I merely nodded my head, for I knew how much the events of our wedding day had hurt her, and figured that she deserved a place in whatever confrontation was to come.

Now the sound of voices was very loud, and all of a sudden they appeared, the villains, coming down the Sissinghurst road, and I heard Charles Kent draw in a breath of astonishment at the numbers of them. The stream of smugglers came and came, some mounted, some afoot, all armed with the most vicious display of blunderbusses, carbines, pistols and hangers. They were all stripped to the waist, with brightly coloured kerchiefs tied about their heads and daubs of blue paint on their bodies like the Iceni once wore. They sang loud shanties and laughed, and it was clear that many were well in their cups, for they were hardly able to walk in a straight line.

Then Kingsmill and Arthur Gray appeared, both on horseback, both attired more sombrely than the men about them, in dark jackets and three-cornered hats. I saw the gigantic Poison, and the ratty-faced man they called Smoker. With horror I saw that Poison held old Silas Moore by the hair. He had been deprived of his clothes and his naked body was covered in the most horrible gashes and bruises. With a kick, Poison sent him face-first into the dust, from which he lifted himself and crawled with great difficulty over the wall of the churchyard and, with his hands covering his modesty, made his way to the church. Soon, dressed in his Sunday vestments, he was among us.

'You are hale enough to fight?' William asked him, and he nodded grimly and took up a fowling piece. The smugglers meanwhile ranged themselves along the road, loading their muskets and sharpening their cutlashes. Then Kingsmill shouted that he was come for our hearts, and Gray yelled out that the Hawkhurst Gang would brook no disobedience in those over whom it ruled, and Poison let out a great and horrible shriek, and the Battle of Goudhurst was begun.

XIII

IT WAS CLEAR from the first that the Gang had spent the night roistering and drinking; they had arrived with no plan, figuring that their superior numbers – I estimated a hundred and fifty of them – and firepower would be sufficient to overcome us. They retreated to the lawn behind Mill House and then the first wave of them came, twenty mounted brigands with knives in their teeth. The wall of the yard was too steep to leap at this point, so they took a sweeping line to the east, where the wall was lower, and their horses bounded over and came towards us. I saw that William had accounted for this eventuality, arranging his barricades so that they might repel attacks from a variety of different directions. The horses came fast and our men maintained admirable discipline, holding off from firing until the enemy were almost upon us and then discharging. I saw several of the smugglers fall, while others wheeled away to re-gather. Seth Layard, one of Charles's stable lads, stood bravely and launched his bayonet into one of the villains, eliciting a great arc of blood and a cheer from our men.

It is hard to write sensibly of battle, it being a most insensible thing. I was, anyway, entirely taken up with my own duties, namely firing upon the waves of the enemy that broke upon us, first on horseback, then scrambling over the churchyard wall on foot. We could see the chief smugglers standing on the lawns of Mill House, bottles of grog in their hands, urging their minions onwards. Elizabeth was most helpful in the services she rendered, ensuring that our weapons were always full of shot, or taking up an eye-glass to survey the landscape for the next assault. At one point I heard Charles Kent let out a curse and saw, coming from the direction of the Starre & Crowne, young Edward Kent, a fowling piece in his hand, running at a fast clip across the ground. He took up a place behind one of the barricades and began to fire with the rest of them.

With the time approaching eight of the clock, there was a lull in proceedings, during which we permitted the enemy to retrieve the dozen or so of their dead, while we patched up our own injured and celebrated the fact that we had not lost a single man. Esau Beswick had been slashed across the cheek and Ashley Scotcher had taken a musket ball in the shoulder, but neither was grievously harmed, and both had a swig of rum and said they were well-set to continue.

We then rejoined battle. The enemy decided that, having failed with their tactic of repeated charges on foot and by horse, they would now endeavour to overwhelm us through the weight of their numbers. So there came a great surge of smugglers over the wall, and it was indeed a most fearful sight, for there remained upward of a hundred of them, all bellowing & clashing their cutlashes on the gravestones as they passed. It was clear that the barricades would be overrun, and so

William issued a call for the men to retreat, which they did in good order, moving first behind a cordon near the porch of the church, and then making their way inside and up to the battlements.

We held off firing until the smugglers were nearly at the church. They had ranged themselves behind gravestones and on the far sides of the barricades we had constructed, but there was not enough cover for all of them, and so many were left dreadfully exposed. Then, with all our numbers concentrated along the crenellated battlements and in an excellent position given the elevation and sight line afforded us, William issued his order and we began to fire upon the enemy. I saw that Elizabeth had taken up a pair of pistols and was unloading them with great skill, dropping down beneath the parapet to reload after each discharge. Young Edward Kent cheered with every smuggler that fell and soon the bodies lay thickly upon the ground, with many dead and others horribly wounded and letting out most pitiful groans and imprecations. I saw a good number of the villains turn and flee, taking with them the horses that were tethered by Mill House.

After this there obtained a period of stalemate, whereby those smugglers that remained, perhaps fifty in number, including Gray & Kingsmill and the other principal villains, were well-enough concealed by the gravestones to be immune from our bombardment, while not braving more than a cursory attempt to mount any further attack upon us. So it was that, after perhaps twenty minutes in which shots were exchanged without any noticeable effect on the outcome, William called me and Charles Kent over to him, and suggested that it was time for us to undertake a more offensive line of attack.

The majority of our group stayed on the battlements to provide covering fire, while we three, and with us the large and lumbering Mayor Mortlock and Esau Beswick, descended into the church. 'Our advantage must lie in surprise and dexterity,' William said to us. 'We rush them and try to inflict some damage on their numbers, then we return and go again. Run low, run hard, trust in those providing your cover.' I looked at Mayor Mortlock and wondered at his ability to run in any fashion, let alone as directed by our General. But then the logic of our orders took over and we were out of the porch and into the bright morning. I held my sword in one hand, a pistol in the other, and I began to run.

The smugglers had not been expecting our appearance, and whether it was the size of Mortlock and Beswick, or the sight of our weapons, or the terrible cries that issued from us (not least, I confess, from me), but the enemy seemed most discomfited by our arrival, and a new contingent departed running, several of whom were hit in the back by our covering fire. I cannot tell you the joy that seized hold of me to see this, and then to realise that I was thick amongst the smugglers. I saw that my comrades were alongside me, with William locked in a close-fought clashing of swords with Arthur Gray, and Charles Kent pursuing a fleeing Kingsmill before hurling himself upon him as if he were in a football game, and pounding him with his fists until the brute was quite insentient.

Now all of our Goudhurst Band descended and

rushed upon the enemy, who were fleeing in the most disordered and panicked fashion. I saw one of the brigands turn and fire at Esau Beswick, who fell, while another hid behind a gravestone and dealt the already much-wounded Silas Moore a deadly blow with his hanger. Otherwise the fatalities were all on the side of the smugglers, and those that did not flee were either cut down or surrendered themselves.

I hacked and slashed at a few of the fleeing smugglers, and, coming round a barricade of gravestones, saw that the ratty Smoker was just before me. Quicker than thought, I thrust my sword into his guts and then again in his chest, where I met orts and organs and there was the most gratifying crunch of blade against bone. He fell, his face contorted, a gurgling sound coming from his mouth.

I turned about to see the giant Poison step round the side of the barricade with his great blunderbuss aimed at my head. I confess I did shut my eyes, and heard the report of the firearm discharging, but I felt no pain. I opened my eyes once more and watched as his face, only half-visible behind his beard, registered first surprise, then a kind of dawning horror, and he sank to his knees. As he fell, I saw Elizabeth behind him, her pistol still smoking. There was a hole in the back of the great brute's head. I took her in my arms then, and for a brief moment we embraced as we had when we were very much in love, and I felt the child within her through the thin wall of her belly, and I loved it because it was part of her, and made all sorts of resolutions that are not of any import to this story.

Then, all of a sudden, I felt a creeping presence behind me. I turned and saw Arthur Gray, a long red slash down one cheek, a pistol in his hand. There was a wild and raving look to him: his hat had come off and his hair fell in matted strands about his face, blood had dyed his shirt and, when he opened his mouth to speak, I perceived that several of his teeth were missing. 'We are not done yet,' he said, leering horribly. I placed myself before my wife, who was herself cowering against the gravestones. Now Gray raised the pistol, pointing it directly at my head. I held up my sword, aware of how useless it was in this situation, but pleased to make some sign of defiance. I prepared for death, hoping at least that Gray would be apprehended before he could attack my wife.

Gray pulled the trigger and the pistol let out a little *phut*. He pulled again with the same result, before hurling the weapon to the ground and drawing out a vicious-looking dagger, its blade all crusted with blood. Muttering to himself and spraying a fine mist of blood from his mouth, he took a step towards us, and at that point a figure came flying over the gravestones as if swooping down from the air. The man landed atop Gray and cast the dagger from his grasp, before pressing a pistol into the smuggler's neck. It was William Stuart who had come to our aid, and I saw that he was much affected by emotion to have the smuggler king within his grasp, for his chest did rise and fall most swiftly, and I could see that the hand that gripped the pistol shook as mine did where I gripped my sword. I was close enough to hear the words that the two men spoke to each other, although

William's voice was most strange, being high and quite unlike his habitual register.

'You are frighted,' Gray sneered. 'You cannot look me in the eye. You will not pull the trigger. You are soft, you who held yourself as the leader of this band of fops and yokels.' With this last, a laugh that broke into a cough.

A silence, then William took off his hat and brought his scarred face down very close to Gray's. The smuggler let out a curse, and I could see that he recognised William, for a visage that had appeared provoking was now transformed into one of bafflement & dread. In that peculiar, high voice, William spoke words that I fathomed not at all at the time, but would come to understand later on. 'I will not kill you, Father,' William said, and I saw Gray start at the word, his eyes near leaping from their sockets. 'I have nothing in my heart for you but hatred, for what you did to my brother, to me. You will hang, and I will see you drawn and gibbetted.' William looked up. 'Arnold,' he said, his voice returned to its normal tone, 'go search me out some rope, friend. Mr Gray requires elevation.'

I heard a cheer go up from our men, and thought at first that it was directed at William's apprehension of the Gang's leader, but then I saw coming in from the Sissinghurst road an assemblage of red-coated men on horseback, and with them rode young George Kent, a broad smile upon his face. The soldiers were fanning out about the graveyard, muskets drawn, and there were a few small skirmishes while the Gang were apprehended.

Those smugglers that had not yet been caught or fled were rounded up and detained in the church's crypt until they could be transported to more permanent incarceration, the soldiers staying to guard them. We urged the soldiers to take particular care over Gray and Kingsmill, the latter most terribly swollen and bruised from the beating he had received by Charles Kent. Gray, now tightly bound, was apoplectic with rage, calling out for his lawyer, offering money to any that would free him. He sobbed between shouts and looked for all the world not like the master of a deadly group of brigands, but rather a small, petulant child.

XIV

THIS IS THE end of the story of the Battle of Goudhurst, as recounted by one who was there. It may be thought that I have made too much of my own role in the proceedings, and that may be so, but we are always the heroes of our own stories, are we not? I tell all this as closely to the truth as possible, but am sure that others might render it differently. Mayhap one's best sentence is one's best self, and so a book such as this may generate a kind of supreme adulthood. As for what happened next, there is little to say, save some particularities that might help to provide a more satisfyingly conclusive ending to my tale.

The smugglers we had apprehended, of which there were fifteen in number, were tried at Chichester. Twelve were transported to the Americas, while three were sentenced to death: Kingsmill, Gray and another, who went by the name Half-Coat Robin and was found guilty of the murder of Jarvis Lambert and his daughter on the evidence of Lambert's wife. Such was the depravity of their actions that they were returned to the Weald to be executed.

I stood, at three of the afternoon on that day in August, with my wife beside me holding our baby girl, whom we had named Goody, in her arms. My friend William Stuart was next to her, and we were there in the crowd as first George Kingsmill, then Arthur Gray, were strung up and hanged by their necks, twitching like slaughtered beef until they were dead. I watched William as Gray spasmed himself deathwards, but I could read nothing in his pock-marked face, and anyway little Goody had started to bawl and I took her from her mother and hushed her. We celebrated their passing most joyfully at the Starre & Crowne and then later with Charles Kent at Pattenden. William, with whom I had struck up a great, if enigmatical, friendship, and whom my wife declared to find the most charming and convivial of all the gentlemen of the village, was sombre afterwards, and I saw him leave the public house early and go to stand in the graveyard, looking up into the summer sky.

Half-Coat Robin was hung on the cricket pitch at Horsmonden, and it was not long afterwards that I heard the children in my class singing to each other the rhyme that has now become quite familiar:

> *On Horsmonden Heath*
> *There hangs a thief.*
> *At Goudhurst Gore*
> *There hang two more.*

Several days after this final reckoning brought to an end the most violent reign of the Hawkhurst Gang, William Stuart appeared at my door. Little Goody was asleep upon my chest and I begged his forgiveness for not rising to greet him. Elizabeth smiled enormously to see William enter. I had not looked at William closely without his hat before, and saw that he must have been a handsome man before the pox caused him such disfiguration. His wig was well-made and hid all but a few strands of fine blond hair beneath. We spoke on inconsequential matters for some time, and yet I could tell that William wished to disburden himself of something, for he sat very straight and kept casting his eyes this way and that, starting at the least sound.

It was a Sunday and the Widow Brown & young Ezekiel had been out picking damsons in the wood, and when they came in I felt a profound shift in the atmosphere in the room. The Widow looked at William with excessive frankness, until I was forced to ask if they were acquainted. It seemed to me that everyone knew this man from some former time save me. William nodded his head – her head – slightly and, taking young Ezekiel upon his knee – her knee – where the child did sit most happily, he said that she had a tale to recount to us. Then she began to speak – he began to speak – and, having always a pencil and paper beside my favourite chair in this room, and not being overly discomfited by the child across my chest, I noted down his story – herstory – which was a most wondrous and fantastical thing.

'I'd left the curtains open that night, the drapes of

my bed too,' she began, 'so that the fire in the Hundred Place painted the walls of my chamber with fading reds . . .'

Epilogue,
writ by Goody Brown / William Stuart

I THOUGHT THAT I should be permitted to conclude my own history, seeing as it has been so jumbled and corrupted by dear Arnold. It was only just before he died, some six or seven years after the events that came to be known as the Battle of Goudhurst, that I became aware that he had been shaping my story into the form of a book. What was more, it seemed that he mistrusted my own recollection of my adventures with Prince Charlie in the '45 and so had written to my friend Johnstone de Moffatt, the Chevalier, to seek corroboration. I find I like my friend's version of events better than my own (or that which posed as my own, filtered through Arnold's pen) and so have included it herewith.

I continued to live at Goudhurst for several years, going regularly to visit with the Nesbitt family, making the firm acquaintance of young Ezekiel, of whom I did grow very fond, rebuilding between us the bonds that had been broken by my departure from his early life. I continued to attire myself as a gentleman in public, but in the farmhouse I left off my hat and wig and let my hair hang down. My mother produced a salve which she applied to the weals and scars on my face and body, and which much reduced their hideousness.

I returned to Winchelsea several times during this period, a journey that never failed to move and sadden me. I rode past the ruins of Paradise, which none had sought to build upon, and all throughout the town, where memories were inscribed in the cobbles, on the trees. Mayor Parnell and his wife suffered at this time a most lamentable accident, where their coach was driven off the road at Icklesham and over the cliffs, killing them both and their driver also. It was said that a masked rider was seen in the vicinity not long before this, but I can say no more of that. Jurat Garland, the chamberlain, was found dead in one of the less-visited tunnels of the Under-Reach, long after the search party sent out after him had given up hope. A certain Mr Spence, who had replaced me as Cellarman when I departed, was never found at all.

After Arnold sickened and died of a grippe, I went to live at the farmhouse with my mother, with Elizabeth – my dear Lily – with young Goody and young Ezekiel, the latter of whom was now growing into a bright, well-featured young man. I took to sharing Elizabeth's bed with her, and we regained the closeness that we had enjoyed in the distant past, when she and I had both been such very different persons. My fastness with Lily did not go unremarked upon in the village, which was a place much given to gossip and insinuation. So it was that, when Lily's father died and, notwithstanding the coolness that lay between them, left her a goodly sum in his intestement, we decided to return to Winchelsea.

We enlisted builders to construct Paradise anew, with a glass-house for my mother, a music room for young

Goody, who showed some gifts in that direction, and a study for Ezekiel, who was much taken up with his books and whom we wished to send to school in Canterbury. Within six months, the house was ready, and so we bade farewell to Goudhurst, whose people cheered us off with many thanks for the services rendered unto them.

It would take another book to tell of the years that followed, and I have neither the time nor the inclination to write one. I returned to Winchelsea as Goody, and attired myself as a woman when in the town, but at home preferred to clothe myself in articles that were more manly than otherwise, recognising that I felt most comfortable neither as woman nor man, but in the space in between. Like many, I suspect. I did receive several letters from Johnstone de Moffatt, but chose to leave them unanswered, being in a state of perfect happiness and companionship with Lily.

So I bring this mongrel record of a hybrid life to a close. I could, of course, tell you of the smuggling that went on again beneath the streets of Winchelsea, and of young Ezekiel's role in it, and young Goody's, and how Lily and I became richer than almost any in the land. But I am tired now, and I wish to wander a little before dusk. For I find that more than anything, I love this place and its surrounding country, love the Under-Reach and the wild woods, the marshes and lofty cliffs. I love the bay and the Brede. My mother is now buried here and, when I go, which will be soon, I suspect, I will go happily beneath the earth of this fair town: Winchelsea.

THE END

Acknowledgements

ELIZABETH MACFARLANE VISITED the smugglers' caves in Hastings and came back with the idea of a grown-up *Moonfleet*. I hope this is close to what she was imagining. Numerous friends have helped me as the book developed. Particular thanks to Alex and Katie Clarke for the best view of the moon on Rye Bay. Chris Clothier advised on the ships and sailing. His book, *Sea Fever*, is a blissful thing. I was lucky to spend a day with Carey Marsh, who brought the sea and sailing alive for me. Oliver Chris has been a great friend to me and the book. Neil Gower's maps, as usual, are worth a hundred thousand words. Thanks to Sadie Holland for midwifery expertise. Ian and Enid Frow introduced me to the eerie beauty of the marshes and their churches.

I had tea in Winchelsea right at the start of this project with Malcolm Pratt. His books on the town are superb. Thanks to Kent Barker and his magical book *The Smuggling Life of Gabriel Tomkins*. I was also greatly helped in my early research by the wonderful people at Winchelsea Museum. Jo Turner in particular was full of the most amazing information. I am also

Acknowledgements

grateful for the help of the Goudhurst & Kilndown Local History Society and particularly Gill Joye. Thanks to Sean Gilder who provided friendship and introductions in Goudhurst.

In Scotland, Louisa Lindsay welcomed us to Rothiemurchus and was incredibly helpful and encouraging. Thanks to her mother, the late Philippa Grant, who delivered the Chevalier de Johnstone to me fully-formed.

Thanks to my early readers – Walter Donohue, Tom Edmunds, Eleanor Fitzpatrick and Anthony Preston.

Thanks to Steven Desmyter and Rosanna Konarzewski for your great support.

Thanks to Karolina Sutton at Curtis Brown – you are amazing.

It's a joy to be part of the Canongate family. Thanks to the wonderful Joanna Dingley, to Simon Thorogood, who was both good and thorough. Thanks to Leila Cruickshank, Vicki Rutherford and Anna Frame. Thanks also to Gabrielle Chant, for an immaculate copy edit.

I finished this novel on my last ever morning in my grandfather's house in Princeton. He was always my first reader and the book doesn't feel quite finished without him giving his characteristically unvarnished verdict. I will also miss my mother-in-law, Annabelle Simpson, who was the only audience member at the worst-attended literary festival I ever spoke at, and whose support was generous and unconditional.

Thanks, finally, to Al and Ray, who came up with far better titles for this book, and to Ary, my great love.

The True History of the Hawkhurst Gang

FORGET EVERYTHING YOU thought you knew about smuggling. You've been reading too many stories. If you believe the books, smuggling was a West Country affair, with row boats tacking up Cornish coves, the smuggler on the run from a brutal Navy, only wanting to act as a maritime Robin Hood, disbursing the spoils of his nocturnal voyages to the villagers around him. The popular imagination has smuggling wrong in location, in scale and in the pureness of the smuggler's heart. The smuggler wasn't Ross Poldark, he wasn't *Moonfleet*'s Elzevir Block, he – and it was almost always a he – was a more evil and organised figure than that. He also, in all likelihood, lived in Sussex or Kent.

The first time I heard of the Hawkhurst Gang was on a visit to Winchelsea with my grandparents as a child. We were walking along the Udimore ridge, looking down over the wide sweep of the Brede Valley, when we came to Dumb Woman's Lane. My grandfather told me how the lane had been named: a local publican's wife who lived there had seen the notorious smugglers of the Hawkhurst Gang pass in the night. This was the late 1740s, the height of the gang's notoriety and a time when the government was offering ever more glittering incentives for those willing to 'peach' on the smugglers – to turn them in to the authorities. The publican's wife told the Revenue Men what she'd seen and was duly rewarded. That night, a group of smugglers came to her house and ensured she would never peach again – by cutting out her tongue.

This is what you need to understand about the smugglers of the eighteenth century: they were brutal, they were highly organised, they were vastly wealthy. When William Baldock, head of the Seasalter Gang, a group of smugglers on the north coast of Kent, died in 1812, he left an estate valued at the equivalent of a quarter of a billion pounds in today's money. Arthur Gray, a former butcher who along with the vicious Kingsmill brothers, George and Thomas, ran the Hawkhurst Gang, built Seacox Heath, just to the north of Hawkhurst, one of the largest and most luxurious private homes in the country. The gangs exerted a rule of terror over the villages of the Kentish Weald – the wooded hills that straddle Kent and Sussex – maintaining their power through bribery, intimidation and even murder. When Daniel Defoe visited Deal in Kent during the early 1700s, he said that it seemed that the whole town was taken up with a single pursuit: smuggling. Kent and Sussex were a smuggling economy, because of their history and their geography.

To understand how smuggling took hold of the southeastern corner of England, you need to go back to the 1200s, when the country was a poor and backward place. Wool was its most valuable commodity, and wool was where smuggling began. Whereas the later history of smuggling saw illicit goods carried from the Continent to England, the direction of trafficking in the early years was all one way. English wool, and particularly the wool of Romney Marsh, was highly prized in Europe, the weavers of Flanders and Tuscany valuing it for its long fibres and the ease with which it could be woven. Wool was England's first export to be taxed – Edward I raised taxes from £3 to £6 a sack in order to finance wars with the Welsh and the French.

By 1300, England was exporting 30,000 sacks a year. The steep taxes that were levied, twinned with the proximity of the Continent to the marshes on which much of the wool was raised, made smuggling inevitable. The wool smugglers were called Owlers – perhaps because they plied their trade at night, perhaps because of the hoots they gave as warnings, but most likely a local contraction of 'Woolers'. In 1350, Edward III attempted at once to stimulate English industry and move against the Owlers by banning the export of wool and incentivising Italian weavers to come and work in London. By 1390, there was three years' output of unsold fleeces rotting on the quaysides of the south-eastern ports. Exports began once more, and the Owlers returned.

The 1400s saw the first attempts to enforce the payment of export duties, with the establishment of customs houses at key ports. There were tide waiters, coast waiters and land waiters, searchers and weighers, all tasked with cutting off the smugglers at various stages of their journeys to France and Flanders. One of the problems faced by this nascent customs system was that the Channel ports had long enjoyed near-independence from the country's government, with the Cinque Ports of Dover, Hastings, New Romney, Hythe and Sandwich, and the ancient towns of Rye and Winchelsea enjoying freedom from taxation in return for providing their feared and brilliant sailors and boats to the Navy in times of war. By 1600, there were 160,000 sacks of wool being smuggled annually, with the punishment for those caught being either execution or the cutting off of the right hand.

The Civil War, though, led to a revolution in the English tax system, and the emergence of what most people think of when they hear the word smuggling. In order to pay for the cost of the war (and no doubt a reflection of the Commonwealth's puritanism), excise duties were imposed on a range of luxury items, including coffee, tea, cider, spirits, salt, leather and soap. Suddenly, what was one-way traffic became a two-way process, where wool went out but, increasingly, untaxed goods came back in.

The eighteenth century was the heyday of smuggling in Sussex and Kent. You had rival gangs who wrestled for power, with first the Mayfield and Alfriston Gangs in the ascendant, then the Groombridge Gang, then, in the 1740s, the Hawkhurst Gang, led by the sinister Arthur Gray and the Kingsmill brothers. For the whole of that decade, until the Battle of Goudhurst that marked their final defeat, the gang ruled over the Weald. They made vast amounts of money, committed unspeakable deeds, and were an efficient and well-managed criminal organisation.

The government tried repeatedly to crush the smugglers – in this century of strange and distant wars they needed the revenue to pay their soldiers – but numerous strategies, from lowering taxes to gazetteering (listing wanted smugglers in the *London Gazette* and offering staggering rewards for those who were prepared to 'peach') bore little fruit. By 1747, there were a whole host of new and punitive laws in place targeted at the smugglers. You faced the death penalty for wearing a bee skep on your head as a disguise, or a 'wizard's mask'. You could be transported to the American plantations for 'hovering' offshore or muffling the hooves of your horse.

The smugglers grew bolder and more brutal, openly defying the authorities. The Hawkhurst Gang had a consignment of goods confiscated by the Revenue at Poole Customs House; undaunted, they marched west and stole the goods from under the eyes of the customs officers. When the Revenue came after them, they tortured and murdered one of the officials. Gray and his men grew vastly rich, dabbling in politics and gaining enormous local influence. So many goods were coming in that there would be fairs on the sands at low tide; villagers washed their windows with gin; the church at Snargate on the Marsh smelt strongly of tobacco – the priest allowed smugglers to store their goods in the crypt.

Living in the Weald, on the outskirts of Hawkhurst, I'm aware every day of the fact that I'm walking in the footsteps of figures who have attained an almost mythical status in this rolling and rural corner of England. Bringing them to life in *Winchelsea* wasn't hard because they feel so alive to me now. They are deeply woven into the history of this place, and every time I drive down Dumb Woman's Lane, or past Goudhurst Church, or in front of Seacox Heath (now the country dacha of the Russian government), I think of the rogues and villains who once struck fear into the hearts of the inhabitants of the villages of the Weald.

Questions to Discuss in Your Book Club

Do you want to start a book club? Are you a part of a book club but can't decide on your next read? *Winchelsea* is the perfect book to kickstart your club and stimulate discussion. Here are some questions to help you get started.

Q1

Goody is shocked by violence at the beginning of the novel. What makes her turn to the life that she does? Is revenge the only force to blame for her actions?

Q2

One of the most important elements of *Winchelsea* is the setting – from the East Sussex coastal landscape and underground network of tunnels to Culloden Moor and the Highlands. How are the characters' sense of identity affected by their physical locations?

Q3

What is the effect of the narrator being the age that Goody is? How does seeing things through her eyes shape the novel? How is this complicated by Arnold's involvement, and the inclusion of the Chevalier's memoirs?

Q4

Alex Preston has said that this book is a 'grown up' response to *Moonfleet*, the classic adventure book written by J. Meade Falkner. In what ways is *Winchelsea* a classic adventure story? How does it animate its historical period and events?

Q5

Goody is described as most comfortable 'neither as woman or man, but in the space in between', and dresses in different clothes throughout. How is she treated differently by others based on her outward appearance?